A love letter, of course! The kind Sasha is so good at writing! And sent from the beach where she is frolicking with the Other Woman! She's making love to the Other Woman and writing love letters to *me*, talking of our future together, of how *much* she misses me!

I recall her saying, one day last spring, "We are two single people who are married to each other."

Such statements made me believe that there was hope for us, in spite of the untenable situation we were then in, that perhaps she had begun to want what I wanted, a common life, a home, the future of which she writes so eloquently now.

Then she added that she felt the same way about the Other Woman. . . .

Marcia S. Andrews' *A Summer's Tale* speaks to everyone who has ever been in love . . . but especially to those lesbians who have been hurt time and again. If there's any difference between lesbian and heterosexual love, Ms. Andrews explores the question with incisive candor and profound respect.

A Summer's Tale

Marcia S. Andrews

timely books

p.o. box 267
new milford, connecticut 06776

A SUMMER'S TALE by Marcia S. Andrews

An original Timely Books publication.

First Edition — December 1986

Jacket design and typography by Linda Benveniste, New York City.

Acknowledgements

Rich, Adrienne: *The Dream of a Common Language*, W.W. Norton Co.,
      1978

Joyce, James: *Ulysses*, Modern Library, 1942

Eliot, T.S.: "Burnt Norton," *Four Quartets*, Harcourt, Brace & World,
      Inc., 1943

———   "Little Gidding," *Four Quartets*, Harcourt, Brace & World,
      Inc., 1943

Library of Congress Catalog Card Number: 86-51051

ISBN 0-931328-10-1

Timely Books
P.O. Box 267
New Milford, CT 06776

PART ONE

Miriam woke suddenly, nauseated, and stared into the darkness of the room, trying to slow her rapid breathing and pounding heart. She rose quietly, put on the gray chenille bathrobe that had fallen to the floor at the end of the bed, and sat down at her desk by the window. Opening the right hand drawer slowly, she removed her journal, and found a pen.

I'm standing outside an abandoned institutional building of some sort, like a boarding school. Or the concentration camp barracks I visited in Dachau. Beside me is a woman with whom I want to be lovers, though she isn't familiar. Looking for a private place to make love, we climb through an open window on the first floor and begin walking down the halls of the building. The floor is covered by two or three inches of muddy water but we ignore it. Finally we find the shower room and decide to use one of the stalls. Just at that moment I see a man in the room with us, lying in the water on his back. He's wrapped in bands of white material, like a mummified corpse. The muddy water is rising and has almost covered his face. Surprised, I ask him, "Why are you lying in this dirty water?" He replies, "Oh, it was difficult at first, but I've gotten used to it." The water begins to rise more rapidly then and I see that it is, in fact, sewage. There is garbage, unrecognizable debris, and feces floating in it. My potential lover and I escape from the shower room just as this filth reaches our knees and the stench of it nearly overpowers us.

This dream reminds me of one I had while married to Martin. I was having a lot of nightmares then, but the most terrible and vivid of them involved a scientific lab with an experimental pressure chamber in it. Martin and I are taking turns going into this chamber. The one outside increases the pressure until the one inside signals to stop. When my turn comes and I signal him through the large plate glass window to let me out, Martin continues to increase the pressure. Panic-stricken, I pull at the locked door and pound my fists against it frantically. Though I find it more and more difficult to breathe, I scream at Martin, who ignores me. I realize then that, with coldhearted deliberation, he is slowly destroying me. Martin can't hear me through the heavy steel door, but I

7

continue to plead for mercy; he refuses to meet my eyes. As my lungs begin to collapse and I grow weaker, I lean against the glass that separates us mouthing the word, "Why? Why?" The meaning of the dream was clear to me when I woke, sitting upright in bed bathed in sweat, but I didn't act on it until much later.

Funny about relationships. How they never quite work out, I mean. There is never quite the mesh one hopes for at the outset. Something is always slightly askew in the last snapshot. Sometimes it's in the eyes, a certain line of boredom around the mouth, or a gesture of concern that you suddenly realize is missing, has actually been missing for quite a while. You can't always put a finger on it exactly, but you know.

A couple of times I've thought I had it made. Everything was right, came together with no hitches. I was totally involved, in tune. Then that last snapshot revealed I'd been wrong all along. The one I loved didn't feel "that way" at all. In point of fact, the woman I love now has another lover and I've been pretending it's all right.

Miriam turned slightly on her chair to glance at Sasha, still asleep in the double bed across the room. It was almost dawn. She could hear birds beginning to twitter outside in the bushes along the freeway walls, and the clock ticking. The street lights of Portland were brighter than the stars. An occasional long-distance semi passed down the freeway, its red taillights glowing in the dark. The sky before her was slowly turning to cobalt blue.

When I met Sasha, I thought she was like some bright flower opening, some gift I didn't deserve. I was overwhelmed by her beauty and liveliness. I came alive again myself.

The first week we were lovers she bought me a copy of Adrienne Rich's book, *The Dream of a Common Language*. She opened it and quoted from "Splittings": "I choose to love this time for once/with all my intelligence." I was flattered by Sasha's serious, yet romantic, intent and astonished to find in that slim volume of poetry what I'd been imagining for years, the dreams for which I hadn't found adequate words. I wanted the common language and the sexual intensity both, everything, all of it. Determined to turn these dreams into realities in my relationship with Sasha, I made the mistake of thinking she and I shared this vision. I discovered, as the months went by, that we didn't share the definition of a single word, let along anything as complex as a language.

Being with Sasha was often like being with a child and made me feel like a parent. She could break down my resistance by crying and she cried easily. I didn't realize I was being manipulated that way until about six months down the road. We were arguing about something — pick a word, any word — and at a certain point in the argument I watched Sasha's face flush. Tears filled her eyes and ran down her cheeks. I saw for the first time that I was sleeping with a little girl. After I'd given in or compromised, as usual, on whatever the issue was, I asked her, "Do you ever cry when you're alone?" We were lying on my bed and I was cuddling her close to me the way I always did after we argued.

"No," she said. "Do you?"

After a pause, I replied, "Often."

"About what?"

"Oh, the miserable state of the world, I suppose. Starving people. Rape victims. My clients in the nursing homes and mental hospitals. Animals mutilated by experimental scientists. My fear of failure. Lost innocence. My mother." One of the reasons I've been so hurt and made so defenseless by the impending end of my relationship with Sasha is that I've told her things about myself I've never told anyone else. She's taking all that knowledge away with her, into a life with someone else, someplace else.

She must have realized then why I'd asked my original question.

"Do you think I try to manipulate you by crying?"

"Yes," I replied. "What are we going to do about that? We didn't do anything about it and, though I sometimes felt powerful and then guilty about the power, I started building safeguards. Maybe I should have reread *Lolita*.

It seemed to me that Sasha wanted what she didn't have and couldn't appreciate what she did have. She argued the theory that fidelity was a form of oppression and that lesbian partners were unloving to require it. I tried to accept this because I wanted Sasha but deep down I knew it was ridiculous. In practice, Sasha considered fidelity a concept I should live by but which she could ignore. In social situations she could flirt with the other women, which she did, and I could watch.

One night my phone rang very late. I was asleep. Sasha was in a nearby phone booth. She'd been out drinking with friends and had dropped by my apartment. As usual at night, I had the deadbolt on the door so that her key was ineffectual. She hadn't been able to wake me by knocking and was nearly hysterical. "What's going on? Why didn't you let me in? Who's with you?"

I tried not to sound angry or irritated but, after all, she was the one who wanted to sleep with other women, not I. Later I sat cross-legged on the bed and watched her undress. "Look, if this is non-monogamy, it's got to go. This is crazy."

She agreed but resented my unwillingness to tolerate her inconsistencies. This became another divisive issue in the end. Sasha always reserves a part of herself for the possibility of other lovers, or at least for romantic fantasies about them. While I was yearning for a complete immersion of my total self in another, I loved a woman who could only give part of herself away.

Obviously little common ground can develop in a relationship that is almost entirely sexual, even when delightfully passionate and physically satisfying. Sasha is a naturally romantic type and I, I've discovered, am inordinately susceptible to those charms. On our first anniversary she suggested that we buy each other rings, and we rolled around in my double bed that night whispering connubial desires to each other: "My sister, my spouse!" I've always underestimated the power of the erotic. No more. It kept me in a relationship that proved, early on, not to embody the psychic bond and intellectual affinity I wanted.

There is no excuse though for the fact that I tried to change Sasha. I wanted her to be not just charming and beautiful and clever which she is, but also an emotionally honest and consistent lover which she isn't. I wanted her to share my values, my interests, and my goals. I was relentless, believing that since she wouldn't do what I asked her to do, she didn't love me.

When Sasha and I got drunk, I accused her of lack of love in one form or another. "You never make time for us, Sasha, for us to be alone together. You're always including a hundred other people!" I said, exaggering the source of my irritation.

This was another old complaint and Sasha had learned how to defend herself against it. "That's not true, Miriam," she said, approaching her winning point slowly and with certainty. "What about last weekend? We did nothing with anyone else."

"One out of ten!" Being put in the position of scorekeeper made me feel cheap and unloving, of course. I didn't realize until recently how unwilling Sasha was to be viewed as half of a couple. I guess it limited her options.

"You've had too much to drink." Sasha removed the glass of brandy from the arm of my chair. "You're getting irrational."

"So are you. You say you love me —!"

"I can't live my whole life around you, Miriam!"

"But that's what *you* want from *me*, isn't it?"

Sasha usually put on her coat and hat at that point, sniffling, and got as far as the door. Then one of two thing happened: either she came back of her own volition or I called her back. The reunion was tearful and ecstatic. Nothing was resolved. The next day I was emotionally exhausted and disgusted with myself. Neither of us forgave or forgot the unkind words.

After Sasha received the letter that she'd been accepted into a graduate program in Massachusetts and decided to go alone, things rapidly went downhill between us, degenerating into more frequent arguments and slamming doors. Our ability to achieve mutual satisfaction was limited even more stringently to sex. We shouted at each other in private more than any of our friends suspected. In public we drifted away from each other while monitoring the other's movements around the room as if gathering evidence. No on would ever believe that Sasha was capable of mean behavior. She was so "nice" around our friends, so warm and solicitous, a regular Polly-

11

anna, while I, angry and threatening and never able to control my feelings, sounded like the Wicked Witch of the West.

Three months ago, in March, nearly simultaneous with the first of Mt. St. Helens' blasts, Sasha first spoke to me of her serious interest in the Other Woman. Apparently they'd already been spending some time together. Over tea, Sasha said. Rage and jealousy churned within me and I considered beating Sasha's head against the wall in an attempt to change the direction of her desire by force. Sasha is the only person to whom I've ever wanted to do extreme physical violence and this tendency to fantasize about it alarmed me since I'm essentially a passive person unless physically attacked. Because Sasha is a woman of impulse, I wanted her to weigh the consequences before the irrevocable act.

I needn't have bothered to think through the pros and cons, however. Sasha had already decided not to negotiate. "There is no continuity," she said. "Continuity" was a word we'd argued a number of times but, of course, had never agreed on a definition. Yet the meaning of her statement was clear to us both.

For a day or two I sat alone in my apartment, playing with my fountain pen, staring at the apartment building across the street, and thinking about patterns and the futility of escaping them. We write our own scenario very early on, it seems, and then we play the same part over and over, with various other characters. An old sense of being physically unattractive and unloveable returned to me from childhood. I had failed once again to be beautiful enough, or clever enough, to win permanent approval and·love. I wondered if there was something hidden from me that I was trying to uncover by this repetitious and apparent waste of time.

Then Mt. St. Helens exploded, shaking the earth, taking lives, burning the forests around it, blocking the rivers with mud. Roads were impassable in places, visibility zero. Scientists quoted in the newspapers spoke of faults under the Cascades and of land masses colliding with the ocean floor. I knew better. The earth was angry, like some ancient goddess. We had lied, been deceitful and destructive toward her, been unfaithful to her dictates, the Laws of Nature, much too long. This was a punishment. The ash drifted over Portland, lying on the ground like a late snow. It clung to skin, hair, clothing, was brought into the building on shoes so that the floor of my apartment was always gritty, blew through cracks in the windows and lay on the tabletops. The air, and possibly the city's water supply, was polluted. The days passed slowly and there was no sun. The atmosphere had been affected, perhaps permanently speculators said, by the hot ash and steam, and there would be no summer at all. People on the street or in cars wore masks to protect themselves from the ash. To breathe was hazardous.

I was unable to breathe anyway, suffocated by an acute sense of rejection. At the social services office where I worked part-time, my assignments lay neglected as I ran to a restroom stall to cry. I could not get solid food past the lump in my throat and began to lose weight. My complexion looked pale and clammy. My hair felt too oily though I was washing it daily. I gathered everything that Sasha had ever given me and put it on the back, very dark, shelf of my closet. I removed her ring, a jade band, from my right hand. Anticipating the sympathy of my friends as they became aware of the separation, I rehearsed myself to speak only of cheerful, innocuous topics. At home alone, however, I could not work on the novel I was trying to write. I could not listen to music. I could not read. I wrote poems instead, long poems about death, violence, and the earth's anger. The uncluttered white environment of my small apartment, that I had designed to be light and airy, now felt cold and empty. I waited for Sasha to call. The phone did not ring and finally I unplugged it so that it had a good excuse not to ring. March had slipped past me and April had begun. It didn't matter.

I wondered how long I could go on, barely holding the powerful forces of emotional and physical collapse at bay, before my whole life dissolved around me. Already the edges of tables and doorways had begun to loom at me, razorsharp. My skin felt increasingly vulnerable to the human touch. My insides quaked constantly and threatened to rise into my throat at any moment, like they do the day after a night of too little sleep and too many drinks. And, in fact, as was probably ob-

13

vious to those around me, I wasn't sleeping very much, rising each day to an ominous cloudy sky, and I was drinking a lot more than I should. The combination of lack of sleep, the inability to keep food down, and the resulting migraine headaches caused me to view the world somewhat surrealistically. Words came to me from a great distance and I knew I was responding inappropriately in conversation. I laughed at the wrong time, at the wrong things, at someone's dog getting run over by a truck, for example. On the other hand, if I saw children playing happily together in a park, I wept.

Then the postcard arrived from Simon in London saying, "I'm leaving the bookshop in my partner's hands for the whole summer. Will be at Les Bluets early in June. Come to France! Come for the sun, the clean air, and the good red wine." His invitation was like a lifeline thrown to a drowning person. The next day I renewed my passport, withdrew my savings, and bought a plane ticket.

At the end of April Sasha was back. I sat in my rocking chair glaring at her, a wounded animal plotting its moment of retaliation. She began her half of the dialogue with tears in her eyes. "Oh, I've missed you, Miriam. I've been in so much pain over all this."

Anger rose in me like the lava I had described in my poems. I shot out of the chair. "Don't tell me about your pain! I've gone nearly mad while you've been fucking around!" I moved toward her in two large steps, my hand raised. "You, bitch!" Stopping myself only at the last moment, I went into the bathroom and slammed the door behind me. While leaning against it, I reviewed the things she'd said and done that had angered and hurt me, bolstering myself against her tears and the eloquent pleas I knew she'd make for herself. I stayed there until I thought I was calm enough not to do any harm to her but also not to succumb to any residual desire.

When we'd been sitting opposite each other in silence for about two minutes, she said, "Miriam, I'm still in love with you. I can't help it. I can't live with you and I can't live without you! What am I supposed to do?"

I stared at her, expressionless. She'd cut her hair, as she always did when we were fighting, symbolically declaring her freedom. It make her look too masculine and I didn't like it. Then, before I could stop the words, I heard myself reply, "I'm still in love with you too. I haven't changed."

She knelt on the floor between my knees and we held each other for a long time.

Finally we looked into each other's eyes and I said, "Sometimes when I look at you like this, I think, 'I've loved this woman for at least a thousand years, and still do, and always will.' "

Sasha nodded in agreement. "Yes...yes, I know." She was staring at the watercolor of me that my friend Rebecca had done when we were in college. "You look so vulnerable in that picture," Sasha said, "but there's strength in the eyes."

I didn't ask until the next morning what she intended to do about the Other Woman. What she intended to do, it turned out, was be a good lover to both of us. Oddly enough, in spite of my past protests about the kind of relationship I wanted, I accepted this proposition. I was needy, I suppose, and my sense of worth was supported by the realization that the Other Woman hadn't been enough.

My crazy belief persisted that, with some commitment and compromise, Sasha and I could achieve a stable and creative life together, even in the face of an intensity we were unable to control, the fear of being overwhelmed, and the panic of self-loss. Though flawed, I wanted it to go on. Now I see myself still clinging desperately to the shreds and tatters of what I once mistakenly considered a much more whole fabric.

I was even willing to accept that Sasha would leave me to go to graduate school.

Sasha wanted freedom. "I need to strike out on my own, Miriam," she insisted. "I've never really been a single person in a strange place. I just want to be a hermit for a while, read and study, be totally alone."

I had no trouble respecting this. I'd often felt the same way and had had no hesitation about following my own inclinations.

Yet when I told her I was leaving for Europe in June, she was irritated. "Well, you've had one foot on the plane as long as I've known you," she accused me, as if it were solely my fault from the beginning that the relationship hadn't worked.

"There was a point at which I was willing to take the foot back off," I reminded her, "but you wanted to be alone, wherever you went."

She was silent. She knew I was right.

I wondered if Sasha viewed one of her lovers as primary and the other as secondary, though I considered such categories embarrassing and, besides, I was still basking in the glow of renewed passion. When I finally asked, jokingly, if she'd prioritized her two lovers, I got the shock of being told I was secondary. I remembered someone saying once that the essential dynamic of a relationship cannot be changed. Sasha and I have functioned as a mother-and-daughter team, almost from the start. I was expected to provide a constant level of love and support, but was hated when I refused any request or challenged her willfulness. She constantly tested the limit of my love, found it, then mocked me for my selfishness and ran away. She didn't believe me when I said I would not operate from the basis of unconditional love. There were certain things that, if she intentionally did them, I wouldn't forgive.

Then came the day she told me she had asked the Other Woman to go with her when she left for graduate school. This was after I'd told myself and her that I didn't want to live without her, after she'd said that she couldn't live with anyone else's needs but her own, after I'd accepted her relationship with the Other Woman and my reduced status, and after she'd said she wanted to go alone. I kept quiet a moment, trying not to show my hurt and anger, trying to maintain some degree of composure.

We were lying in bed. "That will make it rather difficult to be a hermit, won't it?" I asked.

Sasha turned away. "I knew you wouldn't understand!"

"What I now understand is that you don't want *me* with you!" I moved around so that she had to face me.

Her eyes were frightened. "You're just too much for me. I can't breathe or feel free around you anymore."

"You're such a liar, Sasha! That's why you don't feel free!"

"I admit I'm inconsistent," she said, "but I've never lied to

16

you."

"Bullshit!" I shouted. "There are many ways to deceive and you've mastered them all. Reread that essay." That essay being Rich's "Women and Honor: Some Notes on Lying." I was still hoping, even then, for some shared insight because I hadn't yet realized how desperate she was to escape our relationship nor how frightened she was of actually doing it. Sasha is right though. She doesn't lie. She just doesn't tell the truth.

"Go ahead, hit me! I know you want to!" She looked at me full of defiance, very much like a child wanting to be punished.

She'd baited me like this before. I'd never hit her, though I'd often wondered how she'd react if I did. This time though I struck out, rather blindly and undirected since I didn't really want to hurt her. I felt my hand make contact with her naked shoulder. She tried to put her arms around me almost immediately, but I pulled away, appalled at both of us, and she hid her face in the pillows. After awhile we made love anyway and I decided that her self-hatred must be nearly as great as my own.

When I stopped being angry about this latest rejection, I had to agree, at least to myself, that I might have left Sasha first if I'd found as convenient and willing a replacement as she apparently had. A week later Sasha changed her mind about taking the Other Woman with her, and the Other Woman, devastated by this reversal, contracted some undiagnosed disease of the stomach coupled with severe depression, and lost her job. Though it diminishes my sense of uniqueness, the knowledge that I'm not the only victim of Sasha's erotic universalism sometimes makes it easier to bear.

When Sasha and I made love, she still said I was her one and only. "You're the one I love." When I questioned her about the meaning of the words, considering that she had another lover who was primary, she admitted that she felt the same way about the Other Woman. How is that possible? On occasion I found that I could actually enjoy the momentary, transient pleasure of such bullshit. Yet the contrast of that activity with the search for truthful meanings, that for me is

17

part of being a writer, confused me. Sex became an empty activity as I retreated into fantasy to enjoy it. We were engaged only in "sweaty grapplings," as I'd often referred to sex during my heterosexual years. I took a lot of unnecessary baths. My body was telling me a truth my mind wouldn't recognize. Self-disgust grew as I continued to deny what I really wanted. I yearned for an innocence I'd lost somewhere. I've always believed that to lose innocence is to lose faith in the essential goodness of the human heart. No corner of my life was warm and secure, a place where I could crawl in and be comforted. I was still unable to work on the novel I was trying to write. Finally I told Sasha I could no longer be her lover.

"What about being a friend?" she asked, her lower lip trembling.

"We've never been friends, Sasha." My voice sounded hard and cynical to me. "Please leave me alone."

In May, on the day I gave a final poetry reading for friends in Portland, the mountain exploded again. Sasha was not at the reading, saying it would be too painful to hear me read when we weren't even speaking to each other. I was shaky and nervous until the moment when I spoke the first line of the first poem. While my personal life was disintegrating around me, I wouldn't allow myself to fail publicly. I had an attentive audience and no one suspected the devastations taking place within.

Sasha laughed and rolled over in her sleep. The street lights were extinguished one by one. From her desk Miriam could see across the freeway to the house where she and Martin had once lived. She could also see the house where Sasha had lived with a previous lover. It was a landscape full of sad reminders.

I don't blame anyone. There can be no fault, no blame, for our own decisions, as Sasha has always reminded me. And of course, to be fair, I must admit that I've been on the other point of this triangle too. I've had my share of being passionately loved and not returning it in kind. I don't think there can ever be a greater crime. It's worse than murder, however

18

accidental. It kills the spirit.

Miriam heard Sasha rise leisurely from the bed, stretching and yawning. She knew Sasha would walk toward the desk where Miriam sat writing, lean over and wrap her arms around the hunched shoulders. Miriam shut the notebook quickly and laid her head back between Sasha's bare breasts.

"How's it going?" Sasha rubbed her chin against Miriam's hair.

"Slowly." Miriam turned in the chair and Sasha bent over her mouth. It was a long, deep kiss. Miriam thought of suggesting that they go back to bed but felt she no longer had the right to ask. Nothing happened spontaneously between them anymore. They made appointments to see each other, and Miriam was careful not to call Sasha's apartment at what might be an awkward moment.

Sasha caressed her cheek and strode away toward the bathroom. She had gained some weight the last few months but it made her voluptuous rather than heavy. Her short hair was disheveled by sleep, emphasizing the new boyish look Miriam disliked.

The water running into the bathtub told Miriam that Sasha was definitely out of bed. In the kitchen Miriam flushed three small cockroaches down the sink while she waited for the coffee water to boil; she remembered her dream. "It was difficult at first but I've gotten used to it." That was one of the major problems between them, she decided; Miriam never quite got used to things while Sasha needed constant variety.

Why am I still trying to satisfy a desire that is apparently inextinguishable but doomed? In these terrible dreams I'm enduring a symbolic self-annihilation every night. During the day I'm living a form of moral suicide, destroying my sense of personal integrity. I've tried to analyze my reaons for this irrationality. Is it Sasha's warmth and affection that attract me, her romantic and spontaneous offerings of champagne and roses, her erotic charms? All of these enticements are dispensed at her whim, unpredictably, as in some Pavlovian experiment, and I keep going for it. Because I am so susceptible, am I a masochist or weak-willed? When she is gone, I miss these superficial pleasures. Yet, surely, my delight in them cannot totally explain the obsession.

19

Tomorrow I leave for Europe, and now I'm worried that this trip is just a convenient escape from a problem I'm too weak to solve. I'm relying on time and distance to rescue me, not just from Sasha, but from my agonizing compulsion to analyze what we have and haven't been to each other.

Three days ago Sasha appeared at my door, returning a book I'd left at her apartment. Sasha is also persistent when she wants something badly enough. It was easy too, knowing I'd be gone so soon.

As on so many other mornings, Miriam and Sasha sat facing each other across cups of hot coffee. Miriam had quit her job a week before to prepare for the trip and planned to spend this last day in Portland writing. She wondered if Sasha would be seeing the Other Woman as usual and tried to be intelligently detached from that possibility. The three members of the triangle had discussed their situation, endlessly it seemed to Miriam. Everything was tacitly understood and outwardly accepted by all parties involved, but Miriam's stomach muscles tightened involuntarily and she felt nauseated again.

Sasha reached across the table and slid her shorter fingers between Miriam's long white ones. Without looking up, she murmured, "Last night was very nice."

Miriam nodded. "Yes." By mutual consent, reluctantly given on Miriam's part, they had considered it their last night together. It had been surprisingly wonderful, in spite of Miriam's dissatisfaction with the state of the relationship. They had made love with as much desire as in the days before Sasha's sexual wandering and Miriam's jealousy. "But I wish I could understand how you do this." Her voice was reduced to a whisper by emotions she was having difficulty controlling.

"What?" Sasha's frown was one of puzzlement and innocent concern.

"Be so passionate about two people at the same time. It doesn't seem possible."

Sasha smiled a bit self-consciously. "But I'm doing it."

"For a moment Miriam considered confronting the smugness of the reply, then shook her head. "It's contrary to the whole idea of romance."

"For you."

"For me absolutely. Besides, it would take too much energy."

"It gives me energy."

"While I've been nearly drained by my job and writing and relating intimately to one person." Miriam listened to a fire engine approaching along the freeway. After it sped past, its siren wailing into the distance, she looked at Sasha again, tired of the too familiar dialogue. Then she smiled, challenging Sasha with a new insight. "When I have something good with a person, I want more of the person, not more of the thing."

A silent moment passed as they gazed at each other over the impasse of their contrary words and intentions. Having come to the acknowledged conclusion of their time as lovers, neither was quite prepared.

Sasha set her cup down so clumsily that some of the coffee spilled into the saucer. "Sometimes I think we should just run away together. Then I think, 'No, we both have things to do.' Then I think, 'What for?'"

Miriam made no reply to this interior monologue of Sasha's. The answer was obvious to her but she knew it would be rejected.

"Would you like to have dinner together at Marcel's Bar and Grill, about six?" Sasha asked. "I don't want this moment to be our last, I guess."

Sasha's large brown eyes were contradicting what Miriam knew to be her own best interest. Another meeting would only prolong the pain.

Sasha was wearing the purple silk shirt Miriam had bought for her. No particular occasion for the purchase, it had just looked like something Sasha should wear. The neckline plunged. In her imagination Miriam watched another pair of hands as they unbuttoned the shirt the rest of the way down. She knew she was masochistic to indulge herself along such lines, and banished the picture by tracing Sasha's left eyebrow, the crooked one, with her finger. The ache where her heart was had returned. "It's going to be hard whenever we do it." Tears began to well up but she didn't want to cry. There was a lump in her throat and her voice sounded husky and nasal.

There were tears in Sasha's eyes too. "Do you hate me?"

Miriam sighed. "Of course not. Well, maybe sometimes, a little. I have to be honest with you."

"So do I, don't you see? That's why it's been like this. These things just happen."

Miriam rested her elbows on the table and twirled a spoon on the white linen tablecloth. "Oh, I know! And I also know all the platitudes, all the rationales that people use to justify everything they want to do."

Sasha sat back in her chair sharply, obviously on the verge of anger. "You're so good at condescension, Miriam. I happen to think the question of non-monogamy in relationships is important and valid."

"You mean infidelity." She was satisfied with the disturbance that passed across Sasha's face when the word registered.

Sasha's eyes were flashing danger signals that said "Do Not Proceed." "That's a subjective value judgment. It's unfair."

"Oh, I don't think it's unfair at all, though I'll admit it's a value judgment. Do you have something against values?" Miriam knew that Sasha always rejected any very definite moral strictures but she felt unusually reckless.

"I feel like I'm being attacked," Sasha replied simply.

"Sorry." Miriam poured them both more coffee. "I know it's a bit old-fashioned but then I've discovered lately that I am. And besides, what have I got to lose?" She raised her eyebrows at Sasha and got no answer but a cold stare. "I like such words — honesty, truth, honor, fidelity. I want to write about them. What else is there? Musical beds?"

"You really despise me." Sasha's chin was trembling.

Miriam decided to relax her internal defenses for a moment. She looked squarely and earnestly into Sasha's eyes. "No. But my sense of personal dignity has been outraged. It seems to me that you tend to avoid any struggle, or self-denial, in favor of overly easy solutions."

"I don't think this has been a particularly easy time."

"Have you been unhappy?"

"Sometimes."

"What would have made you happy?"

Sasha shrugged. She looked genuinely miserable. "You and I having dinner together tonight would help." Sasha glanced suggestively into the dark cleavage where Miriam's bathrobe had fallen open.

Miriam smiled. She was beginning to recognize the more pleasant forms of manipulation for what they were. "Sure," she finally agreed, "that sounds fine." She knew she was making a mistake, but maintaining her position consistently was not yet possible.

"Will that give you enough writing time?" asked Sasha, standing up from the table. She seemed concerned about Miriam as a writer, but Miriam wondered if Sasha ever recognized that there was a real person

22

doing the writing whose ability to concentrate could be adversely affected by sudden and extreme changes in the emotional climate.

"Will it give *you* enough time?" Miriam looked away, embarrassed to be revealing so candidly the direction of her thoughts. She passed a hand across her cheek which felt hot and damp. "Sorry."

Sasha blushed slightly too. "Actually, darling, I was planning to spend the afternoon at the Portland Town Council collating the newsletter. Lucky you with no more job!" She swallowed the rest of her coffee and carried the cup into the kitchen.

Miriam sat hunched over the table, her face in her hands, already engulfed by sadness and failure.

"Oh, Miriam, please don't. It only makes everything worse." Sasha, with her jacket on, her bag hanging from one shoulder, was ready to leave. She crouched down, pulled Miriam's hands away from her face, and kissed her.

For a moment they leaned their foreheads together, as if making one last attempt to communicate nonverbally, then Miriam stood up. "How can it be worse?" she complained. "I don't understand any of this, I don't! Why is this happening? What went wrong?" Miriam heard her voice rising with hysteria and was embarrassed again. She didn't like to view herself as a poor loser.

Sasha held Miriam's hands tightly in her own as if she could impress on her, through the skin, the superiority of her own perceptions. "It's not necessarily ending. We might be together again someday, after we've done what we both have to do."

"Oh, Sasha!" Miriam raised her hands in exasperation. She'd decided recently that Sasha's ambivalence about enduring relationships must make separation less painful. Sasha had vague, easy answers that Miriam couldn't share. "I have no faith in that," Miriam replied, staring at Sasha's shoes opposite her own bare feet with their bright red toenails.

When they looked at each other, Miriam's eyes, communicating her disbelief, saw the sympathy in Sasha's and she turned away. After a moment she heard Sasha leave the apartment, closing the door firmly behind her.

Later Miriam sat at her desk trying to write, drank another cup of coffee, then drew lines in the dust on the wide windowsill.

I know it's too late to salvage this relationship in any form.

The wreckage has already been recycled. From the beginning I've been so preoccupied with the possibilities that I've let all the major cue lines go right on past me. I can make a world out of words but have a hell of a time maintaining a viable connection with one other human being. Much easier to ride along with it, take it in stride, tripping over my own feet from time to time, and slipping in the mud.

Finally she surrendered to her utter lack of enthusiasm for fiction, as she had done nearly every day since March. She lay down on the bed and entered a haunted sleep. It was one o'clock in the afternoon when she woke, tossing between the pillows.

I have been dreaming of them again — my mother Judith, and Martin, and Sasha. Those Fates again, like the vengeful Furies, pursuing me. In profile they look so similar, the high cheekbones, the Roman nose, the delicate fine-boned archness.

Judith should have been their mother, not mine. she wanted a son when I was born. Martin would have been a gift from the gods. Maybe that's why I could never please her. Yet that's too simple an explanation. Rather, my mother, like me, had no capacity or inclination for motherhood. I remember falling asleep as a child crying and repeating over and over, "No one loves me. No one loves me." Do all children do that?

I was never certain from one day to the next whether my mother cared to look at me or not. She often said, "Go away. I'm busy." She didn't seem busy to me, just staring off into space like that. I do it now though. I've puzzled and hurt lovers by staring off into space instead of into their eyes saying, "I'm thinking. I'm working on a story. I've got this idea." Sometimes I appear to be listening but it's only the scenario in my head I'm seeing and hearing. How can I be a good writer and be devoted to someone else? And vise versa.

Sasha and I had a conversation in bed once (our harmonious exchanges occur there, the only place we never disagree) in which she asked me to tell her about my mother. It was early morning and we were relating our dreams as we often do. Sasha's head was resting on my shoulder and I was mainly pre-

occupied in winding my fingers through her thick curls.
"She was a terrible mother," I replied, "but a wonderful lover."

Sasha raised herself abruptly on one elbow and looked at me, a mixture of shock and amazement on her face, then realizing from the grin I couldn't control that I was teasing her, and burst out laughing. "Well, it wouldn't surprise me!"

But it surprised *me*. In fact, I didn't know where that reply had been hiding. In some subconscious desire? Now I'm sure of it. The truth is my mother was a terrible lover too, inconsistent, and that's the kind of lover I've been choosing all my life. Our connection was intense, volatile, and I'm convinced, passionate. She had lofty principles of integrity and dignity that she couldn't live by, and I violate mine all too often.

" 'Don't be common,' my mother always said. 'There's nothing worse.' "

"Oh, there must be something worse," Sasha teased. Sasha has a storehouse of such responses for various situations, like Hallmark's occasional cards. Initially I thought it was cute. After awhile the superficiality of it began to grate. A certain degree of unpredictability in response is essential to the maintenance of respect in any relationship.

My mother had no qualms about entertaining her friends with amusing anecdotes, usually embarrassing to me, from my childhood. By the time the significance of this really began to enrage me I was in college, bringing young men home to dinner on Sunday afternoons. Though I accused her in private of betrayal and lack of respect, she continued with the stories. I stopped bringing my lovers home for gourmet meals, preferring to entertain in my one-room apartment over rice, sliced tomatoes, and cheap wine.

Martin and my mother were enchanted with each other, of course. He waited on her like a white knight, bowing. She was coy and admiring.

Early on I also began to see the personality similarities between Sasha and my mother, and my weakness for them frightened and irritated me. She herself was not to blame but once in an argument I flung out at Sasha, "I wish you and my mother could have known each other! You could have charmed each other to death!" For nearly two years Sasha has charmed me, and nearly to death. There are times when I am intoxicated by her, rendered unconscious. I can dimly perceive some perspective on another reality for myself, but it must begin with freedom from Sasha and, more basic than that, from my mother. At this fragile point in my life, I'm afraid that I am only grasping the superficial facts that so often mask the truth.

In comparing personal histories with other women, I have found that my mother was common herself in one way. As I approached adulthood, she wanted me to stop being eccentric, wayward, and nonconforming, and "settle down to something."

We often drank together, though she stopped after the first glass and I went on to finish the bottle in spite of her half-hearted protests. I think now that she took some pleasure in my drunken illnesses out under the quince trees and the stars that whirled overhead. One time I began to talk about writing, which I hardly ever did then, pacing up and down the living room throwing out ideas for stories that I thought would dazzle her with their insight and clever plot lines.

"What makes you think you can be a writer?"

Her interjection stopped me in mid-sentence. We looked at each other and the moment hung silent in the air. I could reason with the question but not with the mockery in her eyes. I brought my nearly empty wine glass down on the table with so much force that it shattered and a long thin shard imbedded itself in my hand. Enjoying the unoriginal metaphor of the suffering artist and the crucified Christ, I laughed as the blood dripped onto the deep pile beige rug. "What difference does it make if you use a hammer or a pen to drive in the nails?" I asked.

My mother was appalled at the blasphemy of the comparison rather than the melodramatic pose and, even more so, at the soiling of the wall-to-wall carpet. She poured half a bottle of iodine into the palm of my hand and took a wet sponge to the fresh blood stains at my feet.

"For this, O dearly beloved, is the genuine Christine: body and soul and blood. . . ." The opening scene of *Ulysses* has

26

always been one of my favorites. While I alternate between tears and laughter and grasped my wrist hard to stop the pain, I tried to talk to her intelligently about Joyce's novel.

With my hand sore and bandaged, I couln't even *pretend* to be a writer for the next few days.

I finally abandoned the attempts to win her approval and several years later she began to die of cancer. I was angry, thinking it another form of parental punishment for wrongs I hadn't committed. The irrevocable nature of my mother's predicament didn't affect me much until her hair began to fall out and her eyeballs turned yellow. She had always been very vain so I knew she wasn't faking. I read articles by Kubler-Ross hoping to achieve some necessary equilibrium.

It was during this time, as she lay dying in my grandmother's house, attended by a hired nurse, that she told me about my father and brother. Simply put, the man she had always told me was my father and her first husband was neither one. In fact, I am a bastard. Not that I mind — some great writers were bastards, after all. What I minded then was the twenty-seven-year-old lie, a truth that everyone in the family had known and collectively kept from me. All the years in which I'd told my mother everything, kept nothing back, she'd withheld the truth about my own father from me. In terms of communication, it was just as well she was dying because she would never have been able to utter another word to me that I would have believed. It seems that I also had a brother, three years younger than myself, who was privately adopted by a wealthy family in the city. I thought of Martin, so far away, so lost to me, and the subliminal connection between us when we were together. We'd come psychically from the same womb, eternally predestined, siblings, incestuous. After my mother's revelation and its emotional implications registered, I turned away from her and left the house, slamming the door behind me. I offered no understanding, no compassion. I shared nothing personal with my mother after that day.

I didn't realize until much later that the second chances we always think we'll have in life are, in fact, forbidden by time and death. At the right moment I neglected to say the words of love and comfort that might have healed the breach be-

27

tween my mother and myself and then it was too late. Not death, but the refusal to love, is the great divide between us all. And there is no way to change the truth of that.

Miriam left the apartment and stepped out into an unusually warm day, even for June. Portland's summer, always late in arriving, had, as predicted, been further delayed by the eruption of the mountain. Dry volcanic ash, like a light dusting of baby powder, was blowing along the sidewalks. Attempts by the city to vacuum the streets had proven as unsuccessful as everyone had known it would.

She had dressed with some care in gabardine slacks and a soft cotton shirt, not because she was trying to impress anyone but because, after three months of looking as dowdy and depressed as the mental patients with whom she'd worked, she had decided it was time to rebuild her self-image. On the freeway overpass she paused to remove the navy blue cardigan and tied it loosely around her shoulders. Squinting against the sun, she glanced northward, in the direction of the mountain, but a vague smoky cloud cover obscured the lava dome from view. As if she hadn't slept in days, her eyes ached in the glare and she put on her dark glasses. Under her arm she carried a leather-bound notebook. She never went anywhere without that impartial yet compassionate "ear," the only one she could trust with her current private, often embarrassing observations.

She walked toward Marcel's Bar and Grill by the longest route, along the river. She had always loved water and boats. Being near them generally improved her mood. Strolling slowly down the embankment, she could watch the cargo boats go by and feel as transient as she believed life was. She wondered if growing up in a port city made one shiftless and unstable. Yet she longed for stability. On the eve of her departure for Europe, she yearned for a home, for something good that would endure. Recently she had begun to notice that time was rushing by. She feared that she wasn't accomplishing anything, that, no matter how long she lived, she would never create a piece of work that would satisfy her, let alone anyone else. She wrote too slowly and not well enough.

She sat by the sea wall on a bench where she could watch the sailboats as they tacked back and forth across the river. She had a particular admiration for them. They were more vulnerable and fragile than their sisters, the hard fast motorboats, and more dependent on a favorable wind.

Martin was an accomplished sailor and we sailed together on the Willamette River often. He was the most beautiful man I'd ever seen, tall and slender with wavy brown hair that made him look Byronic, and serious brown eyes. What I especially liked, after I discovered it, was that the rest of his body was nearly hairless. He was unable to grow either a beard or a moustache. Physically he was the next best thing to a woman, if I'd been thinking in those terms then.

We were in several literature classes together. He was becoming a scholar and I was losing interest in academics. For a long time after we met, we flirted with each other in the cafeteria between classes, very careful not to touch but spending long hours, over lukewarm coffee, discussing the significance of love and death in the American novel, and the growing incidence of international terrorism. Later he told me he was afraid to touch me, to initiate anything, because he knew we'd drive each other crazy. He was right about that anyway. We discovered that separately we had each created a mental world immediately understood by the other. This instant telepathy was the initial attraction for us both. The line between literature and life, between written dialogue and casual conversation, didn't exist for us. We could reinterpret for each other a seminar discussion or a drunken barroom argument easily, as if we spoke an unknown foreign language, and exclusively, as if everyone else in the room were deaf. Our joy and delight in this secret communication became the way we could hurt each other most effectively too. We could devastate each other publicly without anyone around us being aware of the inner torture. Martin would turn to the nearest man and initiate a discussion of Watergate. I retreated into poetry. In private he denied that he understood my meaning. I've found this to be a truism about relationships: What gives you the most pleasure in the beginning will eventually give you the most pain. There are always more than enough indications of what the source will be.

What contributed to this intensity between us was the belief, on both our parts, that we'd been born for each other. I

29

now consider this unlikely, if not a bit archaic. When we met, we were both studying the work of William Blake. His concept of the Zoa and the Emanation — the two halves of the persona split at the moment of creation and searching the universe for each other through all time — described our feelings perfectly. Actually, most lovers probably feel somewhat that way, at least in the beginning, even if they don't verbalize it in such esoteric terms.

In my relationship with Martin fidelity was never the issue it's been with Sasha. I don't think it ever occurred to either of us. The real continuing problem between me and Martin was my interest in writing, because it was an activity that separated my mind from his. Compared to now, I hardly ever wrote but it infuriated him anyway. Not only could he not bring himself to support my desire to write but he occasionally made it difficult for me to do it. Words that I managed to put down on paper became a wedge between us, and he would never comment on anything one way or the other, just hand the poem back to me with a sad look on his face as if I'd somehow betrayed my commitment to him. He was afraid I'd eventually write about him, about us, and I am, of course. Nothing is so sacred to me that it can't be considered material. Besides, how could I not write about the one who was once the other half of my own soul?

When the words between us got bitter, he began to express his resentment about my writing more directly. "You don't need me at all! You've got your fucking poetry, haven't you?"

It wasn't true, of course. I needed him. As much as I've ever needed anyone. The need died though as I struggled, nearly suffocated by his anger and fear, to write something, anything.

Miriam lifted her face to the sun. At four-thirty it was still high, glinting on the surface of the water through which the boats were moving slowly and silently, as if in a dream. A slight wind kept the sails full and on the boat closest to the embankment she could see two crew members dozing on the bow, while another stood relaxed at the helm eating a sandwich. She was reminded of the many Impressionist paintings she'd seen in so many museums — sunlight on water, eager

30

bathers, picnicking families. Someone else's happy romance, pleasant memories in shades of green, blue, and gold.

My mother loved color and form, was very particular about distinguishing between shades of colors. I think she wanted me to be a painter like herself, but I was hopeless. I couldn't compete with her in the creation of beautiful objects and gave up on it early. Even now I have a hard time persisting when I'm not achieving some measure of success. Except in love and writing. Why do I continue to write? To survive. Why do I continue to love? It was Martin who answered that best.

During the last summer of our three years together Martin and I went abroad, disillusioned by American imperialism though the Vietnam War had officially ended, and bored by the hollowness in the intellectual community we frequented. Our own relationship was obviously breaking down and the cracks widened in the daily strain of travel in foreign places. Yet I held on stubbornly with all the committed strength I could gather and tried to ignore the tension. I was still in love with Martin and wanted to believe we could resolve the problems with effort. A silence, both psychic and verbal, settled between us with an almost irreversible vengeance.

In Greece we decided to spend our time on an island rather than in Athens. By that time there was little shared joy in what we were seeing anyway, and our dissatisfactions with each other seemed to have drained the energy from us both. We chose Chios because the ticket agent at Piraeus said tourists rarely went there.

From the ferry dock on the island we took the only bus, which went up one side and down the other of the volcanic mountain that forms Chios. The bus carried nearly as many animals, mainly chickens and pigs, as people. Boxes and bicycles and suitcases were strapped to the top and the whole menagerie swayed and bumped along on roads that, in this country, would be closed to all motorized vehicles. At each village the children ran out to the bus, clammering for the mail and newspapers and the attention of the passengers.

We left the bus at a village called Volisous. Immediately Martin and I were surrounded by the children. With our

Levi's and backpacks we were so obviously not Greek. Because it was nearly two miles from the village to the beach where we wanted to camp, I sat down to drain the large blister that the leather strap of my new sandals had made on one heel. The children wanted to watch that too and crowded around me, pushing and shoving each other, staring at the long needle I was injecting carefully into the blister. Maybe they were hoping I'd cry. Then, from one of the nearby houses, an old woman in the usual black dress and scarf and heavy cotton stockings of Greek peasant women rushed up to me with a bowl of water and gauze bandage. Before I could stop her, she had bathed my foot and was wrapping the bandage around it. I glanced at Martin, certain that he would be sharing my amazement at this unexpected and sympathetic gesture, but he was looking away from me into the distance.

That evening we walked back into Volisous to have dinner at the only taverna. We ate the sliced tomatoes, the fried potatoes, and broiled chicken in silence. I entertained myself by watching the men in the doorway of the taverna playing a game with large marbles.

During his second beer, Martin spoke across the great chasm that had opened between us. "Miriam, I think we should separate when we get back to the States."

I looked at him unbelieving, suddenly chilled in the warm evening air, panic tightening my chest. "But why?" I asked stupidly.

Martin raised his eyebrows critically in reply. We both knew the answer, and I knew that anything else I said would sound like a cliché. Such moments permit little sophistication.

I let the tears slide down my cheeks as I mumbled over and over, "Please don't do this, Martin. Please."

The men in the doorway of the taverna stopped playing their game and watched us instead, glancing at each other from time to time. I was embarrassed but unable to stop crying and pleading. Finally I wiped the tears away with my soiled napkin and related the nightmare of the pressure chamber.

It didn't win Martin's sympathy, however, merely confirmed his perception of our marriage as totally failed. "After such an obvious warning, you wanted to stay with me?" In his voice I heard a genuine concern for my soundness of mind.

I nodded, miserable but encouraged by his apparent sincerity.

"You have an unregenerate heart," he concluded, looking at me almost tenderly, as he hadn't done for weeks.

Since then, during the last five years, I've come to recognize that I am not a casual lover and that I take my loves as seriously as I do my writing. They are inexorably connected, both surfacing from the deepest part of my being. Many theories have evolved regarding the similarity of sexual and creative energy. Some say they detract from each other. Some say they complement each other. I find them often in conflict, yet equally desirable.

As we continued to sit in the taverna drinking beer for another hour, I sensed that Martin would reconsider if I said nothing further to persuade him. I was determined to change his mind by giving whatever he wanted, including silence. He seemed to be trying too, making insignificant but humorous comments about the day's events. Something I had done was the right thing, and I was relieved enough not to ask myself what it was.

Just as we were deciding to leave, remembering with weariness the two-mile walk to our campsite, the old woman who had attended to my blister earlier in the day came to our table and insisted on inspecting my foot. The painful sore was nearly healed by the salty sea water in which Martin and I had been swimming all afternoon. When she was satisfied, she stood up and looked at me for a long moment. Her black eyes were watery, dark and mysterious like tide pools. Her skin was covered with interwoven wrinkles like the threads of a tapestry. A woman of indeterminate age, she revealed in her face the encounters with time and struggle and loss that lay ahead of me, waiting patiently for me. We recognized something in each other too, as if we knew each other's lives, not the details of course, but the essence. I fell in love with Greece at that moment, and I began to separate from Martin in my mind.

Martin and I did a lot of night-sky watching that summer in Greece, still so warm at midnight that I could sit outside wearing a sleeveless dress. We got drunk together slowly, night after night, sinking down into a shared, very sad resignation. It became clear to me that our failure to love each other well, to create a reality from a possibility, for whatever the reasons, was an offense against some higher order of existence. I believed it was a violation of the purity, beauty, and order of that island with its blue water meeting a paler blue sky, its blindingly golden beaches, its square whitewashed houses, its kind and generous people. I never spoke to Martin about it. Even now I don't like to dwell on it much. It comes back to me most often when I am considering a metaphor for purity, or an unpossessable kind of beauty, that blue, white and gold world still shimmering somewhere in the sunlight, bright and free.

A noisy game of Frisbee had commenced behind her, and the waterfront was rapidly being populated by office workers diverting themselves between a day on the job and a hot bus ride home. Directly in front of her, obstructing a previously uncluttered view of the river, two young men who had removed their shirts were leaning against the stone embankment. They were talking animatedly, gesturing, with cans of beer in their hands, toward the sailboats. She couldn't hear their conversation but an occasional "Hey, man!" drifted her way and intruded on her recollections.

She stared at the broad suntanned shoulders, the narrow hips in faded Levi's and wondered why the wide maternal build of some women was so unattractive to her, what it might mean. She disliked large breasts, heaviness of any sort, admired most of all the body of the classical dancer, light yet powerful, like a panther.

The two men turned suddenly, almost in unison, strolled toward her bench and sat down, grinning, one on each side of her. She knew what was coming and was annoyed rather than frightened. She didn't want to relinquish the bench just yet but knew that she probably would.

"Hey, baby," began the one with short greasy blond hair. "Want some beer?" He spoke with a drawl that was slurred with drunkenness.

"No, thanks." Miriam continued to watch the sailboats.

"How about a nice smoke then?" said the other, pulling a joint from his shirt pocket. She didn't look at him either but saw that his hands were grimy. He smelled of sweat and day-old boozing.

"No, thanks."

"Well," said the blond, "we don't seem to be able to satisfy this young lady at all, Joe." They both laughed.

Joe leaned toward her, putting a hand on her leg and squeezing it slightly. "How about you satisfying *us* then?"

She turned toward him finally, and saw that his teeth were yellowed and one in the front was missing. She stood up and took several steps away from them, then turned around. "Why don't you satisfy each other instead?"

As she walked away, one of them yelled after her, "Fuck you, bitch!" They laughed and hooted together, slapping their thighs.

She continued walking along the seawall, trying not to be angry, wanting the beauty of the place to erase the ugliness created by the people there, and to comfort her one last time.

Like so many intense relationships, mine with Martin evolved into a struggle for power. One afternoon, during the spring we were planning to leave the United States again, we drove to the Gifford Pinchot National Forest. In the car with us were two helium-filled balloons with the words "Love" and "Joy" printed on them. This was 1976 and the Age of Aquarius was still giving posthumous birth to such sentimental gestures. Martin had bought the balloons from a Vietnam veteran with no legs who wheeled around downtown Portland talking about Jesus.

It was one of those warm balmy days in Oregon between the long rainy months that lead up to a damp summer, a day that suggests it's possible to have a life without raincoats and mufflers. Martin was unusually cheerful, whistling a popular lovesong and smiling at me periodically. Until we left the freeway he let his hand rest on my thigh and I covered it with my own. I was confused though by this high-spirited mood, unexpected and almost untimely. Our life together since the trip abroad had been maintained through routine and lowered expectations.

On a narrow winding section of the road up the mountain, where he had to slow to twenty miles per hour, Martin glanced at me. "Have you ever wondered how it would be if we had a kid?"

I was surprised. He knew I didn't want children. "No, Martin, I haven't." The thought of finding myself one day trapped in the center of a nuclear family always sent me into an emotional tailspin.

When we reached the deadend of the mountain road we had chosen and parked, I took the balloon that said "Love" out of the car and Martin took "Joy." I think now that we both knew exactly what we were doing but it seemed then that he only accidently let go of the string in his hand. We watched silently as "Joy" floated away from us into the blue sky. We watched it for a long time, until it disappeared, then looked at each other and at "Love."

"Don't," Martin said, just as I let the string go.

"I have to," I insisted. "When 'Joy' leaves, 'Love' must follow." I didn't blame him at all because the opposite is equally true.

Martin stared for several long moments into the distance at the neighboring mountain peak toward which "Love" was moving. Then he got back into the car and turned the key in the ignition.

That night we lay in bed and got high. We were both too emotionally bruised to touch each other. Besides, in contrast to my relationship with Sasha, life with Martin wasn't particularly sexual. It's an irony and an understatement to say that *our* relationship existed primarily in our minds.

Martin turned to me suddenly and said, "You know that time on Chios?"

I nodded, immediately alert.

"I had no intention of leaving you. Really." He reached out and gently laid his hand on my arm.

I lay still, shocked, barely breathing, as I realized that my tearful begging, my humiliation before those Greek men in that taverna in Volisous, had been enough to recharge Martin's flagging sense of power over me.

After a pause Martin added, "Please don't leave me either."

Such a straightforward request was unusual for Martin. I couldn't look at him or speak. If I hadn't been stoned, I might have tried to explain but in the end I was glad I didn't. Nothing could have healed that wound by then. Instead I watched the candle flame throw flickering shadows on the ceiling. I might have responded more honestly if I hadn't been paralyzed by my long-repressed anger. "Of course I won't leave you," I replied finally. It was easier and I really didn't know it was too late.

What had been initially an intense and ecstatic connection ended peacefully, uneventfully for me, like a defective fuse.

Miriam entered the cool dimness of Marcel's Bar and Grill and removed her dark glasses. She was relieved not to recognize any of the customers. The interior of Marcel's was less sleazy than most of the gay bars in Portland, with its natural wood paneling, Boston ferns, and classical music. Yet this conformity to trend also gave the place a characterless quality. Only the artwork above the booths was distinctive, usually male nudes that, in Miriam's opinion, reduced the atmosphere to a slightly more refined offshoot of the nearby men's bathhouse.

Miriam ordered a beer and took it to the brick courtyard in the back. Sasha would know to look for her there since Marcel's appealed to Miriam only in warmer weather when she could sit outside. Unlike the indoor area, the courtyard was a haven of rustic disrepair. The stone floor was uneven and caused the wooden tables to rock. The chairs were the uncomfortable metal sort used in high school auditoriums. In the eaves of the roofs above, pigeons were cooing to each other. There was no one seated at any of the picnic tables and Miriam chose the one by the small fountain where a stone child of uncertain sex and age poured water out of a fish's mouth. It was pleasant, one of the most pleasant things she could think of at the moment, to sit outside with a drink, waiting for the sky to turn its myriad, subtle shades of blue and then disappear into the darkness, waiting for the stars to reappear.

I have a friend who likes to say that people marry their own pathology. Sasha is the only person I've ever consciously wanted to marry. The proof is that, besides my mother, Sasha is the only person I've ever allowed to call me "darling"; it makes me feel owned. Perhaps I thought a public declaration would make her faithful to me.

I will now agree with the theorists that the desire to marry

37

is a desire to possess and be possessed totally, no matter how loving, gentle, and concerned it superficially appears. At least for people like me who are basically non-compromisers. My desire to possess and be possessed by a woman who, like my mother, is physically beautiful, emotionally inconsistent, and unable to be possessed has created a disaster for both of us. If I ever find myself wanting to marry anyone again, I'll know it's time to run.

Miriam looked at her watch. It was six-fifteen. Sasha was late. Six hours obviously hadn't been enough. Miriam went to the bathroom. As she sat there staring at the blackboard in front of her that was meant for graffiti, she remembered how Sasha always carried a piece of chalk to write messages to her when they were at Marcel's together. "Sasha loves Miriam." "Miriam, I love you. Sasha." The blackboard was empty of messages today. Miriam was grateful that Sasha wasn't writing her love for the Other Woman. She wished she could flush her nausea down the toilet.

When she returned to the courtyard, there were two lovers at another table, staring into each other's eyes over glasses of champagne.

Sasha and I fell in love in a bar, staring into each other's eyes, just like that. Moral: Never put any faith in a relationship that begins in a bar. Of course, since I spend a lot of time in them myself, I suppose this could happen again, but I'm on guard against it now.

The loved one is so idealistically attractive at the outset, perfect in mind and body, but by the end is disgustingly flawed. A clear, unwavering awareness of this process would probably make it difficult to fall passionately in love. I don't want to love blindly again, trying to please a beautiful and inconsistent woman, the way I tried to please my mother and never could. Yet being passionately in love is one of the great joys of human existence. Sasha's laugh, for example, is like a sweet-voiced bell that is still ringing in my head.

Miriam looked up from contemplating the foam in the bottom of her beer glass to find Sasha sitting across the table. Her watch said six forty-five.

"Sorry." Sasha looked sincere. She always did.

"It seems like we're saying that to each other a lot lately." Miriam refilled her glass from the pitcher Sasha had brought with her to the courtyard. Again one of those unpleasant accusatory remarks came to mind, and this time she was successful in squelching it before it slipped out.

Sasha reached across the table and took Miriam's hands. "You seem far away," she whispered.

Miriam didn't look up or reply. She already had a vague premonition of the dialogue that was closing in on them.

"Your hands are so cold," continued Sasha, "on such a warm day too." Her voice was soft and conciliatory, what Miriam called "the compensation tone," the one Sasha used when she wished she were elsewhere, with someone else, or felt guilty about something she had done or was planning to do.

Miriam raised her eyes and looked into Sasha's as candidly and coolly as she could. "Rigor mortis," she explained. "My soul is dead."

"Oh, Miriam!" Sasha laughed softly at this bit of melodrama. After a pause, when Miriam said nothing more, Sasha added, "I do love you very much, you know."

"But there's no hope, is there?" They were both operating from force of habit, Sasha with her declarations of love and Miriam with her doubts. Even if Sasha said "yes," Miriam knew that she could never really trust her again, not enough to take the risks of commitment.

Sasha stroked Miriam's right hand with her own. "Not unless you can accept me the way I am."

Again Miriam remembered the man in her dream drowning in shit. "And to do that means not accepting myself the way *I* am. I know." She looked away at the ivy growing tenaciously between the broken bricks of the courtyard wall and sighed, uncertain still of her strength against the charm that had seduced her before into agreements she knew she couldn't keep. "My plane doesn't leave until noon. You could stay with me tonight."

Sasha's lips tightened immediately in a negative response.

"Why not?"

"Because we said last night was the last."

Miriam leaned forward. "We can change what we said. You do — often."

Sasha took her hand away from Miriam's. "I'm going away too, to

39

the beach."

"Revolving doors, huh?" Miriam commented sarcastically. "I guess I thought all your talk about a future together meant that my wishes would be given consideration."

"They are, but I have other plans and I won't change them for you."

"Not even for the last night we can have together for a long time?" In spite of their agreement, and all the disagreements, Miriam couldn't quite believe that Sasha didn't want this too.

"No."

Miriam saw the waiter approaching to take their dinner order. "I'm not hungry."

Sasha smiled warmly at the blond young man in the apron. "I don't think we're ready to eat yet. Thanks."

"Okay." He returned the smile and glanced at Miriam. He raised his eyebrows at them, a silent comment that said he was aware they were having an argument. "I'll just come back a little later then."

"You just do that," muttered Miriam as the waiter slid over to the love-struck couple and took their order for another split of champagne.

"I meant it about keeping in touch, darling. I'm missing you already," Sasha said sadly.

Miriam was looking at a spot just above Sasha's head. She wanted to be free of this relationship now much more than Sasha had in March. She wanted to be really free. She lowered her eyes to Sasha's and, though there was a knot in her throat, managed to keep her voice level. "I don't want to keep in touch. I want it to end tomorrow when I fly out of here."

"You're retaliating like that because I won't give you what you want," complained Sasha.

"And aren't you? Haven't you been doing that all along? Protecting yourself from getting too involved with me by being involved elsewhere? Or am I being presumptuous? Sorry!"

Tears began to slide down Sasha's cheeks, but Miriam was, at last, too exhausted to placate or console her. She sipped the rest of her beer and once more considered whether Sasha had refused to love her, or was merely incapable, or if she herself was unworthy.

When they finally left the bar, without eating, and stood outside to say good-bye, Sasha clung to her. "I can hardly bear to let you go."

Miriam thought of saying, "Don't then," but she knew Sasha wasn't prepared to go that far. She walked only half a block, then stopped to watch Sasha walking away, light and jaunty as ever. She watched her until she disappeared into the dusk and smog of the city.

"What makes you think you can be a writer?"

Such moments.

It crossed my mind to call her name, to call Sasha back, to tell her that I loved her in spite of everything. But why? And do I, really? You can't call anything back. And I really wouldn't want to. I couldn't go through it again. And it would happen like that with Sasha, again and again.

They say that maternal attachment is the strongest human tie. As I stood there, I remembered how, after I started college and moved into my own apartment across town, my mother knew whenever I was in the middle of a crisis and would call: "Something is going wrong in your life, darling. I can feel it. Tell me." By contrast, I hardly ever called her and went to see her even less. I was too busy. My life was full of other people. It occurred to me how lonely my mother must have been. They say it's natural for a mother to feel abandoned when a child leaves home, but I was her only child, just the two of us for eighteen years. An aching desolation lives in the heart when a familiar and still desired touch or tone of voice is suddenly gone from your life.

I realized then, standing on the street corner like a daydreamer, that my mother will never call me again no matter how wrong my life goes, that I'd lost irretrievably, without ever appreciating it, something unique. I saw what it was that I've been so desperate to find, what I wanted both Martin and Sasha to be for me: someone who could make that same connection, someone who could break into the solitude of my heart the way my mother did.

Miriam wandered around the apartment that was empty of her personal possessions. They were packed in boxes in a local mini-storage unit. She had found a sublet for the summer, one she hoped she could trust with the larger pieces of furniture. For a long time she lay smoking on the double bed, trying not to think of Sasha and the Other Woman driving to the coast. Finally she poured herself a water glass full of brandy.

41

No one will be able to create with me the kind of closeness that my mother and I had in spite of our passionate conflicts, and I must stop searching. It's self-defeating because my mother, while she was very beautiful, was also manipulative, while she was emotionally spontaneous, was also inconsistent, while she was clever, was also sarcastic. I was never able to win her approval or to feel loved by her. Yet from her I learned what love is, a love that cannot be fulfilled.

I must also stop looking at the lights on the hill over the houses where we all lived such senseless lives. What I said to Sasha is the truth: I am dead inside, spiritually lifeless. I don't know why I'm trying to write; I have nothing worth saying. I can no longer trust my perceptions. Everything is relative. Nothing makes sense. The difference between life and fiction is that fiction makes sense. Maybe I can disappear into one.

As soon as I finish this brandy, I will try to sleep. It's very, very late. The freeway is almost silent. Tomorrow I'm flying to Europe. Sasha was jealous of my love for Europe, as if it were another woman taking me from her. When I spoke of it, either in terms of the past or the future, she would grow silent and turn away from me. I stopped talking about it but, like a third party in a triangular love affair, it continued to hover around the edge of my consciousness and she knew.

In the morning when Miriam woke, too early and hung over, in that place between awareness and sleep, that Never-never land where she could imagine almost anything, her best lines of poetry, the face of a lost love, she laid an arm across the other side of the bed and found it empty. She opened her eyes. Of course, she reasoned with herself. Sasha wouldn't be there for her anymore.

"There is no continuity," she whispered to the one thin crack extending itself across the white ceiling.

PART TWO

Rebecca drove Miriam to the airport, rehearsing aloud for last minute approval, the details of her own flight still a month away. "So I land in Lyon, then take a bus. . . ." She had recently begun putting henna on her hair and Miriam was admiring the reddish-brown sheen that was more obvious in daylight.

"Right," said Miriam. "And then a taxi to the farm."

"What will the weather be like? I'm not bringing much, you know. I want them to be the right things." Rebecca was a fastidious dresser, always perfectly groomed. It had taken some persuasion on Miriam's part to convince her to leave the hairstyling equipment behind.

Miriam watched a fine drizzle begin to coat the windshield. "I'll write as soon as I get there and let you know."

Rebecca had never been outside the United States and spoke no French. She was nervous and uncertain of her ability to cope. Miriam wanted to be reassuring but for the first time she was apprehensive about her own flight. At the point of departure, of physical separation from her accustomed environment, she was not experiencing the joyous sense of rootlessness and unattached adventure she'd relished five years earlier.

Rebecca was Miriam's oldest friend in Portland. They'd gone to college together and, with other friends, had shared a house during those years. While Miriam was still foundering through her last year with Martin, Rebecca, always a step ahead of the crowd, re-defined herself as a radical lesbian separatist and gave away all her books and records by men. Like many others, she had gradually moved to a less extreme position and was now considered, by many of her former friends, to be not politically correct.

What touched Miriam deeply about Rebecca was her loyalty. In any conflict, though she might not agree with Miriam's reasoning, she would listen compassionately and stand beside her in public situations. Whether participant or observer, through the good times and the failures, she knew all the facts of Miriam's adult life, and more of the nuance than anyone else. Since March Miriam had avoided most of her friends, re-treating into that crazy solitude where she could indulge her anger and rejection, yet maintain a public image of cool transcendence, but in Rebecca she had confided all the embarrassing details and her feelings about them.

Rebecca herself was secretive and disturbingly private. Miriam felt that she never had access to her friend, that Rebecca did not share herself with equal openness. During the last few months especially, Miriam had sensed an even greater distance between them and was surprised when Rebecca accepted her rather offhanded invitation to visit Simon's farm while she was there.

The check-in line at the airport was interminable. Just in front of Miriam an Arab student returning home had three hundred and fifty dollars' worth of excess baggage to be tagged and, with the aid of confused friends and relatives, was trying to negotiate the price. Most of the other passengers seemed to have several hyperactive children in tow. By the time Miriam's one bag was taken from her and she'd been assigned a seat, she had the start of a migraine.

There was just enough time for a drink in the lounge. As Miriam stirred the ice around the Manhattan, preflight panic, which she'd never experienced before, invaded her — a fearful suspicion that she would lose her life in the attempt to escape, that even if she survived, the attempt to escape would be fruitless. She'd had terrifying nightmares of running and being caught in the months that followed her mother's death. Death. She knew that the plane would crash.

Rebecca sipped a glass of Perrier water. "Little early in the day for bourbon, isn't it?"

"I guess I'm tense." Miriam's hand shook slightly as she lit a cigarette with Rebecca's gold-plated lighter.

"I'm glad you're getting away for a while. You obviously need a rest."

"Yeah, I suppose." Miriam smiled wryly at Rebecca, grateful for the concern and appraising the way she had, with her Christian Dior eyeglass frames, razor-cut hair style, and raw silk pantsuit, of looking so casual and relaxed. "The novel has been a strain. I didn't realize when I began how much hard lonely work it would be. I've been weighted down by it."

"And by Sasha." Rebecca wanted honesty. Another quality Miriam liked in her was this unwillingness to insult the intelligence of those she loved. Yet Rebecca had a tact that allowed her to be direct without tipping anyone's self-concept too far off its axis.

"I suppose she's had something to do with it." Miriam scanned the other women in the lounge — the business executives, the wives, the secretaries — and wondered if any of those choices would be easier than her own. "What bothers me is realizing I've been so lacking in perception. I feel foolish. My pride is suffering — not my heart, necessarily."

"Ouch! That's a bit pompous, isn't it?"

Miriam knew Rebecca was right. In fact, her heart was shattered.

Rebecca smiled. "You know, everyone who knew you and Sasha considered you an established couple except Sasha."

Miriam smiled back wryly, nodding.

"Why not fall in love with a potter or a weaver?" Rebecca asked lightly.

"Sure," Miriam said, "I'm open to anything. How about a plumber or a politician?" Miriam laughed. "Or a man?"

Rebecca gave her a quizzical look, began to say something, then fell silent. After a moment she said, "You've had a certain kind of love with Sasha, Miriam, passionate, ecstatic, overwhelming — and destructive. There are other kinds of love, you know."

"I suppose."

"When you've been away from Sasha awhile, you'll see," Rebecca said reassuringly.

"Yeah, I suppose."

Rebecca laughed. "Will you stop saying that?"

Miriam laughed too. "My vocabulary has been substantially reduced lately by an overdose of bullshit."

Rebecca reached across the table and squeezed Miriam's hand. "Try to relax for a while, okay?"

"Oh, don't worry. I intend to do exactly that — red wine and all." After a moment she laughed again, shaking her head. "Last week sometime we argued about whether the whole is equal to or greater than the sum of its parts. I said, 'Equal to.' It felt like a matter of life and death."

Rebecca did not reply. They both knew that the correct answer would not necessarily be the truth.

Miriam finished her drink with some reluctance. "I'd better board."

She discovered with a sense of predestined fatality that her seat on the crowded charter flight was directly behind a woman with an overly tired, fussy, and periodically screaming child. The one drink had only increased the pain building in her head and she was impatient for the flight attendant to come around with the trolley so she could get some aspirin.

After I accepted Simon's invitation with a cablegram, I wrote him a long letter in which I tried to explain that my mental outlook was not good and why, without saying anything too disturbing, and that I needed a haven from serious thought. His reply indicated that he would be overjoyed to see me at last, since he'd invited me every year with no result. He didn't ask any questions. I've found that most people are really very understanding about the emotions that arise over the end of intimate relationships. "Separation anxiety," as it's called in the world of social work, is one of those universal experiences.

It's a tribute to something substantial in the human spirit that Simon and I have maintained our friendship at all. We haven't seen each other in five years and, though our letters have been sporadic, a bond must have been created during the time Martin and I spent on Simon's farm, Les Bluets, and obviously we haven't wanted to let it go.

Martin and I were on the way to Switzerland when we met Simon and Richard. Between buses in Annonay, we chose an outdoor table at a cafe near the station and ordered coffee. While I wrote in my journal, which I insisted on doing daily though it bored Martin, he rolled cigarettes. After a few minutes two men sat down at the table next to us and, assuming from our clothing and gear that we were English-speaking, began talking to Martin. They were both British and introduced themselves as Simon and Richard.

Richard was from Edinburgh, a heavyset man with a goatee and brown hair that was beginning to thin. It was a warm day and his face was flushed, but I came to know that this was a characteristic caused by his excessive drinking habit. Simon, who had moved to London from Australia, was small and wiry with blond hair that was turning gray prematurely. He reminded me then of an elf and that image was reinforced as I spent more time with him. His blue eyes flashed with enthusiasm when he talked and his sudden laugh was infectious.

One hour and many glasses of brown beer later, Simon invited us to stay awhile on his nearby farm. Both of the men had flats and jobs in London, but lived in France as long as possible during the summer. It was Simon's greatest pleasure to play host to as many friends and travelers as he could entice to Les Bluets.

Richard leaned toward me across the table with a smile playing around his mouth. "We've been best friends for years, but, to tell you the truth, we're alone there now and getting a bit tired of each other."

Simon shook his head sadly. "It's a fact! Even Richard, the world-renowned storyteller, is running dry. Last night he tried to tell me one I'd already heard."

"Can you imagine such a thing?" asked Richard, still surprised at himself. "Won't you both come along and help me save my reputation? I badly need the inspiration of unspoiled ears."

For Martin and me as well, the invitation provided a timely rescue from each other's exclusive company, and quite drunk, we were easily persuaded. Besides, our new acquaintances were so eager and amusing it was impossible to refuse.

Simon was almost as heavy a drinker as Richard and they were both aspiring writers like myself. The conversational philosophizing with Simon kept Martin entertained, while the writing interested me. I was impressed the first evening when, after a few glasses, Richard began reciting from memory the ballads of Robert Burns. Each evening we took turns reading our poetry to each other in front of the fire.

"I like your work, Miriam, but you can't read worth a damn," Simon commented after a few days, when he was comfortable enough with me.

We all laughed and I blushed. "I know," I said.

"And you're full of shit!" Richard shouted at Simon, then burst into loud drunken laughter.

It is an idyllic time in my memory, one I enjoy relating to friends who have never been abroad when I'm trying to convince them to go. In fact, it was the best two weeks of that entire summer, that fateful journey. Fateful because nothing about my relationship with Martin was ever quite good for me afterward.

Initially I formed a much closer bond with Richard than I did with Simon. Richard and I shared a love of poetry that was stronger and a desire to write professionally. We left the discussions of world affairs and economics to Martin and Simon, and took long walks during which Richard taught me the names of the local wildflowers and guided me through abandoned farmhouses.

The night before Martin and I were leaving there was a full moon. At ten o'clock, both feeling restless, Richard and I decided to walk to a bar in Garance, about a mile away. For a while the only sound was our footsteps falling softly on the tarred country road.

Finally Richard broke the silence. "You and Martin aren't getting along so well, are you?"

"No. Is it that obvious?"

"A bit. Maybe I'm just sensititve to it."

I nodded. "No doubt."

"You could stay on here, you know, through the summer."

I was surprised at the suggestion. "Without Martin?" Then I remembered the times when I'd wanted to leave Martin but hadn't known where to go that was far enough.

Richard stopped walking abruptly and took my hand. In the moonlight I could just see his face and the sincere devotion that glazed it. "I think I'm falling in love with you is what I mean, Miriam."

I panicked. "Oh, no, you can't, Richard!"

"Miriam, I could stop drinking and really write if you were with me all the time." His voice was insistent and he spoke uncharacteristically fast. He began to put his arms around me but I moved away, trying to be gentle in refusing the embrace.

The starry sky, the cool clear darkness, even the smell of the grass were suddenly suspect, a lovely background that had lured me into a trap. I was a foreigner in a landscape I knew well. When I spoke, what I said to Richard was what I needed to say to extricate myself from an awkward situation. "I'm really in love with Martin. And even if it ended tomorrow, I'd probably still be in love with him for a long time."

We resumed walking to the village in silence. There are only two bars in Garance and the one we entered was so crowded, noisy, and filled with smoke that no one noticed us. We ordered two cognacs and sat at a table in the corner sipping them and not looking at each other.

Finally Richard spoke in a low voice, unnecessarily since no one in the bar besides myself could understand English. "Doesn't it mean anything to you that I love you so much?"

"Yes, it means a lot. I love you too. Not in the same way, that's all." I was so nervous that I lit another Gauloise with the one I was putting out.

"Would it have been different in a different time and place?" He was pleading for some strand of hope, something for the future. His eyes were sad and the pale greenness of them was surrounded by bloodshot tissue.

"Of course. But I don't know what the difference would have been." I was prevaricating. Actually, it probably wouldn't have been that different and I should have admitted it. At any rate, I didn't, and still don't, want to save anyone from a bad habit. How is it possible to love someone as much as I did Richard — and I did — and yet be repelled by the thought of physical intimacy? And to desire someone physically — as I did Martin — and yet know that person doesn't return the love? It didn't make sense to me then, nor does it now.

"How can we change the pattern of our attractions?" I asked Rebecca once, "so that we are passionately attracted to people we genuinely love and who genuinely love us?"

"Friends, in other words."

I nodded, only then realizing that that's what it would mean.

"Maybe it's better if we don't," she said. "We'll keep our friends longer."

I had to agree, but I think it's damned unfair.

The next morning Richard started drinking at dawn and had passed out by the time Simon was ready to drive us to the station.

Simon shook his head. "He's got it bad, my poor friend."

Martin laughed. "Does he do this often?"

Simon looked at me as he answered the question. "Hardly ever, like this." As he climbed into the driver's seat to warm up the old Citroen's engine, he reached into his pocket and handed me an envelope. "He asked me to give you this."

In the envelope was one of the most perfect poems I've ever read. What it described was a butterfly breaking out of the

51

chrysalis, the images precise and coherent. Its meaning spoke quite obviously of erotic love. Martin read it over my shoulder.

A half hour later, after we'd said good-bye to Simon, thanking him profusely for his hospitality and promised to write, and stood alone together by the bus we'd be taking out of Annonay, Martin looked at me critically. "The guy's in love with you, isn't he?"

"So he said last night."

"You could stay on with him," he said, echoing Richard's invitation.

I went into the women's washroom in the bus station, re-read the poem, and cried, wondering if, in spite of Richard's drinking problem, I was giving up something precious by not staying.

Last week, as I was packing my poetry books, I found the poem. It's as perfect as ever, as fine as any of the excellent poetry I've read since that summer. I sat there on the floor of my apartment with the worn page in my lap and began to wonder how it would be to see Richard again. He's planning to meet me at the airport and we'll drive to the farm together. We've written only two or three times, superficial letters on my part, drunken ones on his. I really don't know much more about love now than I did then except that there's nothing remotely fair or just about it. That winged baby in the sky shoots his arrows so indiscriminately — and sometimes even with malice. But then, his name is Cupid — not love.

During the crowded turmoil of the baggage claim at Gatwick, and then the long walk down the narrow white corridors with large plate glass windows that overlook the endless airstrips and the planes slowly beginning or concluding their journeys, Miriam was sure she would emerge into a waiting area full of strangers and there would be no one with a familiar face, though Simon had written that Richard intended to meet her. She walked quickly under the customs sign that read "Nothing to Declare," suspecting that she'd be stopped and searched though she had, in fact, nothing to declare, and doubtful that, even if Richard was there, they would be able to find each other in such a throng.

A hand on her shoulder made her turn sharply and she wobbled, suddenly dizzy, barely recognizing the round rosy face as she was heartily hugged and kissed. Holding her firmly by the shoulders, Richard stood back and laughed. "You looked like you were wandering around in a total daze."

"I was." Through the blur of her disorientation, she decided that his three-piece suit gave him an air of sophistication she'd never associated with him. At the farm, where he'd dressed in faded baggy cords and loose shirts, it had been easy to forget that he made his living by writing contracts for London's largest computer firm.

Picking up her bag, Richard steered her expertly through the maze of the parking structure and minutes later they were on the motorway to London. During the hour's drive she nearly fell asleep after his polite interest in the details of her transatlantic flight and her observation that England seemed much the same. London, as they dodged through the heavy traffic, was still a gray, foul-smelling and over-crowded city whose architecture, crooked streets, and abiding sense of history tugged unexpectedly at her affections.

"It isn't the same at all, you know," responded Richard to her sentimental memories. "It's become a disgusting city. A lot more violent since you and Martin were here. Noisy, crazy! And those bloody Arabs!"

Miriam was always surprised at the conservatism of her British friends, their sense of being invaded by the members of the countries Britain had dominated for hundreds of years. It seemed to her that they were simply getting a karmic return now as the oil-rich Arabs bought the pieces of England that the English could no longer afford. "It doesn't affect you personally though, does it?"

"But it does! They hang their bloody laundry out to dry all over Kensington. They have parties all hours of the night. Christ!" He parked the car in the alley next to his local pub and took her arm as they walked over the broken cobblestones. "You see, you're back in town an hour and already you've got me wound up about something!"

Miriam protested her innocence with a laugh as he swung open the door of the pub and they were swallowed by the cheerful noisiness of its afternoon inhabitants. Richard settled her at a quieter corner table while he bought them some lunch. The Fox and Hounds was typical of English pubs as Miriam remembered them — the ornate bar hung with shining glassware and tended by a friendly though probably insolent publican, the small round tables, the neighbors who considered the place another home leaning against the bar making it difficult to order, and the air full of lively conversation and blue with smoke. It lacked the wood paneling, hanging ferns, pool tables, and jukeboxes of the American taverns, nor was it darkened in an attitude of Puritan disapproval but lit instead with beautiful chandelier lamps of multicolored glass. A black and white cocker spaniel dozed by the door waiting for one of the elderly gray-haired men gathered at the bar, all of whom were arguing loudly about "the Irish question."

Miriam studied Richard as he approached the table with his hands full. His hair was thinner and he'd gained weight, but his face still had the sweet, mild-mannered quality she'd remembered.

With a flourish Richard set the food and drinks in front of her. "Have some good English fare, milady."

"If I recall, this is about the extent of it."

"Nonsense! There's fish and chips, isn't there? We'll have some tonight, I promise you." Though he grinned at her, she knew he wasn't kidding. She remembered him saying once that, when in England, he rarely ate anything else.

"Great." Miriam looked down at the crusty mashed potatoes and knew that beneath was a mixture of ground beef and peas. Shepherd's pie was her favorite English dish. For the first time in weeks she began to eat hungrily.

"I was thinking of leaving for Les Bluets tomorrow morning," Richard said between mouthfuls of food. "That all right?"

Miriam nodded. "Couldn't be better."

"You'll miss seeing the new sights of London though," he said, "like the punks."

Miriam paused in her eating to reply, "We have them too, you know."

Richard shook his head. "I was just up to my folks' place yesterday. My younger sister, she's had her hair dyed all different colors, draws whiskers on her face like a cat, wears the strangest clothes you've ever seen. It drives my mother mad."

"Well, I don't think we can expect them to be any better than we were, or are."

They both glanced down at the three whiskies Richard had just consumed with his lunch. "At least we believed in love," he said.

"Did we really?" Miriam asked. Their shared smile had a cynical edge.

"So — how's the writing going then?" he asked changing the subject.

"Terrible."

"What you need is inspiration. That's why you're here."

"What I need is a new life."

"We'll see what we can do about that too, eh?" He reached out and laid the palm of his hand gently against her cheek, only for a moment.

When their eyes met, his reassuring and warm, Miriam remembered his former feelings for her with some apprehension. She wondered what Simon may have told Richard about her lifestyle. "How's your health?" she asked, changing the subject this time. "Simon wrote that you'd had some problems." Miriam pushed the last mound of mashed potatoes onto her fork and briefly considered ordering another portion.

"My doctor told me if I didn't quit drinking whisky I'd be dead within a year. And I'm supposed to walk a mile a day," he said as he swallowed the last of the liquor and chased it with special bitter.

"Do you?"

He shrugged. "Oh, you know me, I never take anything too seriously."

Miriam shook her head, reproving him. "Oh, Richard."

"And that was two years ago, mind." He winked at her.

Miriam was amused along with him at this successful evasion of fate and medical prophecy. Relieved not to have lost the pleasure she'd known before in Richard's company, she smiled and clinked her glass against his.

Richard turned pragmatic though as they left the pub. "You look tired and I should get back to the office."

His flat was large enough for a single person, moderately comfortable, but, as she would have suspected had she thought about it, there was a chaotic tangle of clothes littering the bedroom floor, a kitchen of unwashed dishes and empty beer bottles, and stacks of books on the living room chairs. Since he'd offered it to her, she collapsed onto his unmade bed. Though exhausted, she slept fitfully, entering the past as a bad dream.

There was a scratch on Sasha's cheek. I ran a finger along it. "What's this?"

"Oh, an earring did that. A little pink rosebud," Sasha explained, smiling.

"With sharp thorns that got too close?" I knew it was the Other Woman's earring. I'd seen her wearing them.

Sasha sighed and put her arms around me. "I have treated

you badly, haven't I?"

I didn't deny it.

Miriam woke in tears, only slightly refreshed, when she heard Richard's key turn in the lock.

In his favorite fish and chips shop, just off Bayswater Road, they were standing by the counter waiting for their order and arguing about feminism.

"I just don't understand it, you know. This Women's Movement thing. You're cutting yourself off from half the human race." Having changed to Levi's and a corduroy jacket, Richard looked much younger. His interest, though genuine, sounded unsophisticated to Miriam.

"Wait a minute, Richard. It's men who've cut *women* off. It's men who've told women they can't vote, can't go to medical school, can't use birth control! Men are the original separatists!" Miriam had thought this argument through well enough and used it often enough to be good at delivering it and she recognized the confusion on Richard's face. As the dialogue got louder and more intense, she noticed that the Indonesian man frying the fish was more involved with their conversation than with their food.

"Well, *I've* never said a woman couldn't do whatever she wanted!" insisted Richard, defending himself.

Miriam didn't respond. It was the old individualist defense that she'd heard a hundred times. Suddenly she was weary of the topic. Positive change in either political or personal life remained hopeless to her at the moment.

"Am I missing some important point, Miriam?" Richard's eyes searched hers earnestly.

"Yes." She paused, wanting to somehow keep the gap that was opening between them from widening any farthur. "Look, Richard, I'm obviously not separating myself from you or I wouldn't have come six thousand miles and spent a thousand dollars to be with you and Simon this summer, now would I?" Miriam smiled at him and knew that her smile reminded him that there was a bond between them. At the moment, needing the support of friends as she did, she wanted this bond to be stronger than any theory or movement.

They gathered up the fish and chips wrapped in butcher paper and strolled down Kensington Church Street eating.

For four years I've built my life almost entirely around women, socially and intellectually. I find being with men difficult now, even when they are old friends. Their conversation lacks a certain kind of perceptual depth, a reverence for intangibles, even if they are artists. How can I share myself with Richard and Simon when I am so sure they will not understand me?

"You know, Miriam," said Richard after a few minutes of silence, "it's not your sexuality that bothers me if that's what you're thinking. It's your politics."

Miriam had heard this statement elsewhere and believed it stemmed from fear of losing power in an arena much larger than the bedroom, though definitely including it. She threw her fish and chips wrapper in a trash can, considering whether she would challenge him, and decided against it. She knew she was backing off from a real issue but suspected it would come around again. "I'm a political person, Richard, you know that. In 1975 it was government corruption and ecological pollution. The major concerns have changed for me, that's all. We've always disagreed about the value of having a political perspective."

"True enough!" Richard laughed. "You've always been an idealist, and I'm still an apathetic bastard!"

They ended their stroll at The Fox and Hounds where the lively conversation, during which Miriam temporarily forgot her personal preoccupations, continued over many rounds of drinks. Richard's own romantic escapades had recently culminated in a rather unusual marriage.

"Susan's from Australia, you see, and the Home Office wasn't going to renew her visitor's visa. Some problem, I don't know exactly what. So I married her, you know, so she could stay on with her girl friend Margo."

"You married a lesbian?" she whispered, conscious of the crowded table next to them.

"Sure, why not?"

"Noble of you." Apparently Richard was one of those men who could accept lesbianism, but Miriam knew from previous conversations that he found male homosexuality disgusting. Of course, its threat to him was more personal and, for someone as witty as Richard, that made it a perfect subject for jokes.

He shrugged. "Not really. Though it wrecked my relationship with Frances. She's still madder than hell, and won't even speak to me."

57

"She wanted you to marry *her*?"

"Well, we've been going together for years. It was rather a statement on my part, wasn't it?" After a pause, in which it was obvious to Miriam that Richard was distressed by the loss of Frances, he mumbled, "Guess I'm just a rotten sod."

"You could divorce Susan now, couldn't you?"

"That's just it, you see — I don't really want to. Then I'd have to marry Frances, wouldn't I?" He burst out laughing.

"You are a rotten sod then!" Miriam appreciated the irony of the situation but sympathized with Frances.

"Oh, you should have been here for the wedding, Miriam! We did it up royal, formal dress and a fancy meal afterward, the works. Simon, of course, was my best man. Cost a bloody fortune. We all got pissed as rats!" He laughed and laughed, getting red in the face, and finally coughing hard for a few moments.

Miriam tried to envision this odd wedding ceremony though she didn't know either of the women. In any case, she agreed with Richard that the words of the marriage contract were frightening. She wondered if anyone really intended to keep such promises. They asked so much of a mere human being, asked so much of even a great love — if there ever was one. Maybe that's why couples had begun to write their own vows.

Later, drunk and whirling on the cot Richard set up for her in the living room, Miriam dreamed of Sasha dressed as a bride and marrying the Other Woman. Miriam tried but couldn't get Sasha's attention and finally grabbed at the long white wedding veil. She pulled Sasha away just as she began to say the vows. In the dark unfamiliar room Miriam woke suddenly protesting, "No, Sasha, no! You can't say those words to anyone but me!"

They left London before dawn in Richard's old blue station wagon. The streets were silent except for trash cans being rattled by garbage collectors in nearby alleys. In the dim light the city looked medieval and abandoned, fragile yet enduring like the images in a dream.

"Two months of freedom!" exclaimed Richard. "I thought it would never come!"

"Has it been a particularly hard year?" Miriam asked. In faded jeans and an old tee shirt, he looked relaxed already but the tensions of city life hadn't left the space between the eyes that wrinkles easily.

Richard pursed his lips reflectively. "Oh, no, same old crap, I suppose." He pushed back against the seat, stretching his arms.

"I'm surprised you've stayed with this job," Miriam probed. "It doesn't seem to mean much to you."

"It's a job." He shrugged. "I don't mind it. Keeps me in whisky."

They were driving toward the ferry dock at Southampton, passing through the fields and farmland of Devonshire. Miriam had a soft spot for the English countryside, the small villages, the communal pubs. The lush greenness spread out on each side of the road, dotted with an occasional farmhouse, generally the domain of grazing cows. It was clean and fresh, as if newly created, a sensual paradise.

Miriam gestured toward the scenery out the window. "I've thought of this so often. You know what I remember most though? The Devon cream! I've even dreamed about it."

Richard chuckled. "Well, the goal for this summer is to make a reality of our dreams." He swerved off the road suddenly and came to a stop by a produce stand.

With a childlike innocence that Miriam had thought she'd lost, she purchased two baskets of large, almost perfect, strawberries and two containers of Devon heavy cream. As they continued driving, she picked the stems from the strawberries, dipped each one into the cream, and fed them alternately to Richard and to herself. The cream was too thick to drip. Its sweetness coated the unblemished fruit and mingled richly with the surprising tang of each berry as it broke open in the mouth. The taste was just as she'd remembered it. "It's good to know that some things don't change."

Richard nodded. With each mouthful he groaned in appreciation.

Miriam laughed aloud and was amazed at the sound. It had been so long since she had laughed in pure delight. The sun glowed upon the pastures, upon the cows that had produced the cream and, when the last of it had been consumed, she blessed them all silently in her heart. "Decadence," she said, licking her fingers.

"And that is the method by which we shall achieve all the goals of this trip," Richard announced.

Miriam smiled to herself. She removed her shoes and settled her feet on the dashboard. Riding as a passenger in the left front seat of a British car usually made her very nervous; she felt she should be doing something responsible about the steering. Today she closed her eyes instead, sure that no ill luck could befall her when she was full of

Devon cream and in such capable hands.

Purity and sensuality — that's what I'm seeking to balance. Passion that is directed toward good. Passion is not a word that I like to associate, particularly or solely, with sex. It seems more appropriately to be a philosophy of life, a quality of the soul that directs all one's choices. To be passionate about ideas and values, about the defense of freedom or innocence, for example.

When I was in convent boarding school, my music teacher, Sister Mary Gordon, caught me crying one day over some slight done to me by another student. "You must stop showing your feelings so much, my girl. You are too passionate for your own good." I had no reply to this absurdity then, of course, though I knew there was something wrong with her reasoning. How can one be *too* passionate? All the pleasure of life comes through passion. For the ones we love. For what we create.

Even after the boat pulled away and England began to disappear, they stood at the railing of the ferry's rear deck where it was less windy and sipped red wine out of plastic cups. They were attempting to avoid the crowded pandemonium inside as the other passengers found seats and organized their children. The seagulls following in the wake of the ferry dipped down into the foam looking for scraps of food, then cried in disappointment and veered away.

It would be too cold to stay outdoors in another half hour but meanwhile Miriam liked the salt spray on her skin and her hair being tousled by the breeze. She rolled the collar of her turtleneck sweater up to her earlobes and buttoned her leather jacket. "So what are you writing these days?" She knew this was a touchy subject with Richard now and had avoided it so far.

Richard was squinting at the last visible tip of land on the horizon and didn't answer immediately. "Not much. Too busy drinking."

"I thought you were writing patient entertainment programs for some hospital. What happened to that?" Miriam continued to question him, hoping he would talk about writing, spontaneously and enthusiastically, the way he had when they'd first met.

Richard hunched his shoulders against the wind. "My connection

60

there quit her job and I was too lazy to pursue it."

"I'd like to see those stories sometime." She was sure that Richard, unlike herself, wouldn't write fiction about depressing failures and hidden fears.

"You're in luck then. I brought them along for Simon's nieces and nephew."

"There'll be kids on the farm?" Miriam could see her long-awaited rest disappearing between temper tantrums and irrepressible squeals of excitement.

"Three of them." Richard didn't look at her. They were both watching an elderly man in a tweed visor cap throwing crusts of bread to the eager seagulls. "Simon's sister Beth and her family started coming over from Australia two years ago. They're part owners of the farm now, along with Simon's mother."

It was a fact Miriam knew but had forgotten.

"You should see Simon with those kids," Richard continued. "It's like they're his own. Of course, I've seen him with other kids and he's just the same with them. He's a kid at heart himself."

"Why doesn't he get married and have some of his own?" She remembered Simon talking about wanting a family. In his last letter he'd said he was writing stories for children. He was the sort of man who would be an exceptional father.

"I thought he might last summer. He was in love with a woman who owns a florist shop in Annonay — Gabrielle. You'll probably meet her sometime." Richard took their empty plastic cups and dropped them in a trash bin. "I've never seen him like that."

Miriam pictured Simon happily in love and it pleased her. "Really involved, huh?"

"Whew! Bloody unbelievable!"

"That's nice."

"Not really. When it didn't work out, he fell to pieces."

"The pitfalls of love?" They both smiled at the pun, then she added, "Yes, I know about that part of it too."

I once read in a Medieval Literature class someone's treatise on the courtly love tradition. It described in detail the physical signs of love. The lover has a hard time breathing, is distracted, can't eat or sleep, neglects friends, writes poetry. The odd thing is that the physical signs of loss of love are ex-

61

actly the same. How do you figure it?

It was difficult not to notice how Sasha acted around someone to whom she was attracted. She became very nervous, flitting around the room, talking too much, laughing too loudly. Her heart was probably pounding so hard that she was having a hard time breathing normally and the waves of desire were rippling through her diaphragm. I knew, because that was the way I felt about her in the beginning.

"How old are they — the kids?"

"Oh, let's see." Richard smiled, recalling them. "Martha is eight. She's a little firebrand. And Tina — 'the princess,' Simon calls her — is six. Davis is four." He chuckled. "They're great kids, each one such a character. Davis is quite the boy. His nickname is 'Bionic Dave.' "

"Why's that?" She realized how popular Richard probably was with kids too.

Richard laughed. "He likes the image, I guess."

Miriam knew she was frowning. "It bothers me the way male children get so much ego support for being adventurous and inquisitive while little girls are supposed to be quiet, polite, and considerate. Then when little girls grow up, they get criticized for not being adventurous and inquisitive. You see what I mean?"

The wrinkle of serious thought reappeared between Richard's eyes. "I don't think that's what happens, Miriam." After a pause he turned to her again. "You don't care much for kids, do you?"

"Not much. But I'm better than I used to be. Besides, the farm's a big place. I'll find somewhere to hide." Miriam was trying to light a cigarette, and Richard used his hands to shield her match from the wind.

"I don't think they'll bother you anyway. They stay quite busy, what with flower and berry gathering. And chasing each other — and the ducks."

"Simon keeps animals now?"

"Just a few ducks, and chickens for eggs. The ducks will grace the dining room table at some point."

"Oh, God," Miriam murmured.

Richard nodded. After a moment he continued, "Simon would like to do the whole bit eventually — be self-sufficient on the place."

Miriam nodded. "I can just see Simon out there reciting poetry to his cows."

"So can I and I'd like to be right there with him."

Miriam heard the intensity in Richard's voice. She recalled how close a friendship Simon and Richard had, how they valued and admired each other. Like Rebecca and herself, they had lived through the major events of each other's lives. They loved each other unselfishly and that gave the friendship a solid, inviolate quality free of the complications of physically intimate love.

"It's getting a bit chilly," Richard said. "How about some dinner?"

After standing impatiently in a long cafeteria line, they sat down to one of Miriam's favorite French meals — *bifteck au poivre, pommes frites*, bread and butter, and more red wine. They ate in silence enjoying the food. Finally Richard leaned back, stretching his arms over his head, and stared for a moment out the window at the calm black sea. The sun had set while they were eating and the sky was nearly dark.

"I think I'll take a stroll around the deck. Join me?" He stood up, shaking his legs.

"No, thanks," Miriam said. "I want some coffee and a cigarette." When he'd gone, she took her journal from her shoulder bag.

So it's back to France! In Paris, Martin and I had our final argument. He had withdrawn into himself again after we left Greece and my efforts to be cheerful weren't successful.

It was early evening on our last night in Europe. I'd envisioned a leisurely dinner at some small Left Bank restaurant but Martin said he was too tired. He planned to eat the bread and cheese we had in the room with us and go to bed early. I stood at the open window looking down on Boulevard Sainte Germaine, at the lovers walking hand in hand, a man with his arm around a woman's waist. From somewhere down the street a woman's lighthearted laugh reached me. I was angry, defeated again by Martin's lack of enthusiasm.

"Martin," I said, turning to him, "I wish we were better friends."

"How can we be friends, Miriam? We're lovers." He looked at me coolly from the bed where he'd propped himself against the bolster to read an old copy of *The New York Times*.

"I want both." I walked toward the bed intending to sit on

63

the edge of it, to be closer to him if only physically.

"Well, you don't fuck friends."

"You mean you fuck *me*? I thought we made love."

"Oh, shut up, will you? I'm tired of your bitching. If you don't like me the way I am, find someone else." He rolled over toward the wall, turning his back on me.

I grabbed my jacket and the room key and rushed out. I walked to the Jardin du Luxembourg and sat down on the first bench I saw. In my head I continued the argument with Martin as I so often did, trying to impress him with my superior perspective. After only a few minutes, a Frenchman, tall, thin, with a small stroke of a moustache, approached, bowed, and propositioned me. I looked at the man, at his black hair thick with pomade, his suggestive leer. Then I stood up, swore at him in fluent French, which seemed to surprise him, and went back to the hotel. Martin was asleep and I got into bed but didn't sleep. According to Martin I had been living my life as a whore and the man in the park apparently knew it.

In the morning when Martin, only half awake, began to make love to me, I pulled away, got up and stood in the shower for a long time, crying.

Once they were in France, Miriam insisted on helping Richard with the driving; she was still on the wrong side of the car but at least on the right side of the road. They alternated their route between the motorway, on which four lanes of traffic moved at eighty miles per hour and exhausted the driver in a very short time, and the local roads between provincial towns, which necessitated slower speeds but provided more pleasant views.

With the radio on Miriam attempted to recall some French vocabulary, while Richard napped in the back seat. She hadn't remembered the countryside of France being so brilliantly floral. Everywhere she looked were poppies nodding their red faces at her, daisies and bluebells dancing in the mild breeze, and roses growing in the village window boxes. With the car in her control and the sun shining, she was content to drive on this way forever.

They stopped for lunch at a cafe with a balcony that hung over the Loire. Just enough cool air came off the river to keep their table in the sun from being uncomfortable. Miriam ordered an omelette and *pommes frites*; Richard, a filet of sole. They ate companionably, speak – ing only occasionally of pleasant trivialities, sharing their delight in the simple perfection of the food.

As they were finishing the last glasses of a bottle of regional white wine, Richard cleared his throat. "We'll be there by early afternoon tomorrow."

"Good." Miriam was watching the sun reflected in the bottom of her wine glass and feeling slightly intoxicated. "I'm looking forward to this, you know, the three of us together again. I never quite believed it would really happen."

After a pause Richard spoke, not looking at her either, but squinting at a small sailboat that was pushing off from the far shore. "Maybe you don't remember, but it's very slow there. Not much happens."

Miriam laughed. "Oh, and am I looking forward to that!"

Richard smiled sympathetically, then was serious again. "What I mean is . . . I'm not trying to warn you or anything, Miriam, but . . . well, maybe I am. It just won't work at Les Bluets – to be into this political thing of yours, sometimes the way you are. If you go ex-pounding . . . you know what I mean?"

"Do I expound?" She thought he was teasing her because he often did. Then she saw that he'd meant it. "Look, Richard, all I ask for is respect. I don't have any trouble with men as long as there's mutual respect."

He nodded but didn't meet her eyes. "Fair enough then."

It was the first of their disagreements that had actually wounded Miriam. She had consciously been speaking much less politically than she usually did but still Richard saw her as a shrew, something to be reckoned with, controlled. While he drove she leaned back pretending to sleep. Like an overly sensitive child who felt she had been unjustly reprimanded, tears formed under Miriam's eyelids. She had assumed it was her responsibility to renew the friendship between the three of them, and now an uncomfortable sense of being strangers threatened her good intentions and she didn't like it.

That evening they camped in a small wooded area owned by a local farmer. Hurrying to complete the chores before dark, they pitched the yellow and orange tent and started a fire for cooking. Miriam sliced some bacon and onions while Richard warmed the peas. Laughing at his embarrassment, she insisted on taking a picture of him as he cooked their food in a skillet over the low fire. They ate hungrily and too fast, rarely speaking, as they watched the cows in a nearby pasture move languidly toward the barn to be milked. After washing their tin plates at the farmer's water pump, they gathered more firewood, and Richard found the bottle of whisky he'd brought along for the occasion, their first night on French soil. "And to keep the chill off, you know," he assured her.

They sat against a fallen tree log extending their feet to the fire and passed the bottle back and forth. After the exertion of making camp and the hot, heavy meal, they approached the rest of the evening with tired sighs. In the vast dark countryside they could see only each other's faces lit by a fire that crackled and flickered in the breeze, the smoke constantly shifting its direction.

Miriam was relaxing toward sleep. She was tired from the sun, the driving, the unsettling nervousness of change. She noted that the bottle was being quickly emptied. "Richard, will you sing 'Barbara Allen' for me?" she asked.

" 'Barbara Allen'?" Richard's round fleshy face was flushed in the firelight. Miriam looked with fondness at her friend's sensitive mouth and at the strong hands with which he was whittling at a piece of wood with a penknife. "I haven't sung that for ages," he said. "I'm not sure I can remember all the words."

It was Miriam's favorite among the ballads Richard had sung the summer she met him. She knew instinctively that he only wanted to be coaxed a little and touched him lightly on the arm. "Come on, please try."

Richard continued to whittle but after a moment he began to sing. His voice was low and vibrant in the dark like a crooning woman at the cradle.

As Richard sang, Miriam considered the themes of infidelity and death, the process of fate and consequence, which the song illustrated. Its two ill-starred lovers couldn't live with each other or without each other but grew together in death as they never could in life. In the silence following the song, Miriam sat staring into the fire, the bottle of whisky dangling in her right hand.

Richard took the bottle from her protectively. "And what are you so intense about, my dear?"

"I was thinking about unconditional love," The last large piece of wood split in the fire scattering sparks onto their shoes.

"Oh, Miriam," sighed Richard. "Why do you think about such

things anyway? I mean, what does it all mean? Love is love, isn't it? Why categorize everything?"

"Just crazy, I guess," she whispered.

"Simon mentioned that you've had a rough time of it."

"You could put it that way."

"Tell me," he said softly.

Her throat was tight. She was fighting a long, painful cry. "It's really hard for me to give up, I guess, to accept the end of things. Martin called it my 'unregenerate heart.' "

Richard was silent, allowing her time.

She took a deep breath. "I really have been crazy. Cut myself off from everything, everyone. Just not being in touch anywhere. More separate than usual. I mean, I always feel somewhat separate but it's been worse. It just occurred to me that part of me stands outside my life, as I'm thrashing about on the floor with some new agony, and says, 'This is good material!' I'm like a fucking movie camera!" She looked closely at Richard.

He threw the piece of wood he'd been whittling into the dying fire and put the penknife in his pocket, then looked back at Miriam. "You say you want to be a writer, Miriam. So maybe this is an occupational hazard. I mean, Christ, experience − yours, mine, and everyone else's − *is* the material."

Miriam nodded, trying to fight back the tears.

Richard took her right hand and patted it with both of his. He spoke softly. "Miriam, everyone has disappointments in love, and − it's true − they hurt like hell."

"You've always said I take things too seriously," Miriam said, smiling at him.

"Love *should* be taken seriously. While it's happening − *that's* the time to take it seriously," he said. "And afterwards, well, you tried."

"Yeah," Miriam said, looking at Richard and remembering his chrysalis poem. She let the tears run down her face.

Richard searched in his back pocket and offered a large white handkerchief to her. He went on drinking the whisky and watching the fire die. When she'd stopped crying and had blown her nose into his handkerchief, he leaned toward her and squeezed her hand. "You're not cut off and separate now, Miriam. Simon and I won't let you be."

The fire was finally only glowing ashes. Richard poured some water over it. Then they climbed into the tent and slept.

Les Bluets/1

A hand-painted sign had been nailed to a post near the main road. "Les Bluets," it said, "The Cornflowers," those delicate blue blooms that covered the hillside behind the house and symbolized innocence and childhood.

Honking the horn repeatedly, Richard turned the car into the dirt drive that led around the house and into the yard. Even before he had stopped the car, two small girls and an even smaller boy surrounded them shouting and waving their arms.

Miriam studied the features of the old square farmhouse, the cream-colored stone walls of all the buildings, their orange shutters and slate roofs with fluted tiles. As with the Devon cream, she was grateful for the immutable pleasure of this place.

Simon grabbed Miriam as she climbed from the car and hugged her hard. "Christ, it's good to see you!" He stood back. "You look beat though."

"I am. We both are." She managed a smile and controlled her impulse to ask for water and a private place to wash herself. She had expected Simon to notice that her hair was no longer waist length, that she even had a couple of tiny wrinkles around her mouth and eyes. Then she remembered how his enthusiasm often overrode such superficial details.

"Well, come on!" Simon urged. "We're just having some lunch."

Richard greeted Simon with a gentle clap on the shoulder. "Pour me a beer, *mon ami*. That'll cure the fatigue."

Simon looked the same to Miriam except that his blond hair was almost all gray. Though he'd only been at the farm a couple of weeks, he was already tanned and exuded good health. Over the excitement of the children who were trying to climb Richard's legs, Simon introduced Miriam to his sister and brother-in-law.

Beth was small like Simon and had the same slightly crooked smile and laughing eyes. Her hair was dark brown though and hung straight to her shoulders in a pageboy cut. She put her hand out and shook Miriam's firmly. Jack was strikingly handsome and distinguished looking with his jet black hair and beard. In contrast to his wife, he had a tall narrow body.

Lunch was a noisy crowded affair around a long tiled table. Miriam studied the remaining *salade niçoise,* the crusty bread and the Camembert cheese, and decided not to be shy about filling her plate. "This salad's great," she murmured to Simon between mouthfuls.

"My sister is *devoted* to French provincial cooking," said Simon with a wink at Beth. He poured Miriam a glass of white wine. "I made this myself — from the gooseberries that grow on the hill up there."

"Still the gentleman farmer," Miriam teased, sipping the cool wine that was, in fact, delicious.

As she ate, Miriam listened to the conversation around her and the interruptions of the children, tried to answer questions about her flight, the upcoming American presidential election, and the most recent explosions of Mt. St. Helens.

Holding Davis, a frail-looking boy and the only one of the children with black hair, Jack distanced himself from the others, appearing unruffled by the verbal turmoil around him. Davis watched quietly too, his thumb in his mouth, and Miriam noticed that his eyes, gray like his father's, were slightly crossed.

In spite of Beth's protests, Martha and Tina climbed on Richard as he ate, attempting to relate in a few minutes all their adventures since the previous summer. Richard laughed and nodded, encouraging them.

During the year since they'd last seen him, the children had not forgotten Richard's proficiency at tale-telling and Tina, the younger of the two girls, exacted a promise from him for a story before dinner and another before bed. Tina's hair, brown and straight, was cut like Beth's. She was slower in movement than Martha, but coy. Miriam suspected that she got to the same places in the end by less direct means.

Martha, the elder sister, looked like Simon, fair-haired and freckled. She was obviously used to directing the activities of her siblings. She slid over beside Miriam. "We're going to sleep in the loft of the big barn tonight!" she announced.

"Is that right?" Miriam tried to seem interested.

"Oh, no, you're not, my girl." Jack's voice was firm. "That's been settled before and you know it."

Martha turned quickly to Beth. "But you said we could, mum!"

"I said we'd see," Beth said softly pushing Martha's hair out of her face.

"There'll be no 'seeing,' " said Jack. "I said no before and that's what I meant."

Miriam observed that the look passing between Beth and Jack wasn't particularly congenial. Perhaps all was not well in the pastoral paradise, she mused; perhaps she wasn't the only one who might disturb Richard's blissful apathy.

Simon stood up rather abruptly, gathering together a pile of dishes, and turned to Miriam. "Come on. Let me take care of these and then I'll show you your room."

While he ran hot water into the scullery sink, Miriam set her bag in the center of the large main room and looked around her. Though dim, the high-ceilinged, stone-walled room was much cheerier than she remembered it.

"Beth's been quite the positive influence around here, eh?" Simon shouted from the scullery.

A couch and four chairs were placed in a semicircle around the hearth and there was a bouquet of field flowers on the antique writing desk. She recalled Simon's decor of five years before as much more haphazard, a bachelor's sparseness and rugged disarray. She opened the heavy oak doors into the dining room and saw two more bouquets of wildflowers on a wooden table that was so long that it barely allowed passage between its ends and the walls. Like the one in the main room, the floor-to-ceiling cupboard had been stripped and carefully refinished. Her eyes returned to the stone hearth, large enough for an adult to stand in. It had already been filled with kindling for a fire against the early evening chill. Memories that had been sleeping in the past were quickly awakened by the actual sights and sounds of the place; she was recalling the hours she'd spent before that hearth with Martin when Simon touched her lightly on the shoulder.

"Remember how bad these floors were?" he asked. They had been covered with slats of wood, worn and cracked, but were now tiled. "Jack and I did the whole first floor last summer," he commented with pride as they climbed the stairs. "The bedrooms will be next. We had enough tiles left over though for Jack to make that table outside."

Sunlight shone into the central hallway of the second story, and the floorboards creaked under their feet.

"Hey, we have a full bath now!" Simon swung open the door of a small room that featured a shining new bathtub as well as a toilet and sink.

"You mean you've got hot water up here?" Miriam's voice was skeptical.

Simon lit a match under a gas heater, and in thirty seconds hot water was pouring into the tub.

"Oh, Simon!" Miriam exclaimed.

73

"I thought you might like it a bit," he teased.

The bedroom he showed her had been painted a pale blue and recently swept. The wooden shutters were closed against the bright sunlight and the air in the room was warm and heavy. The only furnishings were two single bed frames with mattresses, but a bouquet of cornflowers stood on the broad windowsill.

"Did you pick those for me?"

Simon glanced at her as he turned to leave. "Sure did. When you've rested awhile, let's take a walk."

The bathtub was unusually long and Miriam ran the hot water into it until her whole body was covered up to her chin. Simon had chipped the plaster from one of the walls to uncover the huge rough stones of the original structure. The light through the one small round window was dim. The result gave the room a quality of austere beauty and she imagined herself in a hidden underground hot spring. After she had washed away the sweat and grime of traveling and had shampooed her hair with some unfamiliar brand of herbal concentrate, she lay there in the silence, listening to the murmur of voices downstairs without being able to distinguish one from another.

Sasha is the one who always said she wanted it all. I never could figure out what "it all" really was. But I know she wanted − or needed − a lot of love from a lot of different people, a variety of sensation. And I can see that much of what she's done has been an attempt to satisfy that need rather than to reject anyone in particular. One lover could never satisfy that kind of need, no matter how much love she had to give.

Irritated by this reflection, Miriam was already tense when there was a knock on the door.

"Yes?" She tried to sound pleasant.

"Who's in there?" It was a child's voice.

"Miriam."

"Oh. Well, I have to use the toilet."

"Damn!" Miriam muttered to herself. She guessed it was Tina. "All right. I'll be out in two minutes, okay?"

She pulled the plug and stepped out onto the pale orange tiles that made the floor smooth and cool. As she began drying herself briskly, she realized she hadn't brought clean clothes into the bathroom with her. There was another knock. "Just a minute!" she shouted. She wrapped the towel around her, gathered up her dirty clothes, and opened the door.

Tina dashed past her without speaking. Miriam made a conscious effort not to bang her bedroom door shut in protest and wondered how happy she was going to be living with children.

She found Simon at the table in the yard, wearing a green straw hat and reading a science-fiction novel. In front of him was a large glass of beer, half drunk.

He showed her the cover of the book before marking his place and closing it. "Quite good, this. You've never gotten into sci-fi, have you?"

"No, the future bores me."

"Well, this guy's into the past."

"That's even worse."

Simon squinted at her a moment. "Let's stroll down the road."

They walked past the ducks splashing in the runoff from the creek that was the farm's own natural water supply, past the three long wash troughs, one of which also kept the beer cold, past the small barn. On one side of it the old outhouse, used now only in emergencies, clung to the stone wall. With two blank-eyed windows above the outhouse, the design of the small barn reminded Miriam of a ceremonial mask.

"The kids like to play in there," said Simon gesturing toward its dark interior. "They put on little performances for us, swinging from the rope ladders like Tarzan and Jane."

"At the moment they're probably off somewhere tormenting Richard."

Simon laughed in agreement. "He loves it though, you know."

Wild rosebushes in full bloom wound their way through the ten-foot high wrought iron gates that were locked at night. Miriam picked a rose and stuck it behind her ear as they continued up the drive and onto the tarred main road.

After a few moments of silence, Simon spoke. "So, my dear, how are you now? Your last letter was a zinger." The tone of his voice was the intense and serious one she remembered as being the other side of his exuberant character.

"I know." She sighed softly. "Actually, I toned it down. I didn't want you to take back your invitation."

"Oh, Miriam," Simon protested with a chuckle, "you've always been a bit crazy."

They smiled at each other and Miriam took a deep breath of the clean mountain air. "I'm much better now though," she said, "much better just being here."

They sat down in the grass of a low hill that looked out over the valley. The hillside was covered with the blooms of wildflowers. Butterflies, white and bronze and yellow, darted among them. The only sound was the buzzing of large black bees. Then in the distance Miriam heard the lowing of a cow, the bark of a farm dog at work herding.

She picked a long piece of grass to chew and leaned back on one elbow. The tension in her body had already begun to ease. "It's so peaceful here. It's almost too perfect. Why didn't I come back sooner?"

"I haven't a clue, luv," Simon replied. "I'm glad I kept asking though." He lay back in the grass. "This place is the only thing that keeps me going over there. I have a partner now at the bookstore and we each take two months off out of every year."

She remembered the deep emotion in Richard's voice when he spoke of the farm and she wished he had the same freedom as Simon. Maybe if he had that freedom he'd stop drinking so much and start writing more.

Simon glanced down at the leaf he was shredding. "You know that poem you sent me about your mother?"

She nodded. After the initial shock of her mother's death had struck her and passed, she'd written a long narrative poem about it, a piece that was critical of the Catholic Church, funerals and mourners, and that questioned her own survival.

"You said you couldn't write about anything except her, that everything was connected to her. What did you mean?"

"Actually I was writing a piece about her, about her life, when she went into the 'decline,' as they call it." Miriam paused, uncertain of her willingness to relate the story and of exactly what details she wanted to share right then. "Finally when she could barely talk and couldn't see very well, all she wanted was to hold my hand. It made me sick. Her hands were bony and dry. I didn't want to touch them much. The day they took her to the hospital though, I held both her hands in the ambulance the whole way. Her face was like death already, glazed over with fear and resignation. She knew it was the end. As soon as she arrived, they shot her full of morphine. I stood by the bed for a while."

Miriam paused again and took a deep breath, remembering how her mother had gulped for air before they finally put the oxygen tube in her nose. "I knew what my mother wanted to hear but I wouldn't say it. As I turned to leave the room, she struggled to sit up. Her eyes were unfocused by the drugs and I knew she couldn't see me. 'But where am I going, darling?' she asked me in a hoarse whisper. 'Where am I going?'" Miriam shook her head as if trying to clear it of the scene and looked at Simon. "She went, of course, into a coma. I still have dreams about it. Such a simple sentence for me to say: 'I love you.' The nuns always told me I was too proud."

She gazed out over the peaceful valley. "You know what bothered me and what I still ask myself? Was it because she was no longer so beautiful that I was finally able to refuse her something?" Miriam turned her face away from Simon toward the woods, blinking back her tears. "To take my revenge," she concluded bitterly.

"Christ," Simon whispered to himself. He started to reach toward her, then stopped. "Please don't cry."

"I'm not, at the moment. I have been crying a lot lately though — ask Richard. Disgusting, isn't it?" She knew Simon was at a loss, that such revelations, especially the guilty ones upset him.

"No, it's not," he said, "but it does make me feel rather helpless."

Miriam laid her hand on Simon's arm for a moment. "It's good to be here with you and Richard. And everyone," she added quickly with a smile.

Simon nodded. "I really want you to meet my mum. She's off hiking this afternoon but you'll see her at dinner. She's a super old girl!"

I don't deserve this, Simon's sweet kindness. I know what I deserve: to fail as a writer, never be loved, to have bad dreams about pressure chambers and drowning in shit.

They began walking back toward the farm. Simon rubbed his chin thoughtfully as if he needed a shave. "Say, a friend of yours came by on her way south a couple weeks ago. Ellen somebody."

"Oh, Ellen McElroy! I gave her directions in case I was here. She wasn't sure when she left Portland what her itinerary would be. I hope you didn't mind."

" 'Course not. She said she'd try to stop back this way. I liked her.

She seemed a little hyperactive but interesting."

Miriam flinched mentally, remembering how much Ellen knew about her life with Sasha. "I met her in a writing workshop."

"She said she writes children's stories."

Miriam smiled at Ellen's unaccustomed discretion and flicked a bee away from her face. "Also erotica."

"Well, I hope she turns up again then!" exclaimed Simon, laughing.

Miriam couldn't help wondering if Simon and Ellen would be good together and was immediately amused by the image of herself as a matchmaker. She hadn't been at Les Bluets twenty-four hours and already she was out of character.

Simon walked slowly, his eyes on the ground and his hands clasped behind his back. "Do you ever hear from Martin? Or is that subject taboo?"

Miriam saw that Simon had been saving the question until he could judge her mood. "Not at all. I guess I forgot to write you about it. I saw him last January when he came through Portland. He found my number in the phone book and called and we went out to dinner. He's gotten more conservative — I suppose we all have — and we argued about political ideals that somehow I thought we'd always share." She approached the real surprise of her evening with Martin more cautiously. "We stayed out talking until about three in the morning. Two close friends had died recently. Others had married and now had children. We had a lot to discuss. The truth is, though, that we were enjoying each other's company so much, the way we had in the beginning. We both got very drunk and just let the conversation ramble all over the place, finding a succession of bars that stayed open later and later. A kind of residual attraction surfaced during the course of the night. Sasha went into hysterics over the telephone when I finally got home."

"Sasha's your lover?"

Miriam smiled sardonically. "The labels keep changing on me. She'd asked earlier if she could meet Martin and I'd refused. Just the thought of being in the same room with the two of them, those particular two, made me slightly crazy. On the phone, when she questioned me, I told her that I hadn't been at all attracted to Martin. I wouldn't admit to her that I found any man attractive, even one with whom I'd been so passionately involved once."

"That's a bit weird, isn't it?"

"Simon, I've been living my life as a lesbian for the last four years."

She didn't want to say more. She didn't want to put even a hint of disagreement between them.

He hadn't heard her though. He was standing still, staring into the sky. "There it is! See that hawk up there?" Simon was pointing to a black-winged bird, hovering just above the farmhouse. "It turns up every day and circles overhead like that for about an hour."

"It's hunting for prey, and you're it," she joked.

"No. I think it's a blessing or a good omen."

"And what does that mean?" She sensed that he wanted her to ask.

"It means I'll be able to return here like that bird — again and again until I die." As he looked away from the hawk and into Miriam's eyes, his voice became soft, revealing a secret vulnerability. "That's all I really want anymore."

"Continuity."

He thought a moment, then nodded at her solemnly. "Right."

As they continued walking, Miriam recognized again how it had always been language — the sharing of the right words — that created a bond between her and those in her life who became significant. "I thought hawks were symbolic of ultimate freedom."

"Maybe that too."

"Both things?"

"Why not?" Simon's confident smile promised that everything contradictory in the world was possible to resolve.

At the conclusion of their stroll they were discussing the efforts of the local landowners to control the greed of the lumber industry. Martha came running out the front door of the farmhouse waving a blue envelope. "Did you tell her about the letter, Uncle Simon?"

"Oh, sorry, I forgot what a popular woman you are!" Simon said, laughing.

Miriam took the envelope that Martha thrust at her. From the handwriting she knew it was from Sasha. Her pleasant thoughts of a moment before were instantly scattered and she trembled as she read the return address over and over. Unsure of what her own emotional reaction might be to the contents of this letter, she wanted to avoid questions from anyone about its source. She left Simon watching the flight of the hawk as it returned to the woods and took the letter to her room.

A love letter, of course! The kind Sasha is so good at writing! And sent from the beach where she is frolicking with the Other Woman! She's making love to the Other Woman and writing love letters to *me*, talking of our future together, of how *much* she misses me!

Sasha is the archetypal Woman of Contradiction and she'll do or say whatever is necessary to get the desired result of the moment, Machiavellian. She's creative and original in her manipulations too, like my mother Judith. In addition, she's a genius of romantic verbiage.

I recall her saying, one day last spring, "We are two single people who are married to each other."

Such statements made me believe that there was hope for us, in spite of the untenable situation we were then in, that perhaps she had begun to want what I wanted, a common life, a home, the future of which she writes so eloquently now.

Then she added that she felt the same way about the Other Woman.

Miriam shoved the letter under the jar of cornflowers and went back outside. Jack lay in the deck chair catching the last rays of the sun. He glanced up at her but didn't initiate a conversation and she was grateful. She sat at the table alone, staring off to the left at the spot on the horizon where the Alps would be if she could see them. This particular view of the valley and the mountains had been etched in her memory like a photograph and she had almost forgotten that it was a real place. Over the retaining wall was a field of wildflowers. Down through the center of this field were the two deep tire tracks that had created a public road for the locals to reach the heart of the timber land. The road disappeared into the shadowy interior of the woods directly in front of her. Just at that moment Richard and Simon drove out of the shadows in the Citroen, hauling a load of firewood, and waved at her. Upstairs she could hear Beth bathing the children who were splashing happily in the water.

Simon doesn't see a conflict between continuity and freedom. On the conceptual level I suppose there isn't any. Maybe not even on the reality level, depending on how you define the terms. I've never had difficulty reconciling them within myself, but between myself and another person the difficulties seem to multiply endlessly. Especially with Sasha.

There can be no continuity between me and Sasha. I want the relationship to end. Integrity is to be consistent in your relationship with yourself. I will not answer the letter.

"It's *pastis* time." Simon interrupted Miriam's thoughts by placing in front of her a large glass of the anise-flavored liqueur diluted with water. He picked up her copy of T.S. Eliot's *Four Quartets*, which was the only book she'd brought with her from home, opened it to the first page, and read aloud: "Time present and time past/Are both perhaps present in time future,/and time future contained in time past./If all time is eternally present/All time is unredeemable."

They sat side by side in silence, sipping the *pastis*, and watching the sun go down.

Les Bluets/2

After lunch, Richard loaded the two empty wine casks into the back of the Citroen while Beth explained the various items on the shopping list to Simon. Jack jumped impatiently onto the driver's seat and started the car. The three men were making a midweek trip into Annonay for supplies.

Simon turned to Miriam who was sitting on the lawn chair reading. "You're sure you don't want to come along?"

She paused, momentarily tempted to procrastinate. "No, thanks. I really want to try to do some writing."

"Being dedicated, eh? All right for you then." He swallowed the last of his beer. "We'll be back in an hour or two. Or three if we stop for some cool refreshment in Garance," he added, grinning at Beth.

As he walked toward the car, Miriam called after him. "Simon! Can I use the typewriter in your room?"

"Sure. It's a bloody old monster though, takes some getting used to."

The stairway to the third floor was dark and Miriam had to feel her way until she emerged into Richard's room, bare except for the bed and some clothes hanging on wall pegs. Even there the light was dim because Richard kept his shutters closed. The walls on the loft, like those of all the farm buildings, were constructed of large rocks mortared together in a crude sort of masonry that was common in sixteenth-century structures. The third story was divided into only two large rooms. By tradition now, Richard occupied one of these, and Simon the other. Miriam had to trespass through Richard's room to reach Simon's.

In this second room the sunlight streamed through the open windows and a slight breeze stirred the dust in the air. Beneath one of the windows was a small table and a wooden chair, and on the table, catching Miriam's attention immediately, was an old Royal typewriter. Beneath the other window, its headboard against the wall, was a double bed. A sleeping bag, printed with garish purple flowers, was spread open across it.

She leaned against the headboard and looked out the window, knowing it would be a view of the woods and the yard. Simon's mother Claire was seated at the table in the shadow cast by the large red umbrella, writing. From Simon, Miriam had learned briefly of Claire's determination, after her husband's death, to return to school and become a professional woman. She had just completed her master's degree in psychology and was starting her first job that fall in Melbourne, counseling in a youth clinic. When Simon had introduced them the evening before, Claire had greeted Miriam, shaking hands briskly, but hadn't tried to prolong the conversation, being preoccupied with getting the children's supper. She had retired early.

Life here is simple. There are no questions more pressing than how many loaves of bread we'll need to buy each morning. Not that people here are simpleminded. They have all, voluntarily and maybe unconsciously on the part of some, abandoned the intensity and skepticism that dominate life "out there" in the daily business of the world. There is no newspaper here, no television. For a while I too can renounce with impunity any responsibility for my place in the world, my obligation to be a functioning contributory member of it. I'm just a visitor. I have no obligations except to appreciate the view.

Miriam sat down at the typewriter and inserted a blue airmail letter into the carriage. "Dearest Rebecca," she began, "I'm here!"

Simon was right. The machine had a mind of its own. It was necessary to type slowly or the letters ran together. Miriam didn't really object to this perversity. Her own thoughts were difficult to collect and slow to phrase. In the quiet solitude of Simon's room, she listened to the flies buzzing in and out through the open windows. Above her head, in the beamed ceiling, the termites were making progress. Simon had told her he was planning to treat the wood eventually but it was a costly remedy. She could hear the children playing in "the ruins" next to the big barn. "The ruins" were actually the foundation of an old farm building that had been allowed to decay years before. The escalating sound of angry voices indicated that a fight would soon erupt between Martha and Davis over some important matter; but Miriam knew that, at any moment, before the threat of blows and tears became a reality, Beth would go out to mediate the struggle.

When she'd finished her short, informational letter to Rebecca, Miriam remained seated at the typewriter, staring at the stones in the wall. She figured if she stayed there long enough she'd begin to write.

In March when Sasha slammed the door on our life together and disappeared into her love affair with the Other
Woman, I'd been working on a novel for a year and had nearly
finished a first draft. I wrote the next chapter twice and threw
both versions in the wastebasket. As in other times of mental
distress, I wrote poetry, but I knew I wasn't doing what I
should be doing.

When Sasha returned, I let her keep me in bed when I
should have been writing. When she went back to the Other
Woman and I looked at the novel again, my enthusiasm for the
plot, the characters, had completely evaporated.

Hoping for a revival of interest, Miriam had brought the manuscript
with her. She opened its hard black cover and read the first paragraph.
It bored her. She saw some punctuation changes she could make. A
half hour later she caught herself drawing lines with her finger in the
wood particles dropping from the termite holes above. Exasperated,
she slammed the cover shut again. Probably she was deceiving herself,
and should go back to graduate school and become a teacher. She
knew she had no self-discipline and worried that she had no ability
either. Most likely she'd fail as a writer just as she'd failed as a lover.

Though reluctant to leave the protective solitude of the third floor,
Miriam put the manuscript and letter in her room and went outside to
join Claire. Simon's mother was a swarthy-skinned, white-haired woman who looked, in spite of her sixty years, stronger than any of them.
Like Simon she radiated energy and enthusiasm.

Claire smiled up at her. "Hullo, Miriam. How're you doing?"

"Just fine, thanks." She studied the misty horizon.

"No Alps today, I'm afraid. We might be lucky to see them only
once while we're here."

"Yes, I remember." Miriam was uncertain of the appropriate topics
for discussion with Claire, aside from superficial pleasantries. She
wished Simon were there.

"We're going for a walk to 'the viewpoint,' me and the children,"
Claire said suddenly, as she sealed the letter she'd just finished. "Want
to come along?" Claire's blue eyes sparkled even in the shade of the
umbrella and for the first time Miriam saw the resemblance between
mother and son.

"Sure," she said. A walk with the three children was a diversion that could include whatever level of communication pleased them both. "Is there still a small creek down that way?"

"Yes," replied Claire as her grandchildren came bounding across the yard. "We call it 'Davy's Waterfall' now, don't we?" She gave Davy a tweak on the nose.

As Miriam ran upstairs to exchange her shorts for trousers, she wondered if Davy got so much attention because he was a small shy boy with crossed eyes or because he was the only male child.

They set off with the three children, turning left at the wrought-iron gates away from the main road, and followed another path that was nearly overgrown with waist-high grass. Beetles, grasshoppers, and various other insects, disturbed by so many feet, jumped out of their way, sometimes flying against the arms and faces of the children. Miriam was glad she'd worn hiking boots instead of running shoes. They emerged finally at the tire tracks and could walk more easily on the hard-packed earth, though it was made uneven by patches of mud still not dry from the previous night's rainfall.

From the yard Beth called out, "'Bye! Have a good time!"

They all turned around and waved at her as she sat perched on the retaining wall, a cookbook open on her knees. "Good-bye, mum! Good-bye!" the children shouted back, and then ran ahead chasing each other and were soon lost to view.

"Don't go too far!" shouted their grandmother.

"Beth didn't want to come?" asked Miriam.

Claire didn't answer immediately. "Beth needs some time alone," she finally replied, then paused again. "I think married people spend too much time together. They should take separate vacations."

"That's still considered a bit revolutionary," laughed Miriam. "Did you suggest it?"

"I did actually," said Claire. Then she smiled sideways at Miriam. "Didn't go over. I was told, politely of course, not to meddle."

"You don't strike me as a meddler, Claire," Miriam reassured her.

The roadside was decorated with scatterings of buttercups, poppies, and Queen Anne's lace, a myriad of colors against the green. Miriam enjoyed the physical sensations caused by intense sunlight and its heat — the warm dampness of her skin, the beads of sweat at her hairline. She smoothed down the fine brown hairs on her arms with the moisture, and licked her upper lip to taste the salt. Soon they were out of the sun though and had entered the shady woods, but the air remained warm and still. When the limbs of the plane trees met over their heads like a bower, the world became translucent green. Miriam was trying not to think of Sasha and the past, trying instead to concentrate on the present, on her good fortune to be in such a splendid place with friendly companions.

Claire broke the silence between them. "How does it feel to be abroad again?"

"Absolutely wonderful! It always does. I've spent a lot of my adult life traveling over here. Sometimes I think I'm a bit of a bum at heart." Miriam stopped speaking rather abruptly, afraid of revealing too much too soon.

"But how did you afford it?" Claire's tone was curious rather than critical.

Miriam was suddenly aware that she wanted Simon's mother to like her. "I've never really spent money on anything else. When I was working, I saved most of my money for travel — and then I went." She sighed as she dismembered a piece of Queen Anne's lace. "But I can see all that coming to an end. I want a home now, a permanent place, where I can settle down and write. I guess I'm tired of it all." She had to smile when she heard herself using Sasha's phrase.

"It's hard to settle down alone," commented Claire. The older woman was squinting into the distance, as Miriam had often seen Simon do, lost in private thought.

For a moment Miriam stared at Claire's face, weathered by the Australian sun and wind. "It's hard to do a lot of things alone," she remarked.

Claire's brow wrinkled. "Actually, since my husband died, I've found that I enjoy my solitude. I've been by myself for ten years now, except for the summers, and haven't wanted it to be any different so far."

"Too much solitude makes me tired," complained Miriam, though her sense of isolation had lessened during the last few days. She laughed at herself. "I guess at this point in my life everything's making me tired."

"Boredom?"

"No, I know that kind and it's not that. It's more a kind of despair that anything will ever be better than it is. It makes me want to give up and do nothing."

Claire's response was a thoughtful murmur. They went on walking in silence for a while, deeper into the cool woods. "Maybe doing nothing for now is just the thing then," Claire said finally. "Sometimes I think more can be learned by accepting than by struggling." She smiled at Miriam. Then, missing the children, she called out. "Martha! Tina! Davy! Where are you?"

Martha's voice came back at once. "At 'Davy's Waterfall,' grandma!"

A few moments later, around a bend in the road, they found the children wading. It wasn't really a waterfall, but a swift stream from some hidden source that bubbled and churned around several boulders just above a shallow pool, so very clear that the pebbled bottom and the moss on the undersides of the rocks were visible from where Miriam was standing.

"And where are your shoes?" demanded Claire sharply.

"Over there," Tina replied, pointing to a nearby log behind which the three pairs of shoes were piled.

"Well, let's go on now, shall we?"

"Oh, grandma, please," Martha begged, "this is such fun!"

Davy pushed a large rock into the water, splashing both his sisters. Tina squealed with fear and delight.

"Davy, that's enough," admonished Claire. "Come along, all three of you. *Now*, please!"

With groans of protest, only halfhearted though because their feet were turning blue, the children put on their socks and shoes. Within seconds they'd forgotten the pool and, running ahead, again disappeared down the road.

"I'm amazed when children obey," said Miriam. "I mean, what could you do if they didn't?"

"I think their obedience is guaranteed elsewhere, fortunately for me." Claire nodded self-confidently. "And they know I mean what I say. I never had any trouble with Simon or Beth either, and I never had to paddle them."

Miriam remembered being physically punished often as a child and not knowing why. She still didn't. She hadn't been a disobedient or untruthful child. She'd saved her outburst of nonconformity and rebellion until she was too old to punish.

"I found it easy to love my children though," Claire continued. "And I tried to be consistent, someone they could count on."

The subconscious, confident knowledge that he was consistently loved — was that the secret of Simon's generosity of spirit and his faith in other people, wondered Miriam.

Martha came running back with two bouquets of bluebells and handed one to each of the women.

"Well, thank you, Martha, that's very thoughtful." Claire stuck her nose gratefully into the blooms that had no real perfume.

"They're lovely," agreed Miriam. She was even more surprised when the little girl took her free hand and walked along beside her. After a few moments Miriam looked down and discovered Martha studying her with a calm serious expression.

The girl's wet bangs, needing to be cut, hung down between her eyes and she pushed them back impatiently. "You know what?" she asked, then replied without waiting for an answer. "You're awfully pretty."

Miriam laughed, feeling herself blush. "Well, thank you."

Without another word Martha dashed away to find her brother and sister.

"Now what was that all about?" Miriam glanced at Claire, both amused and puzzled by such a display of interest.

Claire was giving her a semi-teasing, semi-affectionate look that Miriam recognized as one of Simon's. "Don't you think of yourself as pretty?"

"No, not really. My mother was the one — she was beautiful." Miriam considered herself only passable in terms of looks. This was a natural conclusion, since people had often stopped on the street to admire Judith. Miriam accepted her own wavy black hair and violet eyes as a freaky combination, like a birth defect.

By the time the women arrived at the rocks that had been named "the viewpoint" and sat down to enjoy the scene below, the children had thoroughly explored the area and wanted milk and cookies.

Claire sighed. "Wouldn't you know it?" She remained seated a few minutes longer, while the children danced around her feigning hunger, then agreed to start back. "I really did this for the exercise anyway."

"I think I'll stay here awhile," Miriam said. "I'll catch up with you."

"All right," said Claire, patting Miriam on the shoulder. She was taken away laughing by Tina who pulled on her right arm while Davy hung on the left.

Miriam continued climbing, up to the highest point where she had a full panoramic view of the whole valley. It spread out before her as if she were the goddess who'd created it, and she looked down with loving protectiveness on the pastures and animals and farm buildings, all so much like Les Bluets in design. For a while she watched a goatherd taking his lively animals across the road, aided by a brown and white dog who nipped at their heels to keep them in line.

This place reminds me of Smith Rocks, a desert formation in eastern Oregon that Sasha and I visited on a camping trip about a year ago. From a distance the enormous pink-hued rocks, rising suddenly and majestically out of the barren landscape, looked mysterious and surreal to us both. The stark, harsh purity of the place created an atmosphere that was transcendent and, paradoxically, sensual. As we approached, I heard music, a high-pitched, flute-like melody that pulled me almost involuntarity toward the crevasses. Sasha said the music was only the desert wind blowing through the rocks. Her voice came to me from a great distance, as if I were under water, a formless murmuring drowned out by strange, siren-like singing. We explored the rocks as thoroughly as we could; every passage ended in darkness and we had no flashlight. I found myself wanting to press my body into the stone, to be absorbed by its mystery and abstract beauty, to disappear into the crevasses so that I could find the singers.

Sasha, catching my sensual mood though she didn't hear the music, suggested making love there. She found a sheltered spot by the river that bordered one side of the formation. It was a very hot day, like today, making the skin warm and damp, just as mine is now. In our passion for each other we were oblivious to the uneven, rough ground and the insects and dust. Naked and sweaty, we slid over each other's bodies in slow, languid movements. The moment, like the place, became surreal and unreal, and every desire seemed possible to satisfy. I wanted to press myself into Sasha as I had the rocks, and disappear. I didn't tell Sasha that I believed the eyes of the invisible musicians were watching us through the narrow crevasses. They were still singing but it was a song I couldn't understand.

Afterwards I wondered if the message, for I was sure it was a message, would have been clear to me if I'd been alone. Now I'm alone, and I still don't know what words those stony mouths were uttering.

That night after supper Richard read from *Winnie the Pooh* to the children, who were already in their pajamas. On the couch beside him but only half listening, Miriam stared into the fiery hearth. She was slipping away from the reality of the present aided by a second glass of Armagnac, which was taking effect rapidly after her several glasses of wine with the meal. Though aware of an occasional murmured comment between Claire and Simon, she was glad that none was directed to her.

She was pondering Martha's unexpected observation earlier in the day. Children were supposed to be honest to a fault, but Miriam still believed that beauty was a province ruled by her mother Judith, and one in which she herself could never live. Male lovers had sometimes told Miriam that she was beautiful; but, according to Judith, men had vested interests in saying such things. Sasha had often told her she was beautiful and Miriam had believed *her* because, for Miriam, to be beautiful was to be loved and she wanted to be loved by Sasha.

Miriam sighed and noticed that her glass was empty again. When she rose for a refill, the room was quiet. The children had been taken upstairs to bed. Simon and Richard were drinking whisky and staring into the fire. Claire, Jack, and Beth were reading around a gas lamp set in the center of the kitchen worktable.

As Miriam poured more Armagnac into her glass, Beth looked up, then held out her own. Miriam saw that she was reading *Middlemarch*. "What do you think of it?" she asked.

"Wonderful," Beth replied. Putting the book down, she shook a cigarette from the pack on the table and lit it.

Jack, without looking at anyone, reached across the table for the half empty pack of cigarettes and returned to his spy novel.

"It's been lying around here since last summer," said Beth. "I started it a few days ago and can hardly put the thing down."

Miriam nodded. "It's my favorite of her books."

Simon had gotten up to refill his glass too and was standing beside Miriam. "They finally installed a George Eliot Memorial in Westminster Abbey this year," he said to her. "I guess you didn't have time to see it."

Claire put her own book down then. "There was quite a row about it in Parliament — if she was good enough to be in the Abbey, I mean."

93

Miriam stared down into her glass, swirling the golden Armagnac around in the gas light.

"Isn't that ridiculous!" said Beth.

"It was some American professor that pressed it on too," Claire continued, pouring herself more tea.

Richard had finally joined the group around the table. His face was flushed with alcohol and the heat of the fire. "Women should be home washing out the nappies, not writing novels!" he shouted. "No woman ever wrote a *great* novel anyway!"

In the general laughter and protests that followed this statement, Miriam could only stare incredulously at Richard. "That was a disgusting remark," she said finally.

"Ah, come on, Miriam," Richard said, grinning at her. "You know I don't believe that. Where's your sense of humor?"

Miriam took a step toward him. "You always do that, Richard, and I'm really tired of it. I'm tired of the baiting remarks that you think you can get away with because they're funny. Well, here's the news: They're not funny. They're just stupid."

Richard moved away from her toward the door but Miriam followed him.

"Miriam," cautioned Simon.

She ignored Simon and stepped around in front of Richard. "You're afraid of being serious about anything because it's too risky. You hide inside your supposed humor and your booze and we're all supposed to applaud."

Richard looked around the room at the others, then he shrugged his shoulders, grinning drunkenly. "So what else is new?"

Only Jack laughed.

At the door Richard turned and looked at Miriam. In a low voice that only she could hear he said, "I was serious once, remember?" The front door banged shut behind him as he went out.

The room was silent and after a moment Claire and Jack returned to their books. Beth picked up her guitar and began strumming it softly. Embarrassed and stunned by her outburst, Miriam left and huddled before the fire.

Simon sat down beside her. "So what the hell's going on?" he whispered.

Miriam shook her head. "I guess he's still angry."

"Oh, Christ," murmured Simon.

Miriam was surprised but she didn't really blame Richard for that. She was outraged though by his lack of sensitivity toward what he knew was important to her, whether he agreed with it or not. She had wanted to leave her own anger and her political convictions and seriousness behind but he wouldn't let her. He was deliberately making it difficult for them to be friends.

Trying to calm herself, Miriam studied the embroidery on her sleeves and took deep breaths. She was wearing an old caftan that had been left in her closet by a former visitor. Simon had said it looked good on her. It was white with a red and black border around the sleeves and hem. Blood and death, she mused, and was reminded of the chaos from which she had come and that had apparently followed her to Les Bluets.

Les Bluets/3

After lunch Beth and Claire took the children to gather blueberries that grew on the hill behind the farm. Simon and Jack removed their shirts, perspiring in the heat as they worked to repair the crumbling wall. Only Miriam and Richard sat at the table drinking beer and reading. Since their argument they had avoided being alone together and had maintained a superficial politeness in front of the others.

"So, Miriam!" said Richard suddenly, making her jump in surprise. They stared at each other, squinting in the bright sunlight.

"Do you think we can smooth all this over or not?" he continued.

Miriam glanced away toward Simon and Jack who were struggling to position a large stone into place. "I came over here because the three of us were once good friends. I want peace and quiet — and some fun. I don't understand what's going wrong?"

"Why do you have to see everything in such black and white terms?" Richard asked. "You must know by now that life isn't like that."

"I don't believe that human beings are the measure of the universe, Richard," Miriam replied. "There are some realities, some truths, that are greater than we are."

"What makes you think so?" he asked in a detached way.

"Because I'm looking for them," she snapped.

He nodded, smiling at her. "That's the problem, isn't it? That's what's going wrong, Miriam."

Miriam felt like slapping Richard; she knew he understood what she meant but he was refusing, as Martin had so often done, to admit it.

"I think we have to get acquainted all over again, Miriam — taking nothing for granted." The way he looked at Miriam said that included his former love for her. "We've all changed since you were here with Martin," he concluded.

She returned his coolness. "In some ways, we're exactly the same, only more so." They both knew she referred to his drinking.

"Maybe we're less tolerant then."

"We're older."

Then, as they looked at each other, they both started laughing, almost involuntarily, at these analytical musings that, they knew, neither explained nor solved anything. Simon glanced at them and smiled, wiping the sweat from his face.

"We'll never agree about certain things, Richard, and I don't believe in trying to change people."

"Oh, I'd never try to change *you*, my darling!" Richard agreed, laughing.

After a moment of silence, Richard spoke seriously. "We should avoid those 'certain things' then."

"Avoidance," said Miriam. "The story of your life, isn't it, Richard?" Then she reached quickly across the table and grabbed his hands. "I'm sorry," she said. "I'm sorry. That was —"

"Cruel but accurate," he said. "Look, I'll stop 'baiting' you, as you call it."

Miriam sighed. "Richard, if you want to criticize or argue with me, you can do it directly, you know, to my face. You don't need to disguise it as a joke."

Richard smiled, shaking his head slowly. "Miriam, I don't want to argue." He stopped speaking abruptly. "There's a car idling up on the road." When the unseen driver began honking a high-pitched horn, he added, recognizing the sound, "It's the local taxi."

Miriam ran to the gates from where she could see the main road. It was Ellen, who waved excitedly.

"Hello!" Miriam ran up the steep drive and hugged Ellen. "Welcome, welcome!" Though she had never counted Ellen among her close friends, Miriam saw her, at that moment, as a sympathetic ally.

While Ellen paid the taxi driver, Miriam gathered up the various string bags and luggage. "Where have you been?"

"Spain. But I've been on several hot, crowded buses for three days getting *here!*" Miriam could see that Ellen was tired. Her red hair which was thin anyway looked lifeless; her skin was dry and pale.

"Well, what do you want — food, drink, or a good long rest?"

"Something cold to drink. Then sleep."

"Right. There's an extra bed in my room, but let's go have a beer first," Miriam said, shouldering another bag.

"Simon told me you stopped by before, so you've met the family."

"Oh, yes, the whole crew," replied Ellen. When Miriam glanced at her, Ellen smiled. "Quite a crowd."

"I know," agreed Miriam. "I wasn't sure I'd adapt."

"And have you?"

"Yes and no."

The two women were smiling as they entered the yard. Simon and Jack were seated at the table, having mutually decided they'd done enough hard work for the day. Miriam introduced Ellen to Richard.

"This will really knock me out," said Ellen as she lifted the glass of cold beer in salute.

"So how were your travels?" Simon was studying Ellen with interest.

Miriam knew he was remembering that she wrote pornography. She thought of teasing him about it but didn't want to embarrass Ellen or explain just then how he knew.

"Depressing." Ellen's quick glance around at the faces of the three men was unfriendly and defiant, like a caged animal ready to claw an unsuspecting passerby.

The flow of conversation couldn't overcome Ellen's barely suppressed anger and the tension it produced. After a few awkward minutes, Miriam took Ellen upstairs.

"Ellen, are you okay?" Miriam tried not to sound critical in addition to being puzzled.

"Sure. Spain was a real drag though."

"I was there once – only for a few days." Miriam drew the shutters in, closing out the sunlight, and locked them so that a shift in the breeze wouldn't bang them against the sill. "We can have a long talk later and catch up on things. Do you want me to call you for dinner?"

"No, I'd rather sleep," replied Ellen, already pulling off her shoes. "Dinner with a crowd doesn't sound particularly appealing anyway." Miriam heard the harshness in Ellen's voice again, and it worried her. She started out of the room but Ellen grabbed her and wrapped her thin brown arms around Miriam's neck. "It's so good to see you though!"

Miriam hugged Ellen and then stepped back. "You too. Sleep well."

When she returned to the yard, Richard and Jack had disappeared and Simon had returned to reading his latest science-fiction novel. He put the book down when he saw her approaching. "They're hanging new rope ladders in the little barn for the kids. The old ones were getting a bit worn." After a pause he asked, "What's the matter with Ellen?"

Miriam shrugged. "Tired, I guess. She'll be better after some sleep." Miriam noticed a blue airmail letter protruding from Simon's book. "Did you get the letter you were expecting from your partner?" She knew they were negotiating a new lease.

He smoothed the torn edge of letter. "It's from my girl friend Sarah."

"Is it serious?" Simon had never written to her of his romantic interests and Miriam was curious.

"She'd like it to be. Maybe. I want something with someone. Maybe Sarah."

"I know the feeling. It's the nesting instinct. You'd better watch out," she warned.

Simon laughed. "I didn't think you independent women suffered from that."

Miriam smiled wryly. "I've only thought about it seriously the last year or so. No rush, I tell myself. But sometimes I wonder if I need to settle that before I can accomplish anything else."

Simon nodded. The look on his face as he gazed past her toward the woods was troubled. "I watch Jack and Beth though and wonder why I'd ever want to do a damn fool thing like that for!"

"What do you mean?" Miriam probed. "You love kids."

"Sure, I do. Beth and Jack love their kids — that goes without saying — but that doesn't make it easy. Or even successful. Beth was tied down too young and resents it. Jack is bored and restless."

"I guess I haven't noticed that," Miriam admitted.

"They're cooler about it around me and mum," he said. "I guess they've had some real rows at home though. Jack was having an affair all last year and Beth found out about it just before they came over here."

"Oh, shit," Miriam sympathized. "Beth must be devastated."

"Right you are." He looked at her for a long moment. "I wouldn't like it one bit either, and it may end in divorce."

"Well, people go through bad times. Things smooth out." Miriam knew she was saying that to comfort Simon, not because she believed it or because she cared particularly about Jack and Beth's marriage.

"Maybe," he said. Silence fell between them and Simon picked up his book again.

"Would it disturb you if I brought the tape deck out here?"

"Of course not. I can read through anything."

"How about Bach?" She knew he didn't like classical music much, preferring jazz and folk.

He groaned, then laughed. "For you — even Bach."

Earlier that day, while sweeping the dining room, Miriam had found

102

a tape of Bach fugues that had been dropped behind the bookshelf. She dusted off the cobwebs and put it away in the writing desk for safe-keeping. All day she had been imagining the pleasure of the music unraveling around her. Now she brought the tape out to the yard and inserted it into Simon's expensive, high-powered battery-run cassette deck.

This is the music Sasha and I often played on Sunday morning while we ate a late breakfast with a bottle of champagne. We usually ended the meal by stacking the dirty dishes in the sink and going back to bed. I envisioned these leisurely weekend hours as something we would have together for the rest of our lives.

After we separated, I woke each Sunday morning, remembering that the accustomed ritual with Sasha would not, could not, occur because she was enjoying it with someone else. I also knew that she was probably just as happy as she'd been with me.

And why not? What kind of love, what kind of lover, wishes the beloved to be miserable?

Miriam stopped writing and stared unseeing at the thick, dark green forest of pine trees in front of her. She heard the children come running down into the little barn where Richard and Jack were still working. Beth and Claire strolled together into the yard with two pails of blueberries, wiping the dust from their faces and demanding beer. Tina accompanied them, walking sedately and carrying a yellow plastic bowl full of berries in her arms.

Claire took Beth's pail from her. "I'll bring out some more glasses," she said stepping into the front hallway.

"Hey, princess, you did pretty well for yourself!" said Simon, giving Tina a hug. Then he ran toward the trough for another cold liter bottle, swooping Davy into his arms on the way and throwing him, squealing, into the air.

"I picked all these myself," Tina said proudly to Miriam.

"That's great. May I taste one?" Miriam asked, reaching toward the bowl.

"No!" protested Tina. "These are for mum's surprise dessert!"

Beth laughed as she looked at Miriam. "That was my bribe!"

When Martha saw the tape recorder, she wanted to listen to the Sesame Street tapes she'd brought from home. To Miriam's relief, Beth stopped her before she could race into the house to get them. "Not now, dear, we'll finish listening to this first."

Claire, arriving with her hands full of glasses, agreed. "Yes, then you can take that tape machine to your room and listen 'til your heart's content."

Tina was sitting on the edge of the table, her feet dangling, as eager as her sister for the Bach music to end. "Mum," she said, "I wish we had a TV here."

"Oh, God, anything but that," moaned Claire.

"I hope we never even get electricity up here," Beth said.

"Ditto." Simon grinned at the kids as he opened a cold bottle of beer. "No telly in this house to rot your sweet little minds." He picked up Miriam's glass to refill it.

"Oh, none for me, thanks. I've got to do some laundry." As she retrieved her dirty clothes from the entry hall where she'd left them earlier, she overheard Simon telling Beth that Ellen had returned from Spain.

"How long is she staying?" Beth wanted to know.

"A few days probably."

Because of Ellen's disturbing arrival, Miriam was already apprehensive about her visit. If Ellen continued to be angry and sullen, everyone would blame Miriam for the unpleasantness. Miriam herself didn't want any more unpleasantness than she'd already had with Richard. She shuddered at the possibility of a verbal confrontation between Richard and Ellen. Because Ellen had left for Europe in April, she knew about Miriam and Sasha's original breakup in March but nothing of the final unpleasant encounters. Miriam didn't really want to discuss her recent past with Ellen either but, without some insight, Ellen would have no idea of the strength of Miriam's commitment to peace, quiet, and fun.

Miriam enjoyed washing her clothes in the cold water of the trough even though she could never get them as clean as she liked. Rubbing the hard-milled soap into a soiled shirt and then the fabric against the washboard, she thought of her grandmother who had done the laundry that way every week in the deep stationary tubs of the apartment house where they'd lived when Miriam was small. Now washboards were sold in antique stores and her grandmother's hands had protruding blue veins. Miriam's hands were fragile-looking, the fingers long and thin. They were strong enough, she concluded, but the water was so cold that the bones in her fingers soon began to ache.

She let the clothes soak for a while as she sat in the sun watching the ducks snatch at the pieces of wilted lettuce and stale bread that had been thrown into their pen. She imagined Beth wringing their necks, plucking off the shiny feathers and baking the pale limp bodies, as she was planning to do at the end of the summer. It gave Miriam a sick feeling to know in advance the time and details of another creature's death and the sadness of inevitability touched her as she watched the ducks, one white and two brown, totally unaware of their fate, quacking contentedly to each other in the sunny yard.

The culmination of the evening meal was another of Beth's gourmet successes, a large fresh blueberry tart with heavy cream to pour over it. Cries of appreciation and claps of applause filled the crowded dining room. Miriam ran upstairs to get her camera.

As she opened the closet door, trying not to wake Ellen, it squeaked. "Shit," she whispered to herself.

"It's okay. I'm awake." Ellen was inside Miriam's sleeping bag. She stretched her arms and legs, smiling and obviously refreshed.

"Sure you don't want some supper? It's lamb."

Ellen wrinkled her nose. "I don't eat meat anymore."

"Well," Miriam offered, "we're just starting dessert which is the most beautiful tart I've ever seen."

Ellen laughed. "What's her name? I'll go down immediately!"

Generally Miriam didn't like sexual humor but she was missing this particular lesbian brand enough that she didn't mind Ellen's off-color joke. "Come when you can!" she replied appropriately and went out the door laughing too.

"Okay, in a minute!" Ellen called after her.

In the dining room Miriam took several pictures of the tart before it was cut, with Beth sitting behind it looking hot and tired but pleased by all the attention.

Wearing a bright yellow caftan, Ellen came downstairs just as they were cleaning up after the meal, a task that was a chaotic and often amusing group effort. She greeted Beth, Claire, and the children briefly, in a polite but distant way that disturbed Miriam. Sitting down in front of the fire, she ate the slice of blueberry tart that Miriam had put aside for her and watched the completion of the communal housekeeping chores. Until Miriam sat down beside her with an unfinished glass of wine and asked for more details about the trip to Spain, Ellen spoke to no one else.

"Nothing much to tell except that the Spanish men hassle you constantly, everywhere. You can't really go anywhere or do anything alone." Ellen's high cheekbones were accentuated in the firelight, making her face look pinched and tense.

"I wondered why you wanted to go there on your own," Miriam commented.

Ellen ignored this mild criticism of her chosen itinerary. "I finally met some women in a Madrid bar, but they were into role playing." Ellen laughed loudly. "Can you see me in a black lace mantilla?"

Ellen's half of the conversation could have been overheard easily if all the adults except Claire, who was putting the children to bed, hadn't been playing cards in the dining room. Miriam hoped that her own lack of response on certain topics would steer Ellen clear of them.

"This is a very heterosexual setup here. Aren't you bothered by it?" Ellen's large candid eyes and raised brows were meant to encourage self-revelation.

"Not particularly," replied Miriam. "It's actually more comfortable than I thought it would be." Miriam leaned toward Ellen, trying to keep the content of the conversation between them.

"Do these people know you're gay?"

"Some do; some don't." Miriam saw that Ellen was interviewing. It was her usual style. "They aren't the kind of people who criticize the lifestyles of others anyway."

"I'll bet." Ellen studied Miriam for a moment. "You're so relaxed, Miriam. I've never seen you so nonchalant about things."

"I'm working on it," Miriam said, smiling. "You should try it too, Ellen."

"Meaning I'm being too intense for you?" Ellen was obviously trying to pierce Miriam's calm exterior, to arouse some kind of emotion in her.

Miriam wanted to be honest but also receptive. "Almost."

"Why are you working on it?" Ellen probed.

"Because I need a rest." Miriam swallowed the last of the wine and was about to suggest taking a walk out into the yard.

Ellen flicked her cigarette butt into the fire. "I'd really like a bath now."

"Okay." Miriam stood up. "You'll need some light though."

Jack prepared a gas lamp for them and they went upstairs, the flame throwing eerie shadows against the walls and ceiling.

Miriam lit the gas heater in the bathroom and started water running into the tub. "Would you like me to stay up here in my room while you bathe? It's a bit creepy alone."

"Why don't you just get in too and we can talk?"

Miriam hadn't had a bath that day and, though she wasn't usually comfortable in the nude except with a lover, it sounded refreshing enough for her to agree. Because Ellen was smaller, they both fit with room to spare in the oversized tub. Ellen lay back sighing in the hot steamy water. As she scrubbed herself with the loufa, Miriam caught Ellen studying her with interest and blushed.

"Romantic, isn't it?" asked Ellen, as if mocking Miriam's shyness.

"It could be, I suppose." She and Sasha had taken a lot of candle-light baths.

Again Ellen discerned Miriam's thoughts correctly. "Do you hear from Sasha at all?"

"Yes." Miriam's tone was guarded.

"Do you write back?"

"I haven't yet." Conversations with Ellen often had a tone of persistent inquiry. Miriam had come to accept that characteristic, while others they both knew in Portland had considered it manipulative and offensive enough to drop Ellen as a friend.

"That's good."

Miriam looked at Ellen sharply.

"I mean, you obviously can't trust her. It's always been apparent to me that Sasha isn't in touch with her own feelings."

"Pardon the cliché," Miriam commented. She wanted to change the subject now even more than during their conversation downstairs. Ellen was outspoken and enjoyed touching people's soft spots, and she was rapidly approaching Miriam's. "You can't tell me anything about Sasha that I don't already know," replied Miriam, stepping out of the tub and grabbing her towel from the back of the chair. She waited until Ellen had rinsed her hair. Then, carrying the gas lamp, she led the way back to the room. "I always have some cognac before bed. Do you want to come back down with me?" She took the white robe from its hook behind the door and pulled it over her head.

Ellen had unrolled her own sleeping bag on the other bed and she sat down on it now with a white beach towel wrapped around her. "You know, Miriam, I've always been very attracted to you. We could explore that attraction while we're over here together, free of any judgments our mutual friends might make."

Miriam was surprised by this proposal, not because it was so unsubtle but because it was totally unappealing. "That's not possible," was the only reply that came to her. She turned away as if protecting herself from Ellen's aggressive stare.

"Why not?"

"Well, for one thing," said Miriam, locating her sandals in the darkness of the closet, "I've been thinking of being celibate for a while."

Ellen laughed. "Have you made a vow to the Virgin Mary or something?"

Miriam finally turned around, forcing herself to confront the mockery on Ellen's face. "I guess I'm just tired of all that."

"Come on! What's the real reason?" Ellen was drying her hair with one end of the towel, revealing her nudity too obviously.

"That is *one* real reason," insisted Miriam. "The other is that I care for you as a friend."

"Really? Well, prove it then. Come to bed with me." She reached out, grabbed Miriam's hand and, catching her off balance, pulled her down onto the bed.

Miriam jerked away violently and stood up. "No! Ellen, for Christ's sake! Are you stark raving mad or what?" Though she knew she couldn't be forced, she stepped back.

Ellen snickered. "What are you afraid of? You're still hung up on Sasha, aren't you? That's what I figured."

Ellen had finally struck the soft, still sore spot too hard. Miriam sat down on her own bed to hook the straps of her sandals. "No, I'm not," she forced herself to say calmly. "You're wrong." Miriam was preparing to renounce Ellen as a friend.

"You don't want to fight, huh?" challenged Ellen, clearly not realizing that she'd already lost. "What's happened to you over here? That nice little nuclear family down there, the patriarch and his cook and his brats, changing your mind about things? It makes me sick!" Ellen's eyes flashed angrily.

Miriam picked up the gas lamp and stood in the doorway. "Are you coming downstairs with me or not?"

"Hell, no!" Ellen threw the towel on the floor and turned away from Miriam, unzipping her own sleeping bag. "I'd rather masturbate and go to sleep!"

Miriam spoke very softly to Ellen's naked back. "You're really a bitch, Ellen, and you make me very glad to be here." She turned away sharply and shut the door, leaving Ellen in total darkness.

When she got downstairs, only Simon and Richard still sat before the fire. They were both silent, staring into the flames and sipping their drinks. Miriam poured herself a large cognac.

"Well, what have you two been doing?" Richard asked suggestively.

"Arguing." Chilled and trembling, Miriam sat beside the hearth and put her feet up on the bricks that kept the logs from rolling out onto the floor.

"You've really got the knack, my girl," said Richard in a hoarse whisper.

"Richard, don't be an ass," muttered Simon from his corner of the couch.

"She can't stay," Miriam said after a moment.

Simon was instantly alert, leaning toward Miriam, his glass held loosely in his hand. "You're kidding. She just got here."

Miriam knew Richard was listening, though he was still staring into the fire. She tried to formulate something that would make sense to the two men, something that was the truth but that wouldn't incriminate either herself or Ellen, something that wouldn't take all night to say. Her back ached with the old familiar tension. She'd been feeling so much better mentally and physically, hadn't cried much, had been sleeping well, and was even putting on some weight. Now she saw her hard-won normalcy and health gradually receding in Ellen's presence, Ellen with her persistent questioning and aggression and anger. Miriam didn't want to be a foil for Ellen with Simon's family either and she saw that coming; even in private Ellen was a danger.

Simon interrupted her thoughts. "Miriam, what's the problem?"

She pulled a block of wood that was used as a stool over beside the arm of the couch and sat down on it next to Simon. "I just can't take it, Simon," she whispered fiercely. "I can't take *her*. She's got to leave — tomorrow. I can't explain, but believe me." She couldn't explain in any way they'd understand how perfectly Ellen symbolized everything she wanted to escape from and forget, that she, Miriam, wanted to be only in the present, that Ellen had struck the most painful of

Miriam's raw nerves. She was shaking in spite of the blazing fire at her back. "Ellen won't let me forget, Simon, and I'm so tired of remembering," Miriam groaned. Then she put her head down on the arm of the couch and cried.

Simon smoothed her dark, shiny hair with his hand. He spoke softly and slowly as if to a wounded, frightened animal. "All right, luv. You know what you can live with. Don't worry — I'm behind you, whatever. We'll talk this all out in the morning."

Miriam saw the puzzled look that passed between Simon and Richard. She knew she couldn't go back to her room and lie beside Ellen but she didn't try to explain any further. Simon found a blanket and laid it over her on the couch when he and Richard went upstairs. Without the gas lamp the room was filled with shadows thrown by the dying fire, but Miriam wasn't afraid. She was almost at peace with herself again. The reconstruction of her life would go on. Simon would help her safeguard it.

Les Bluets/4

Someone was touching her shoulder. Miriam woke quickly and confused, remembering as she sat up that she was sleeping downstairs on the couch. The room, in the early light, was cold. In front of her stood Ellen in the yellow caftan with a long brightly colored shawl wrapped around her. Its fringe swept the floor.

"What's going on?" Ellen demanded sternly.

Miriam rose and faced her for a moment not speaking, then began to lay kindling over the dead ashes in the fireplace. She searched for some matches and lit a piece of newspaper under the small twigs. "I want you to leave Les Bluets — today."

Ellen's high tinkling laugh echoed through the room. "Hey, Miriam, I can take no for an answer."

Miriam concentrated on building the fire the way she had watched Jack do many times. "It wasn't that."

"I'll bet!" exclaimed Ellen. "Why don't you admit you're afraid to spend time with me? You've always been cagey about our friendship. Now you're forced to deal with me and you want out."

Miriam stood up and looked at her. "Ellen, I don't want to be hassled about anything right now and that's all you've done since you arrived and you'll go on doing it."

Ellen's voice rose in anger. "You just don't want to give me any of your precious time! Why can't you admit it?"

"All right," Miriam sighed. "In order to give you my time, I'd have to be willing to take part in discussions that are painful and upsetting to me, and I just don't feel like doing that." She sat down on the couch and pulled the blanket around her.

Ellen remained standing, blocking her from the warmth of the fire. "Painful and upsetting, huh? I don't believe this! What's happened to you? You're so different from the way you were at home. What have you got going here? And with whom, I might add?" Her eyes, in the light that was beginning to pour through the unshuttered dining room windows, were accusatory.

"What the hell is this?" Filling the doorway, Jack stared at the two women.

Ellen turned sharply to face him and Miriam jumped up from the couch, surprised. She knew he rose before anyone else and went into Garance for the daily ration of bread and milk. Martha, who was going along that morning, stood just behind her father, her eyes wide with

113

curiosity.

Jack walked slowly into the room toward them. "What kind of game are you playing here anyway?" He addressed his question to Ellen in a low, almost threatening, voice.

Ellen looked at him disdainfully but wrapped her shawl more tightly around her. "My good friend, who invited me to this delightful spot, is now ordering me to leave."

Miriam decided quickly not to let Jack participate in the conflict between herself and Ellen, and stepped forward. "It's okay, Jack. Really. I'd like to handle this myself."

"If you can, then do it," he replied, still staring at Ellen. "You know, you didn't have a decent word to say to any of us from the moment you got here," he continued, pointing a finger at Ellen. "If Miriam asks you to leave, you leave." He grabbed the household expense bag from its nail inside the cupboard and went out with Martha, slamming the door.

Neither of them moved until they heard Jack start the engine of the Citroen and drive out of the yard. Then Ellen smiled cynically. "I'm surprised you didn't let him throw me out, just like this!"

"Oh, Ellen," Miriam said softly, "don't be ridiculous."

Ellen gave her a long cool look before speaking again. "You know sometimes back home, in social situations, I could hardly deal with your behavior. You were so hostile and manifested it in such sarcastic ways." She laughed to herself, shaking her head. "I even discussed it with my therapist. Then you suddenly seemed to change and I thought maybe we could be closer."

Miriam tried to remember those situations and exactly what her behavior had been, wondering how much of the hostility was caused by her unstable relationship with Sasha. She knew she had frequently experienced extreme mood swings during those months. "Why didn't you say something to me then?"

"I guess I thought it wasn't any of my business." Ellen shrugged. "I don't know."

"Well, you certainly seem to think my behavior is your business now."

"Now that Sasha's out of your life, I thought we could be better friends."

"And possibly more than friends," Miriam said, smiling wryly.

Ellen ignored the remark by turning away and staring into the fire.

"You've always made such a big deal about women being honest with each other, à la Adrienne Rich. Is that only for lovers?"

"I assume that honesty exists instrinsically between friends. That's what friendship is." Miriam sighed. "Sex is the great complication, as far as I can see."

Ellen spun around to face Miriam. "Well, that obviously isn't very far!" Ellen threw up her hands in exasperation. "You are totally untrustworthy! I reveal my feelings to you, in the honest way you've always praised, and what happens? I'm rejected and thrown out!"

"Ellen, you don't just reveal your feelings," Miriam argued. "You want audience participation, and I'm not willing." Wanting to end the conversation with some understanding, she reached out to touch Ellen.

"Spare me a reconciliation," Ellen said, pulling away. "I'd rather be enemies. It's more honest."

Miriam sat back, appropriately rebuffed, and abandoned any hope of a more agreeable parting. "I guess there's nothing more to be said then. Simon will drive you to the bus station." After a pause, she added, "I'm sorry, Ellen."

"For what? My behavior?" Ellen shouted. She was trembling with rage. "You're a mess of a person, Miriam, and it's not all Sasha's fault!" She turned and strode out of the room.

Miriam sunk down under the comforter and watched the fire she'd successfully built send its sparks up the chimney.

I looked forward to Ellen being here. I wanted to discuss with her the realizations I've had about my mother, to expose them to Ellen's clear direct perceptions that, in spite of their occasional irritation, have often been surprisingly insightful. And what did Ellen want? Did she come back to the farm specifically to seduce me? A year ago Sasha thought Ellen had sexual designs on me but I didn't see it. Maybe I simply wasn't paying attention. I don't expect passionate attractions to occur between friends.

I've never fallen in love with someone who is already a friend. My love for my friends has an asexual quality, like a shield protecting the relationship from the selfishness that erodes erotic involvements. Friendship is selfless, a higher form of love, and I believe it could be destroyed by sexual passion, that mindless desire to possess.

When Simon returned from Annonay, he and Miriam took a walk up the road.

"Well?" She wanted to know what Ellen had said to him in the car.

Timing his answer like the punchline of a good joke, Simon smiled but let a moment go by. "She thinks you denied any attraction to her because you've decided to go 'straight.' "

Miriam laughed. "That's easier than the explanation I gave her."

"Well, she'll console herself very nicely for the loss of you," he teased. "She bought a big box of pastries before boarding the bus."

In spite of this shared amusement, Miriam's political side, the staunchly feminist side, chided her for her unsympathetic response to Ellen and for her relief now at Ellen's departure. Ellen was right about one thing though: Miriam at Les Bluets was different from Miriam in Portland. She had once held to a certain political line and it had failed to sustain her in hard times. Her resentment about that was pushing her to affirm the right to her own individualism so that now a growing irritation coexisted with the guilt. She was gradually loosening the hold those former political beliefs had on her. She wondered how far she could go.

At the neighbor's pasture she and Simon leaned against the fence admiring the shiny auburn flanks of the horses as they grazed or lifted their heads to stare back with distant wary eyes.

"Are you enjoying yourself here, Miriam?" Simon asked after a few minutes.

She looked at him in surprise. "Of course! It's wonderful! What makes you ask that?"

"Sometimes you get so quiet. I'm never sure why — or what you're thinking."

"And you don't really want to know!" Even while she laughed, she realized that she wanted him to know, that Simon deserved more than an amused response. "I get bothered sometimes. I'm not used to being around men. I stopped socializing with them four years ago. I kept writing to you and Richard, but at home it was different. And I'm not used to being around families either, or kids."

"Sounds to me like you've been living in a bread box," commented Simon, glancing at her critically.

Miriam smiled to herself. "I suppose it does — and was. But then everyone creates a personal social circle that, inevitably, excludes some people from it."

Simon nodded thoughtfully. "I can't argue with that, but it seems like a question of degree, what the variety of composition is in your social circle, how representative it is of the world at large."

"Well, I'm enlarging mine now," she replied seriously, "and sometimes I have to step outside to know what's going on in there."

Simon nudged her shoulder with his. "That still doesn't tell me what things are bothering you."

Miriam paused a moment before answering. "Very simple things actually. Like Beth doing all the kids' laundry and Jack's, plus her own."

"She likes doing it."

Miriam made a face at him. "Yes, I know. Women are such willing slaves. They get all their pleasure in life out of serving everyone else."

Simon nodded, agreeing with her criticism of that patriarchal assumption, but didn't look at her. "All right," he said quietly.

Miriam was reassured by this indication of openness from Simon, so different from Richard's self-justification, and decided it was safe to continue. "I have a vision of the way life could be, Simon – every human being doing everything, entirely independent of each other, so that when two people chose to be together, it wouldn't be to complement each other's needs by role division, but as two whole, capable people respecting each other's completeness and essential separateness yet desiring to live those two lives side by side."

Simon remained silent when Miriam finished speaking, his brow wrinkled in the way that meant he was pondering this idea. She could tell he was skeptical and, after a minute or two, he said, "That's beautiful, Miriam, but a bit improbable."

"I suppose," she said softly. She looked at the horses, noting their serenity. They never had to choose, she thought. "I tried it – or thought I did – but it didn't work."

They started back then and at the bend paused to contemplate the farm below. Smoke from the fireplace in the main room curled out of the largest chimney. Of the five chimneys on the roof it was the only one they bothered to use now.

"Beth doesn't seem to want any help with the cooking either," Miriam commented, returning to their discussion.

Simon shrugged. "I guess she considers it her domain."

Miriam turned toward him annoyed. "Exactly! The only place where she has any power."

117

Simon glanced at her and then away, and she knew he understood what she meant about that too.

"In my ideal world," she said, "Jack would cook half the time."

"And Beth would repair the retaining wall?" Simon joked.

"Yes," insisted Miriam, "and the kids would grow up being able to do both." She sighed, discouraged again. "People always say they want their children to have a better life, and to be better people than they are, but children can only be as good as the people around them, Simon. All growth is a kind of imitation."

Simon began picking the red poppies that stood like signal flags in the tall grass along the side of the road. "Do you think you'd be a good mother, Miriam?"

"Terrible. I'm awkward with children and they sense it."

"Oh, I don't know," he said. "I think the kids like you well enough — for a new face. They know you won't take any nonsense but you treat them as if they're intelligent beings. That's the way my mum is too."

"I like Claire," she said simply. She knew it pleased Simon when the people he liked also liked each other but that wasn't the reason she said it. "I seem to have developed a soft spot for other people's mothers."

At that moment Richard came out into the yard, saw them and waved. They began walking slowly toward the farm again.

"Are things still as tense between you two?" asked Simon.

"I'm not a very good compromiser," Miriam said.

"Yes, I know." Simon chuckled, then fell silent.

"We're trying," Miriam concluded. She thought but didn't say, "for your sake." Their mutual love for Simon was the only unifying factor between Richard and herself now.

As they approached the last curve in the road before the farm, Simon stopped and took her lightly by the arm. "Tell me honestly, Miriam. Do you find it difficult to like me because I'm a man?"

She looked at him speechless, shocked by his doubt. "Oh, God, Simon, of course not!" she stammered at last. "You're one of the best human beings I've ever known." She leaned forward and kissed him on the cheek. "I love you, you know."

He smiled at her. "You mean I'm the one male friend you'll allow into the bread box?"

Miriam laughed. "I don't think you'd be very happy in there. I'll have to come outside to play."

118

They resumed walking, quietly enjoying their private joke. After a few minutes Simon broke the silence. "Maybe I've been taking too much for granted in life, Miriam. I'm a simple man with simple tastes, not a complex thinker like you."

Miriam shook her head at him. "Bullshit," she said.

Miriam sipped her glass of *pastis* and watched Jack and Simon run down the road and into the woods. This race had become an evening ritual that was cheered by the children and deplored by Claire who proclaimed each time that they would both have heart attacks. Beth watched from the dining room window where she could also keep an eye on whatever sauce was the specialty of the evening meal, and Richard, proudly defiant of all exercise despite his doctor's warnings, kept Miriam company with a glass of his own.

Simon may have simple tastes, because he has come to know that they're the best, but he is not a simple man. I've watched him doing a simple task, like mopping the tile floors. After sweeping each room, he painstakingly washes each tile, often on his hands and knees, then opens the doors and windows for the sunlight to chase out the dampness. Performed willingly and in silence, this mundane act, he says, creates a loving communion between himself and the house. This afternoon as he gathered flowers for the dining room table, such a repetitive yet timeless task, I watched him and imagined that it was possible for me to create a meaning for my life too, pure and simple and as brilliant as those red poppies. Like a religious ritual, Simon's ministering attentions to his life here give it a redemptive quality.

I meant it when I told Simon I thought he was one of the best human beings I've ever known. He's kind and gentle and loving — as well as intelligent — and I can't help admiring him. I like to watch him with the others, especially with the children, as we sit here at the table or around the fire at night. Perhaps if I stay close enough to him, all of his wonderful qualities will rub off on me.

That night after Claire and the children had gone upstairs, Beth and Jack sat at the small kitchen table with the gas lamp, reading as usual.

119

Richard, Simon and Miriam, also as usual, sat before the fire, speaking only occasionally.

Miriam was studying Simon's short, stubby fingers resting on the arm of the chair beside her. They were definitely masculine, so very unlike her own. Remembering Ellen's disturbing presence in the house the evening before, Miriam had an impulse to lay her hand gratefully over his. Instead she leaned forward to poke the glowing logs into a fiery blaze. "Simon," she said softly, "you know what I want most in my life?" She didn't wait for him to respond. "I want to be a good person — and a great writer." She knew she'd had too much to drink when she voiced such embarrassingly flamboyant goals, but at least she refrained from adding that she also wanted someone who would support her devotedly on the way to being both.

"You'd better get busy then," commented Richard from his huddled position next to her.

"Am I asking for too much?" she asked him.

Richard laughed softly. "Of course, you are, my love, but then you always have. Being good and being great are mutually exclusive."

"You're full of shit, Richard," Simon muttered, not looking at either of them.

Richard leaned forward. "You think it's a realistic goal?"

"I didn't say that, mate. But ideals have a purpose like anything else. You can never achieve them, but they keep us moving in the right direction."

Recognizing the possible truth of Simon's observation, they all settled into silence again to contemplate it.

As if it had detached itself from her body, Miriam suddenly noticed her hand resting far away on the arm of the couch. As she studied it, at that exact moment, Simon reached out and covered it with his own. The movement was so gentle and unthreatening that Miriam did not pull away as she might have done in other circumstances or with another man. Though her heart began to beat rapidly, Miriam's hand remained there under Simon's and through it she felt the warm moistness of his palm. Miriam had a momentary vision of them sitting there for years, dreaming before the fire, the lord and lady of the manor. Though she quickly dismissed her imagining as silly and impossible, the significance of their two hands touching like that, in such a prolonged embrace, came to her gradually through the next glass of cognac. The potential both intrigued and frightened her. The fire crackled and began to die in the silent room. Outside the wind was blowing through the pine trees with enough force to make the heavier boughs creak. Upstairs a shutter banged.

"Damn!" exclaimed Jack, closing his book. "Those shutters are supposed to be hooked."

"Well, I'm going up now," Beth said, "so I'll check them all."

Jack stretched and yawned. "I guess it's that time."

Beth stood up and Miriam saw that she was looking, not at Jack, nor at the three of them before the fire, but at the two clasped hands. Miriam also saw the curious glance Beth gave her brother as she said good night and was suddenly nervous. Then Jack and Beth left the warm room and groped through the dark hallway to the stairs shining a flashlight before them.

Miriam got to her feet somewhat unsteadily, swallowed the last of her cognac and smiled down at Richard.

"Watch it on those stairs," he mumbled to her sleepily.

"Right," she whispered. Simon was gazing up at her with his head resting against the back of the armchair. They looked at each other for a long moment and again Miriam was both intrigued and frightened. She leaned down and kissed him lightly on the mouth. "Good night, dear Simon. Sleep well."

She climbed the stairs in the dark, finding her way with the help of the handrail. At the top she could see clearly by the moonlight coming through the window of her own room and into the hallway. As she slid into the sleeping bag, she continued to feel the warm pressure of Simon's hand on hers, the quick moisture of their kiss.

Richard stumbled upstairs with much less grace and inadvertently banged the bathroom door against the stone wall. "Christ!" he muttered. His urine pouring into the toilet bowl resounded through the hallway but almost everyone behind the closed doors was dreaming by then.

As she entered the heavy sleep of the intoxicated, Miriam imagined Simon still awake before the dying fire, searching the glowing logs for a face that kept shifting perspective.

121

Les Bluets/5

A second letter arrived from Sasha expressing sorrow and regret. "I can't accept it that we don't have a future together," she wrote. "Should I shoot my wad and fly to France? We could travel somewhere. I'd go anywhere with you, darling!"

Miriam sat at Simon's typewriter arguing with herself. She didn't believe the pleas, having heard them too many times before. Intellectually she knew they meant nothing concrete. They did not mean that Sasha yearned for a life together the way she did. So romantic, mused Miriam, but pure nonsense.

The letter went on: "If I don't come to you, it's not because I'm emotionally involved elsewhere." Miriam wondered how the Other Woman was doing. She knew very well how Sasha behaved when she wanted someone other than the one who was currently at hand. She withdrew. She cried. She was irritable, finding fault with every word and gesture. At that point the Other Woman probably couldn't do anything right.

"I need some time alone, just for a while, to discover who I really am." Though she knew better than to ask, Sasha obviously believed Miriam would be available when she finally found herself. *There's no hope for this relationship,* Miriam reminded herself, *so face it now. You cannot wait for Sasha to grow up.*

Without being nurtured by anything more solid than erotic platitudes, the love within me is losing its energy and all there is now is this pain. Heartache is a genuinely physical sensation in spite of its emotional references, the sensation of a stake run through my chest splitting my heart like an apple sliced cleanly in half by a sharp knife. The love will turn brown and rot just like the flesh of the apple.

Yet her whole body, her mouth, her hands, wanted to touch Sasha. She imagined running her hand along the inside of Sasha's thighs, Sasha trembling and moaning under the pressure of her fingers, Sasha lying between her legs, pressing her down hard. Miriam ached for Sasha's touch too, one kiss, one long, hard embrace, and the longing was so acute that she felt slightly faint in the stuffy heat of the loft. She had liked Sasha's forcefulness, liked abandoning herself to the pretense of masculinity.

Quick loud footsteps on the stairs to the loft broke through her sexual reverie and she was left with only the frustrated desire. Then she remembered that Simon was taking a broken bicycle to the repair shop in Annonay and that she'd planned to ride along.

Davy clomped across Simon's room in his cowboy boots. "Here you are!" he shouted as if she were a mile away instead of a few feet. "Uncle Simon is looking for you!"

"I'll bet he is. Tell him I'll be right down, okay?" She needed some time alone to banish Sasha from her thoughts.

"What's the matter?" Davy's crossed eyes penetrated her adult aloofness bluntly. "You look funny."

"Do I?" Well, I got a letter today that's upset me a little." She smiled at the sincere concern on his face, but continued to sit at the table folding and unfolding the five pages of Sasha's letter.

Finally Davy began hitting her on the arm impatiently with his small hard fist. "Hurry up! Hurry up!" he said rhythmically with the punches.

Miriam noticed Davy was wearing his Superman tee shirt. She'd found herself disliking the boy simply because the men, and especially Richard, reinforced his physical aggression as appropriate and amusing. Though she believed that Davy would ultimately be the real victim of this conditioning, she hadn't openly criticized the adults. Now her own vulnerable state of mind made it easier for her to deal with the child as another human being capable of self-understanding, sensitivity and change. "Davy, don't do that. I don't like it."

He looked at her a moment, confused but defiant, then brought his fist back as if to pummel her again.

She caught his arm in midair. "I *said* I don't like that." She let Davy's surprise pass in silence and then released his arm. "Now — would you like to be friends with me, Davy?"

He nodded cautiously after a moment, as if he weren't quite sure what that entailed.

Miriam paused, uncertain herself if the equal treatment principle really worked. "Well, I think we could be friends, but I like to be treated nicely. I don't like to be poked, or pushed, or shoved, or yelled at. Do you?"

He shook his head emphatically.

"Well, as friends we won't do those things to each other. We'll treat each other nicely, won't we?"

Davy nodded but still didn't speak.

After observing the three children for only a short time, Miriam already knew how to seal an agreement. "Shall we keep this little talk a secret between the two of us?"

Davy smiled this time. "I like secrets," he said.

Miriam winked at him and he winked back. Richard had spent at least an hour the other day before trying to teach him how. "Hey," she said, "I think you're getting it." She stuffed Sasha's letter into her pocket, stood up and held out her hand.

Davy took it, staring curiously up at her as though she might be the keeper of other even more important, secrets, and they went downstairs.

Simon was lifting the broken bicycle into the back of the Citroen when they came out onto the front steps. "About time! I thought maybe you'd been kidnapped," he joked, with a smile for Davy.

Miriam gave Davy's hand a squeeze. "I nearly was." As she watched the boy run to join Claire and his sisters who were playing cards at the outdoor table, she wondered how she could have forgotten, in the confusion of her response to Sasha's letter, that the present was a much happier place.

They promised Beth to be back for lunch at one o'clock and drove out of the rutted yard, scattering the chickens and raising a cloud of dust. Miriam liked the drive to Annonay. The road wound down the mountain and at each curve there was a fresh view of the valley with its farms and pastures.

They stopped for an old farmer who was taking his flock of sheep across the road. He wore the black pants and jacket traditional in the French countryside, but the bandana tied around his forehead was red and white striped. His face was wrinkled, as dry and tough as a piece of chamois cloth, and the butt of a Gauloise hung from one corner of his mouth.

"How do they look so wise?" Miriam whispered as if the shepherd could have heard her or understood English.

"Communing with nature in solitude," replied Simon. Miriam knew this sentimental explanation was one of Simon's favorite jokes on the tourist mentality, and that the shepherd was probably an insensitive bigot who would steal from anyone and call it a gift from God. "If you can get them to talk though," he added seriously, "they tell the best damned stories you've ever heard."

"Better than Richard's?" she asked.

"Don't tell him," replied Simon.

As the last sheep cleared the front of the car and Simon prepared to drive on, the old man tipped his hat to them and smiled broadly. He had only three teeth, yellow and crooked.

Simon turned on the radio and found the station that played American and British popular music. The song that was playing was one Miriam associated with the beginning of her relationship with Sasha. They'd danced to it often. She felt a cold shiver run up her spine and her throat constrict.

"Are you cold?" Simon began to roll up his window.

"No, no." It was a mild morning and, until that moment, Miriam had been perfectly comfortable in her lightweight India cotton dress. She thought she had successfully calmed the earlier disturbance within her, had escaped the pit of depression that had opened before her in the loft room.

Any contact with Sasha, from the memory a song on the radio arouses to an inappropriately romantic letter, is still capable of nearly destroying my self-confidence, of ripping the fabric of the new life I am weaving and revealing that beneath it, I am still mourning the loss of a worthless fantasy. Sasha's absence created a lonely void within me and these unexpected reminders, fatuous as they are, make me unable to fill that void with what is clearly so much better. I am still hopelessly trapped no matter how hard I try to escape. I want to escape!

After a long silence Simon glanced at her. "Is something the matter?"

"Oh, I don't know. I guess so." She sighed and her breath trembled. Hiding her face from Simon's scrutiny, she continued looking out the window at the countryside that became a blur of green and brown. By the time he pulled the car over to the side of the road, the tears were sliding down her face. "Oh, I'm sorry!" she sobbed. "I just can't seem to control this crying, dammit anyway!"

"It's all right, you know, luv." He laid his hand on her shoulder and massaged it gently. "Was it the letter?"

Miriam nodded, putting a hand over her eyes. She could feel Simon stroking the hair at the back of her neck, and turned to face him. "I wish she'd just disappear!" she exclaimed fiercely. "I wish she'd stop existing, in my mind or anywhere! God, I hate that woman! I hate her!" Lodged deep in her chest, the pain throbbed relentlessly as if seeking release.

"Miriam, you mustn't say those things!" Simon put his arms around her has if to muffle the evil wishes as well as to console. "You'll never be rid of her if you keep thinking like that."

Miriam said no more but went on sobbing. He held and rocked her until she was quiet, then rummaged around in the glove compartment for a rumpled but unused Kleenex. While Miriam wiped her face and blew her nose, Simon returned to stroking her hair. "You know," he said thoughtfully, "I think negative emotions tie you to a person as firmly as positive ones." He shrugged and started up the car. "That's not a new theory, and it's been true for me."

After a few moments Miriam laughed softly. "I'll bet I really look like hell."

Simon studied her. "Not great but I can stand it." He took her hand and held it in his lap as he drove.

Miriam suspected that half of her was a fool and the other half a child, but she was pleased that Simon offered her understanding not pity. Strengthened by this support, she was determined to be distracted from her unhappy thoughts, at least long enough to enjoy their outing together.

Self-conscious about her red eyes and sniffly nose, she stayed in the car when they got to the garage. She watched Simon demonstrate the broken gearshift to the mechanic and, when the two men began laughing, guessed it was a foreign language difficulty. They shook hands finally and the mechanic tipped his hat to Miriam.

"Well, that was a first!" Simon exclaimed, jumping into the car. "He's from Brooklyn, New York."

Miriam began laughing too. "Did you feel silly?"

"Fortunately, he only let me get out about half a sentence of my bad French before interrupting." He smiled warmly at her. "How about a pre-luncheon cocktail in Garance, mademoiselle?"

Miriam agreed readily, wanting to prolong the trip. She sensed that Simon did too.

Simon liked to drive the winding road between Annonay and Garance like a sports car racer and soon the Citroen was bouncing along the narrow and cobbled streets of the village. The air in Garance always seemed to Miriam to be laced with gold dust, as if the village were surrounded by active and prosperous mines. She often had the surrealistic sensation of being free of normal confines of time and space while there. Perhaps, she mused, nothing existed outside the public square of Garance; that would certainly settle the question of Sasha.

Simon parked the car under the plane trees that grew in the center of the square. Cafe Benoit was the favorite of the inhabitants of Les Bluets and the white car was often parked in front of it on any day when errands took someone into town. Richard walked there each afternoon for a few draft beers. Everyone called it "the cafe" as if it were the only one in Garance.

They sat on the patio under a black and green umbrella advertising Cinzano and, after exchanging the usual pleasantries with Madame Benoit, ordered two large brown beers.

On one side of the square was the church, a village church like so many hundreds of others across France, but built of the local yellow stone. On Miriam's first visit there with Simon, Richard, and Martin, she had gone into the cool dim structure and lit a candle in a red votive glass for her mother. Standing righteously near the cafe, the clock tower of the church reminded madam's customers how much of the day was being spent in recreation.

Facing the cafe was the one-room post office, with its public phone booth and its single employee, a good-looking young man who spoke some English and tried to be helpful. Next door to it was the mayor's office. In addition to his civic duties, the mayor was Garance's only auto mechanic and could be seen frequenting the cafe in his gray work overalls.

Simon removed his sunglasses and gazed at Miriam a moment. "When you said you loved me the other day, what did you mean?"

"I meant I loved you as a friend." She paused, then added before he could, "Something's changing, isn't it?"

He nodded, emphasizing his agreement with raised eyebrows. "After you kissed me good night, I had to wonder."

"You're the one who grabbed my hand!" Miriam said, laughing.

Simon blushed. "And ever since I did, I've been so happy."

Miriam was suddenly afraid. "You always are. It's a quality about you."

"No, this is different." His eyes were definitely a deeper shade of blue than usual.

"It's different for me too," she said softly, not looking at him. "Until this summer I hadn't touched a man, even affectionately, for years. I thought I never would."

"I love you, Miriam."

He was serious and she believed him. "I love you too, but we shouldn't — not *that way*." Miriam noticed that her right hand was moving back and forth between the patterns the sunlight made on the table as it came through the seams of the umbrella.

"What do you mean 'shouldn't'?" Simon challenged. "You can't deny love. It's a gift."

"I know." *You can't stop it from happening,* Miriam thought, *or make someone love you if it isn't there. No matter how strong your own love is.* She'd tried with Sasha and failed.

Simon leaned toward her and waved a hand. "Miriam? Hello, anybody home?"

She laughed and was embarrassed because Simon had read her thoughts so accurately. "Sorry," she said, wiping the moisture from her beer glass nervously.

"Don't be sorry, Miriam. We both know you're going to get over it, sooner or later." After a pause he continued, "Have you ever considered this? It isn't that Sasha didn't love you — I'm sure she did — she simply didn't love you the way you *wanted* to be loved. And because you were looking for a certain kind of love but in the wrong place, you ended up feeling unloved and rejected." Simon leaned back in his chair, smiling. "You aren't unloveable or undesirable by any means."

Miriam remained silent for a while, wanting the logic of what Simon had said to erase her heartache permanently. Finally she stored both the truth and the pain away, for later when she was alone and could argue with them. "Where do you get all these words of wisdom?" she asked finally, amused.

He shrugged casually. "Communing with nature in solitude." Then he grinned. "From Claire."

"Lucky you," said Miriam.

"Oh, I'm obviously willing to share." He leaned forward and took her hands in his. "Miriam, I don't think it's just friendship anymore. Do you?"

"No, it's not just friendship anymore," she agreed. She was afraid then and, at the same time, thrilled. "There's certainly no other man in my life, not the way you are," she replied, wanting him to know how much she cared without necessarily committing herself to anything.

She wondered briefly what made her sensual attraction to Sasha so much more powerful, if it was based on her knowledge that Sasha could not be possessed while Simon would give himself generously to the one he loved. She looked at him for a long moment, wanting to convey her hesitation as thoughtfulness rather than a denial of involvement. When she imagined sleeping with Simon, she got a combined jolt in her stomach of excitement and panic. Her usual way of coming to terms with sexual attraction was to let it grow and eventually inflame her beyond control. Simon would make it easy for her to acquiesce too soon and then she would be too passive, unequal to his desire. He would be disappointed and she would be sad and guilty. As she had told Ellen, her friends were just that — not lovers. "I need time to get used to this!" she exclaimed, so befuddled that to think any further only irritated her.

Simon laughed. "So do I! Sarah will probably be sending me poison-pen letters — and, for old times' sake, Richard will challenge me to a duel."

Miriam changed chairs and sat down beside him. "Simon, our friendship is more important to me than having a love affair." She knew she was withholding, giving in to fear, and needing reassurance. "I seem to be alienating my friends right and left and I couldn't stand to lose you."

Simon looked at her incredulously. "Miriam, we'll always be friends. Always."

She nodded slowly. She wanted to believe him. Mostly she wanted to believe that it was possible to be both friends and lovers. "Simon," she sighed, "I just don't know."

"Look, Miriam, it won't make me love you less if we don't sleep together. Naturally I'd like to, but it's entirely up to you. I won't put any pressure on you."

"There's the pressure of my knowing that you love me and that you want it, and because I love you, I want to give you what you want," Miriam argued.

"I don't want you to give me what I want. Wait until you want me to give you what you want," Simon replied and the way he said it made it sound final and resolved.

The sun had moved in the sky, escaped the limits of the umbrella and shone on Miriam's face and arms. Her inner turmoil was momentarily pacified by the freedom of choice Simon believed existed between them, and by her belief that he would love her no matter what she chose.

As they sat drinking a second dark beer, the bell in the church tower began to ring the noon hour. It rang so long, preventing them from conversing normally, that Simon finally complained. "Has someone died?" he shouted. "What is this?"

"The 'Angelus.' "

"What's that then?" he persisted.

"A Catholic prayer to the Virgin Mary that's said three times a day, at dawn, at noon, and at dusk." She remembered that she's been particularly fond of the prayer as a child in parochial school, and that it wasn't said much any more.

"And how does it go, Sister Miriam?" Simon liked to tease her about her nunnery upbringing.

Miriam concentrated a moment, trying to recollect. "It's in three parts." The bells paused a few seconds in their ringing. " 'The Angel of the Lord declared unto Mary. And she conceived of the Holy Ghost.' The second part is 'Behold the handmaid of the Lord. Be it done unto me according to Thy Word.' Then, 'And the Word was made flesh. And dwelt among us.' " Miriam smiled. "There you have it."

" 'And the Word was made flesh,' " Simon repeated thoughtfully. "Something profound in that — if you're a writer, eh?" He released her hand and they rose to leave.

Miriam was reminded by his observation that she wasn't writing. Usually she would be feeling uneasy with this lack of productivity, expecting a self-induced urgency to descent upon her like a storm. She certainly couldn't see herself revising the crippled novel and she was too emotionally muddled to begin anything new. It would be easy, she thought, to renounce the persona of the writer at that moment, to discard the word for the flesh.

As they drove away from the square, Simon turned to her. "I'm going to make the salad for lunch whether Beth likes it or not," he announced, and he was smiling to himself all the way home.

Les Bluets/6

Miriam and Simon were lingering over a third cup of morning coffee after everyone else had left the dining room. The children had run out into the yard after gulping their bread and eggs. Jack and Richard were negotiating with the neighbors for some fresh-cured bacon. Claire's voice, mingled with Beth's, drifted down to them from the second floor where the two women were cleaning the children's room.

Simon broke off another piece of baguette bread and buttered it. "I dreamt about your Sasha last night."

Surprised, Miriam looked up from the old copy of *Paris Match* she was casually paging through. "How did you know it was Sasha?"

He shrugged. "Dark hair and eyes?"

Miriam nodded.

"Well, call it a coincidence," he said. He continued to gaze at Miriam, studying her features as if comparing her to the woman in his dream. "She stood between us, *that's* how I really knew."

Miriam played with the bread crumbs on the table near her hands. "She doesn't stand between us."

"You don't believe that," Simon said softly. "Neither do I. I'd be a fool to believe that."

"She's not on my mind so much anymore," Miriam insisted, looking away from him.

Simon smiled wryly. "She'll stand between us until you get the blinders off, Miriam, and see her as she really is rather than as a composite of your own romantic fantasies. It's not easy, I know – I've had to do it myself. You must realize that what you had in the past two years was an obsession, not real love."

"What I felt for Sasha was real love, Simon," Miriam argued.

"I wonder," he replied. "What I think is – we replay with our lovers the power games we lost as a kid with our parents, hoping we'll eventually win. We can never win though until we develop the missing parts of our personalities. Then we'll have real power in our lives."

"And how do you know what's missing?" Miriam asked.

Simon smiled. "You're missing whatever initially attracted you in the lover who doesn't love you as you want to be loved, but to whom you are obsessively attached."

Miriam nodded. "I thought I knew myself so well. I thought I knew what I was and what I wanted. Well, it was easy in Portland, I guess, in my little world."

Simon laughed. "Imagine a world smaller than Les Bluets."

"Yes," Miriam sighed. "Now it's all changed — like that!" she concluded, snapping her fingers.

"Changed by what — just by being here?" Simon looked doubtful.

"No!" exclaimed Miriam, reaching out to lay her hand on his arm. "By you, Simon, by you! You've shown me something new and part of me wants it — very much."

Simon stood up and began to clear the table. "But there's another part."

Miriam stood up too and opened a window. "One thing I've learned already — conflicts follow wherever you go. You can ignore them as Richard does or want to temporarily escape them as I have, but they still hang on, nagging. Even if you get rid of one, there's always another."

"Why does this have to be a conflict," asked Simon, standing in the doorway with his hands full of dirty dishes. "Loving is supposed to be a happy, enthusiastic act, Miriam," he added softly, then turned away and left her alone in the room.

The afternoon stretched hot and sultry before them. Miriam sat at the outdoor table watching Jack cut the children's hair.

Tina, who wore her straight brown hair in a pageboy like Beth, would only let her mother near her with the scissors. She wanted to practice writing the alphabet and Miriam, whose mystery novel was failing to be of much interest, allowed herself to be engaged as a tutor.

"Is this right? Is this a *k*?" Tina's small fist gripped the pencil, bearing down so hard that Miriam was sure she would break the lead before the twenty-six letters were made.

"Just about. Like this, Tina. Let me show you once." Miriam demonstrated the letter in large bold strokes. A frown of concentration dominated Tina's face and she pushed her thick bangs from her forehead as if it would improve her ability.

"Make me pretty, dad," said Martha, trying not to move.

"You're pretty enough, my girl," replied Jack. He was frowning in concentration as he studied the slightly crooked edge of hair above Martha's right eyebrow. "Better to be smart anyway," he added, "it lasts longer."

"Dad, can we get a cat?" asked Davy as he ran his toy car absent-mindedly up and down the length of the tile table, just missing Miriam's hands.

Jack smiled at his son. "Oh, I think we have enough small creatures at Les Bluets, don't you?"

"Where?" demanded Davy.

"Where?" echoed Tina, looking around the yard.

"He means the ducks and chickens, you sillies," said Martha archly.

"No, I mean the three of you," countered Jack. He turned Martha's head back gently and took a final snip from the left side of her bangs.

"Dad, we're not small creatures, we're people!" protested Martha.

"Well, sometimes," said Jack, stepping back to view his handiwork, "people can be like animals and animals can be like people."

The children fell silent, apparently pondering this exchange of personality among the creatures they knew. Miriam wondered if Jack was consciously giving a lesson on the use of metaphor or if it was his usual way of entertaining them.

"You're done, my girl." Jack swung Martha away from the table and into the air.

"Oh, daddy!" she cried, and began giggling, while Tina and Davy observed her flight with envy.

Jack set Martha down on the ground and held her by the shoulders until she regained her balance. Then, with his hand under his son's chin, he studied Davy's hair.

Miriam saw Jack's face soften and thought how painful a divorce and the subsequent loss of his family would probably be for him too, not just for Beth and the children. Yet apparently Jack was the guilty party. Like Simon she hoped that his affair had been caused by infatuation, only infatuation, and that it had passed. What she saw on his face at that moment was certainly love.

The difference between infatuation and love, it seems to me, and the failure to recognize the difference, can be extremely dangerous. Infatuation is actually the stronger of the two conditions. I always think of real love as being very similar to friendship, a quiet peaceful stream that caresses its banks and provides a haven for small forms of wildlife, while infatuation is like a torrent. When you've relaxed your stance on firm ground, it sweeps you off your feet. You never quite know what hit you. Then someone finds you unconscious downstream, your head lodged between two wet rocks, blood

139

running from your nose. Afterwards you crawl back to the shore, embarrassed and in pain and hope the wounds heal fast.

"Well, what kind of animal is Miriam?" Martha demanded of them all, bringing Miriam back rather abruptly from her private considerations.

"Maybe a cat!" insisted Davy, starting to pet Miriam's head.

"I think she's a bit of a porcupine," said Jack, his eyes meeting Miriam's with an amused gleam in them.

The children giggled and Miriam blushed. "A porcupine!" exclaimed Davy.

Jack nodded at Miriam. "Prickly."

She responded to his banter with a sharp look. "Better be careful in that case," she warned. Then she grabbed Davy and tickled him until he screamed and she let him escape.

The moon was full. Beth looked out the window behind her and announced, "There are no clouds, and it's huge, just huge!" Jack and Richard glanced at the large pearly disk in the sky and returned to the last bid. Beth, who had already passed, laid her cards down and approached Claire who was knitting in the large chair before the fire. "Mum, will you take my place for a while? I want to go outside. It's so beautiful tonight."

"Just let me finish this row," Claire said.

"Come on then, mum!" urged Simon. "We can't do a thing with just the three of us."

As she sat before the fire with a cognac, her notebook open but neglected on her lap, Miriam was vaguely aware of Beth behind her putting on a sweater.

"Miriam, come see the full moon!" Beth suddenly insisted.

Miriam could think of no reasonable refusal. She set her half-empty glass on the wood stump beside the chair and, grabbing someone's jacket in the hallway, followed Beth outside.

The yard and the woods beyond were glazed with a milky light. They sat together on the table, feet resting on one of the wooden benches, and watched the moon as it rose high over the valley. Both their faces, in spite of dark tans, were chalky in the lunar brightness.

Miriam recalled a conversation she and Simon had had a few days earlier.

"Beth told me she's disappointed that you two haven't gotten closer," he'd begun.

Miriam wasn't entirely oblivious to the lack of personal communication between Beth and herself. "Well, it's hard to have a good discussion with her," she'd replied defensively. "She's always with the kids."

"Miriam, you know that's not true."

Simon was right, and Miriam graciously admitted her failure in social responsibility. To herself she acknowledged that she was intimidated by Simon's sister, though they were nearly the same age. Beth's domestic skills and her recognized authority as a parent made her seem more experienced in human relationships, the area that presently obsessed and confused Miriam.

Beth lit a cigarette and offered one to Miriam. The match was like a firefly passing between them in the dark. "Do you have any brothers and sisters, Miriam?" she asked after a pause.

"No, I'm an only child. I've mostly lived alone too," Miriam volunteered, "and now it seems the least complicated way to live. I guess I got used to being alone a lot as a kid," she concluded. She sensed that in her uneasiness with Beth she was beginning to ramble.

"So being here with all these people must be a bit difficult," Beth commented.

Miriam sensed a probing curiosity on Beth's part and shifted nervously. "I've never lived communally. I can see it takes more than love and proximity to be successful."

"It's real hard work sometimes," Beth said reflectively as she buttoned her sweater against the chill air.

Miriam suspected Beth was referring more to Jack than to anyone else on the farm, and was wondering if and how they'd decided to stay together when Beth grabbed her by the arm.

"That reminds me!" Beth exclaimed. "I had a very strange dream a few nights ago and I meant to share it with you."

"This must be the day for people to tell me their dreams," murmured Miriam, smiling to herself in the dark.

After a moment Beth realized that Miriam was waiting for her. "There'd been a nuclear war," she began, "and somehow we, all of us who are here now, returned here because we thought it would be safer. You know, the air and water would be cleaner for a longer time and we could grow our food. The main part of the dream was full of details about *how* we managed to survive. And we did, though barely. After awhile all the men decided to leave the farm, to explore what was left of the world. I thought this was silly and told them so, but Jack wouldn't listen to me. They went and I knew they died out there. So we women were here, with the kids, working the land, eating apples and potatoes we'd grown, and drinking milk from our cow."

"Were we happy?" asked Miriam.

Beth looked at her with a self-satisfied smile. "Yes, very happy."

Miriam thought the dream was like much of the lesbian fiction currently on the market, utopian and sentimental, and wondered how Beth would react to such a comparison. Because she'd promised Simon to make more of an effort, and finding herself suddenly relaxed with Beth, Miriam decided to break the barrier between them. From experience she knew she could test, with one short dialogue, the potential for any real friendship. "Are you aware that I'm gay?"

"I haven't been, no," replied Beth without surprise or hesitation. "It really doesn't matter to me one way or the other. I consider myself a feminist, you know, if that means anything."

"It wouldn't have six months ago, but it does now," said Miriam.

"What do you mean?" Beth's voice had that probing tone again, but was sincere.

Miriam was enjoying with a certain degree of self-mockery her recent shifts in political perspective. "Let's just say I've been humbled by experience. Or maybe my obstinacy and narrow vision couldn't survive when confronted by a larger view. Or maybe, as Richard has suggested, we're all just getting older."

Beth nodded, apparently accepting Miriam's intentional vagueness. After a pause she said, "Ever since that night we talked about George Eliot, I've been hoping we'd talk like that again."

"I know I've been distant and I'm sorry about that," Miriam replied. "I've been overly preoccupied with things — old relationships."

Through the one open window in the dining room, they heard Simon's laughter and the pinochle game ending.

"I've been holing up in the kitchen so much you wouldn't have had a chance anyway," apologized Beth.

"I know, and if you don't watch it, you're going to turn into a casserole," Miriam joked.

Beth began to laugh, then stopped. "Maybe life would have been easier if I'd been a chef instead of a wife," she commented bitterly.

After a few moments Miriam said, "Simon told me about it."

Beth shrugged. "Oh, I'm sure we'll work it out, hang in there as they say. Until next time!"

"You mean Jack's done this before?" Miriam had difficulty seeing Jack as the wandering type.

Beth shook her head. "I don't think so, but now I'm on guard." She looked at Miriam, her eyes narrowed in the moonlight. "You know, I really don't want a divorce, but I'd like to get even, make him feel what I've felt. Oh, I'd love it if he really suffered!"

"I know that feeling," Miriam said. She was watching the clouds beginning to gather over the valley.

"You mean, it's not any better between lovers of the same sex?" Beth asked, surprised.

Miriam laughed. "Probably worse, because in that situation you know the psychology behind the games first-hand.

"Like an old friend," mused Beth.

"Like me and Simon?" Suddenly Miriam wanted Beth's opinion, and her approval.

Beth smiled. "I've noticed." She studied Miriam seriously for a long moment. "How does that work — since you say you're a lesbian?"

"Damned if I know." Miriam flicked her cigarette away from them into the darkness. "One thing I do know," she added emphatically, "no other man would interest me."

"He's special, all right," agreed Beth.

Miriam nodded. As she watched the moon, it disappeared for a moment behind the clouds.

I wrote a long narrative poem about the moon goddess during those idealistic first few months as a socially and politically correct lesbian. Later I wrote a love poem for Sasha, comparing her to a shooting star in a sky dominated by a full moon. Traditionally, in the matriarchal mythologies, the moon is the ultimate symbol of the free female spirit.

Is it possible to love deeply and yet remain free?

"I used to think Jack was special too," Beth continued. " 'Love is blind.' "

"Simon keeps telling me that we have to change that," said Miriam.

143

"Love should be inspired. It has to be an effect before it can be a cause."

Beth laughed. "You've lost me but I'm definitely interested. And freezing!" she said with an involuntary shiver. "Let's go in."

They slid off the table and crossed the yard quickly, Miriam following Beth. In the doorway Miriam turned and glanced at the sky once more, just in time to see a black shadow pass across the white face of the moon. It was a hawk, she decided, or a single, powerful hand.

Miriam didn't drink much as they sat around the fire that night because she didn't want to muddle her thoughts. A clear, unwavering decision is what she wanted but it eluded her. She went to bed early but couldn't sleep. The question at the end of her various formulations repeated itself endlessly: "What am I waiting for?" She knew she would do it.

She heard Simon and Richard go up to the loft. Her watch said one-thirty. For a while she lay there imagining Simon inside the sleeping bag with its purple flowers, the moonlight streaming through his window as it was through hers.

Finally she went up the stairs, stepping very carefully in her bare feet to avoid bumping anything and waking Richard. She opened the door to Simon's room slowly. The moonlight was shining directly on the typewriter. She walked over to it and laid a hand on the cold black and chrome body.

"I hope to Christ you're not planning to work at this hour!" Simon's loud whisper made Miriam jump.

They both laughed at the thought.

"Come over here before you freeze to death," he said.

Miriam crossed the room deliberately, fully aware of the moment. Simon opened one side of the sleeping bag and she slid into the warmth.

Les Bluets/7

Slowly, like a mermaid approaching the shimmering surface of the water from deep below, Miriam reached consciousness. Without opening her eyes, she knew she would again be the last one out of bed. The sounds of breakfast echoed through the empty hallways and cavernous room chiding her for another lazy awakening. The relentless sunlight on the bed, radiating through the sleeping bag as if it were an electric blanket, meant it was at least nine o'clock. Soon she would be too sticky and uncomfortable to lie there any longer. She rolled over and flung the sleeping bag back, stretching her naked body sensuously in the sun like a cat. Pointing her toes at the far wall, she saw the muscles form in her thighs and calves and decided that the lean strength of her legs was truly an admirable feature.

Simon had risen an hour and a half earlier to light the fire in the main room and to drive into Garance for bread and milk. She hadn't wanted him to leave the comfort of the bed, reducing the time they had to be secluded and intimate together. She snuggled into his arms, and he held and kissed her, and reminded her of his promise to let Jack sleep in. When they felt the slow stirring of desire between them, he leaped up and pulled his trousers on. "Phooey!" she said, then fell back to sleep almost immediately.

Now, leaning over the edge of the bed, she found her white caftan in a wrinkled heap on the floor. Knowing that Simon would probably not come back upstairs, she stood by the window gazing unfocused into the deep woods and pulled the robe over her head. Distracted by the unexpected pleasure and satisfaction of being Simon's lover, Miriam was somewhat impervious to her environment. She found herself forgetting to rinse the soap from her freshly laundered clothes, occasionally deaf to the questions directed to her, unable to concentrate for long on the lightest of reading material. After the first few days, when she finally perceived these signs of romantic delusion, she laughed privately at herself and decided to enjoy the situation thoroughly.

At least I haven't been suffering over Sasha so much lately, and not just because most of my time and energy is going to Simon. I have consciously banned her to the realm of rational not emotional response. I've been trying to analyze, as Simon suggested, why I found Sasha so obsessively attractive, what she has that I think I'm missing and want to possess by pos-

147

sessing her. I already recognized last spring how like my mother she is, how charming and how beautiful. I wanted to possess Sasha the way I wanted to possess my mother, the way every child wants to possess its mother and never can.

I remember one evening when Sasha and I were dining out with several women friends. The conversation progressed hilariously to the subject of friendships with men. Sasha began to talk of an old friend who was gay and living in San Francisco and with whom she preserved close ties. She joked about how in high school they'd pretended to be married to fool their classmates. Then she added, "Who knows? Maybe we'll do it yet!"

This revelation hit me all wrong. "Thanks a lot!" I said, standing up suddenly. I excused myself and went to the restroom fuming with anger.

Sasha followed me. "What's wrong?" She looked puzzled, and innocent as always.

"Do you ever listen to yourself?" I refused to give her more of an explanation than that. I delivered my punchline, sputtering with fury: "I'm disgusted by you! And myself for putting up with you!" I walked out of the restroom leaving her there with tears in her eyes.

Sasha finally returned to the table, threw some money at me to pay for her food, and left. After a brief embarrassed moment, the others chose to ignore the whole scene and the conversation resumed on a lower key.

I realized later that my anger was the result of a desire for everyone to recognize that Sasha was committed to me, though she'd never confirmed this except during moments of passionate lovemaking and had given me plenty of evidence to the contrary. In spite of all the discouragement, I kept trying to possess Sasha with her charm and beauty, which I believed would finally make me happy with myself.

Rebecca arrived that afternoon, in the same taxi that had brought Ellen. She and Miriam stood in the middle of the road hugging each other hard and laughing until the taxi driver cleared his throat impatiently. Everyone came into the front yard at various paces, the children running, to meet the new American visitor, another friend of

Miriam's. She had no fear that Rebecca would become a popular member of the Les Bluets community if only the others could forget the awkwardness of Ellen's short stay.

"My God, Miriam," whispered Rebecca as they entered the cool hallway with her expensive leather luggage, "you were right. There are a lot of people here." Rebecca, too exhausted to remember any of the names, was nonetheless polite about the introductions.

"Come on, let's go upstairs," Miriam offered, wanting to rescue her friend at least temporarily from the pandemonium.

Rebecca collapsed on the one wooden chair in Miriam's room and the two women looked at each other, happily relieved to have met successfully in such a far place. Miriam had never seen the perfect Rebecca so disheveled, or in such need of a bath and fresh clothes.

"You look wonderful!" exclaimed Rebecca. "You've gained some weight."

"Yeah, I think so. My Levi's will stay up without a belt."

"My God, what a beautiful tan you have!"

Miriam hoped that Rebecca's complimentary observations meant she was improving emotionally as well. "Don't worry — it won't take you long to look great too," she joked. "I've found a few extra hangers for you." She indicated the closet they'd share. "The bathroom is right next door. How's your jet lag?"

"Still hovering around the edges." Rebecca stood up, pacing back and forth across the room. "But, Miriam, I never realized, truly realized, that there's a whole different world outside the United States! I mean, I had to learn sign language in Paris — real fast! I am in a foreign place! I am an alien!" she exclaimed excitedly.

Miriam listened to Rebecca's enthusiastic outburst and was amused. She tried to remember how she'd felt on her first trip abroad, alone with several foreign language dictionaries, seven years before. She watched her friend dancing, exhausted but exhilarated, around the room, and felt a rush of affection for her. Before leaving Rebecca to unpack and rest, she explained a few of the daily routines, then added, "You're just in time for one of the highlights of the summer, I'm told, a catered dinner tonight at Benoit's in the village."

Miriam and Simon discovered that the best time for lovemaking was in the late afternoon. Simon took his bath about five o'clock, as the heat of the day began to pass. When Miriam entered the loft, barefoot and still in her shorts, he was stretched out naked on the bed, eyes closed, a half smile on his face. "Don't forget to lock the door," he reminded her. The lock was a wooden bar that slid across the door and into a rusted metal hook set in the stone wall.

Miriam pulled off her tee shirt as she crossed the room and flung it onto the chair. The breeze coming in the window cooled her skin as she paused to look out. "The hawk is there," she commented.

"Again and again," he replied confidently.

Miriam had finally accepted Simon's interpretation of the bird's daily reappearance and hoped it applied equally to the happiness of Les Bluets that was uniquely her own.

"Do you love me, Miriam?" Simon asked, holding out his hand to her.

She turned away from the bird to look at him. "I always have," she replied simply.

While Beth and Claire were upstairs bathing and dressing the children, the others sat at the outdoor table drinking *pastis* and discussing the courses that had been served at Benoit's the summer before. Miriam noticed that the men had put on their best shirts and shaved more carefully than usual. Apparently even Richard had taken a bath.

"The fish last year, remember? A whole, perfectly brown trout each! And the lemon sauce!" recalled Simon. "I hope we have that again." Beth had been mischievously quiet about the menu she'd ordered.

"They serve it with the head still on, one eye staring up at you," added Richard to Rebecca, as if trying to intimidate her.

"Good!" she replied with a bright smile, refusing to let him win at that game. "The head's the best part anyway."

They were still laughing when Jack pointed toward the retaining wall. "What's that damned cock doing now?" he wondered aloud.

They turned to watch the newly purchased cock picking his way slowly along the edge of the retaining wall. The brown hen, the smaller of the two females Simon had acquired the summer before, was at the far right end, pecking between the stones for bugs. The frustrated attempts of the young cock to mate with this particular hen had been a source of entertainment for several days. The hen either avoided him altogether or, if the cock got too near her, the larger speckled hen would attack him until he wandered away discouraged. This time

150

though, with the speckled hen nowhere in sight, it looked as if the cock might have a fair chance. They watched silently as he approached the hen. After a pause he jumped on her back, wobbled slightly once there, and then, just as quickly, the hen bent forward and the cock fell, squawking, into the blackberry bushes ten feet below the yard.

Everyone burst into laughter, the men hooting and hollering. "Come on, mate," said Jack to Simon finally. "We've got to go rescue the bugger." Not wanting to soil their clothes, the two men tried to coax the cock out of the bushes with sticks, while the others leaned over the wall, still laughing, to offer advice and applaud their efforts.

"He's hiding!" shouted Rebecca. "He's too embarrassed to show his face after such an obvious public rejection."

"If he's got any brains at all, he'll plot a revenge," said Richard.

Miriam looked sharply at him. Richard had hardly said a word to her the last week. He was consciously avoiding her now and Miriam had already guessed why. Her new status with Simon made it unlikely that Richard would ever forgive her past rejection of him or allow them to be close friends the way they once were.

When Beth, Claire, and the children came into the yard, curious about all the noise, Richard immediately told them the story with his usual detailed and humorous embellishments. The speckled hen had come running from the big barn when the cock began his squawking and now the two hens, side by side once more, were placidly searching for bread crumbs beneath the table.

"Well," Beth said, "those two girls have been constant companions for a year already, and now this intruder comes along. You can't expect them to change their ways just to accommodate him."

Rebecca and Miriam exchanged a look. Beth had just earned herself an elevated place in their esteem.

"Besides, he's so clumsy about it all," added Claire.

When Jack and Simon finally chased the cock back into the yard, their faces flushed with the heat and exertion, Simon put an arm around Claire and teased her, "If he doesn't shape up and get down to business by the end of the summer, we'll eat him with the ducks, eh?"

"Oh, Simon, give him a chance! They said at the market he wasn't old enough to mate successfully yet," Beth said defending the bewildered cock who was standing quite still, staring dazedly at the complacent hens.

"But the damned thing doesn't even crow!" complained Jack.

"Fortunately for us all," added Simon, straightening his tie and giving Miriam a smile.

As excited as the children in their best clothes, the adults made last-minute preparations for the excursion to Benoit's. Richard, Rebecca, Simon, and Miriam planned to drive in Richard's car, while the family and Claire would take Simon's old Mercedes. At the last moment Davy climbed onto Miriam's lap as she sat in the back seat with Simon, and she agreed to keep him.

"Tomorrow morning," Simon promised Rebecca, "I'll take you on a grand tour of Les Bluets." He assumed that, as an architect, Rebecca would be interested in everything historical and structural about the farm buildings, and he was right.

"Great," she replied, turning around to smile at Miriam.

Richard met Miriam's eyes briefly in the rearview mirror. "Touring was Simon's favorite activity around here, until lately."

Miriam, refusing to be goaded into a reply or even be irritated, stared out the window at the scenery that was rapidly disappearing in the growing dark.

"After that, if you can stand any more in one day, we'll walk to the rocks. The view of the valley is tremendous," continued Simon, ignoring Richard too, though he took Miriam's hand.

"I'm so glad I bought this new camera," said Rebecca, snapping a picture of Richard's profile. "I had to capture that magnificent frown of yours," she said to him, laughing.

"Can I go too?" Davy twisted around in Miriam's lap to ask Simon, who nodded and ruffled his nephew's hair.

"You can show Rebecca your waterfall," Richard suggested.

"Now, how can anyone own a waterfall?" Rebecca wondered aloud, almost rhetorically.

Miriam smiled to herself, appreciating her friend's characteristic pretense of naivete because its implied criticism was always on target.

"Bionic Davy can own a waterfall!" shouted Richard playfully. "Right there, lad?"

"Right!" shouted Davy in response, too close to Miriam's ear.

"Not so loud, please." Simon touched the boy lightly on the arm. "It's not polite, especially in the car."

"Besides, Miriam might throw you out the window," warned Richard.

"No, she wouldn't, not Miriam," Davy insisted firmly. As if to demonstrate this confidence, he lay his head against her and put his thumb in his mouth. Davy had remembered their "secret" conversation, and Miriam sensed that she'd won a small victory over Richard's macho encouragements.

"Well," asked Rebecca as they pulled into the village square, "what part of the woods do Martha and Tina own?"

"Oh, bloody hell, another one!" muttered Richard, pulling hard on the emergency brake.

Simon laughed. "I should have known."

Davy ran ahead urging Richard and Rebecca to hurry. When they'd locked the back doors of the car, Miriam and Simon walked along more slowly toward the cafe, holding hands.

"What did you mean by that?" Miriam asked him.

Simon laughed with enjoyment. "I like Rebecca. She's going to give Richard a bit of his own back, but in such a nice way that he won't know what to do about it."

By the time Miriam and Simon entered the restaurant everyone else in their party was seated. Not an especially outstanding room, it was typical though of the stark simplicity of provincial dining facilities. No one had expended much time or money on decor. The walls were white, and the cheap framed pictures on them were of the usual chauvinistic French scenes — the Arc de Triomphe, the Eiffel Tower. Miriam recognized one as the ornate facade of the train station in Marseilles. Five long tables covered with white cloths filled the capacity of the room and in the center of each table was a large bouquet of field flowers. What made the place warm and welcoming was the aroma of the approaching feast that drifted into the room from the kitchen. Beth had conferred a week before with Monsieur Benoit, who was the chef as well as the owner of the cafe, and had ordered six courses that began with three trays of vegetable appetizers — cauliflower, coleslaw, pea and carrot salad, stuffed mushrooms. These were met, as was each subsequent course, with appreciative comments and were quickly devoured.

Miriam stopped counting the number of wine bottles on the table, but knew that she herself was rapidly slipping into the state of total amiability she associated with inebriation. The children entertained everyone in the restaurant by holding up the bony spines of their fish simultaneously, snickering into their hands with glee until the adults at the table, in the midst of a confusing flow of conversation, finally noticed. No one reproved them for having bad manners that night.

Miriam met Rebecca's eyes across the table and saw the enjoyment in them. Between the two women rested the wordless understanding of old and like-minded friends. Simon, sitting next to Miriam, only occasionally let his arm or hand brush hers. They didn't speak to each other often, and yet Miriam knew they were in close communication. Between them was growing that sense of intimate and inviolate connectedness she'd desired with Sasha but had never achieved. She heard every word Simon said to anyone else and knew he was listening to her as she spoke to Beth or Jack. Attentively they took turns serving each other food and drink.

By the time the main course of *coq au vin* arrived, Miriam knew she was being seduced by the stability and normalcy of family life. She was unused to feeling so much a valued part of anything, but was able to recognize the potential happiness in it. Like Simon she found herself wishing for an omen of return, to a place and a moment. She emerged from these reflections into a conversation between Richard and Rebecca about the latter's one-night stay in Paris en route to the farm.

"Of course, I had no idea where I was really," Rebecca was saying. "The taxi driver just took me to this place and pointed at the sign 'Hotel.' So I'm standing there on the sidewalk with my bags and this very dark short man in a turban and brightly colored robe — I'm sure he was from some exotic place — came up to me, muttering some strange sounds and grabbed me. I shrieked and he looked surprised and slunk away." Rebecca, still amused by the incident, smiled at Richard and shrugged. He shared her amusement but was more interested in how Miriam would respond.

Miriam knew Rebecca saw the sexist behavior of men as foolish rather than as representative of their sex and could scoff at her misadventures with them, while Miriam continued to be angered by public confrontations even when nonviolent. For her it was a question of injustice as well as sexual abuse. "A similar thing happened to me at home recently," Miriam said. "Right in the middle of the business district, all these types in suits and carrying briefcases, this guy grabs me. When I pulled away, he just sneered at me and stomped off."

"Well," replied Richard refilling the glasses around him, "I wish some woman would attack me on my way to work!"

Miriam considered agreeing with him but instead, hoping he'd see the point, asked, "How about a man?"

"Of course not!" Richard exploded. "Bloody wankers!"

Everyone except Miriam laughed uproariously and Rebecca leaned toward her. "A wanker?"

Even Richard seemed nervous for a moment wondering if Miriam would answer the question. "I'll tell you later," she replied. The tension between Richard and herself had jarred Miriam from her contemplation of familial bliss. *What is life anyway,* she thought, *but very brief moments of utter contentment strung together by spiritual dissatisfaction or physical deprivation?*

At another table a large party, drunkenly celebrating a birthday, began to sing "La Vie en Rose," a love song that was one of Miriam's favorites, linked in her mind with her first visit to Paris. She tried not to let herself get sentimental over it, but as she glanced quickly around the table, she saw that Beth was experiencing the same emotional undertow. The two women smiled at each and blew their noses without embarrassment. Simon took Miriam's hand affectionately and once again she was tempted by the potential haven of kindred.

The dessert of ice cream cake dominated the attention of the children who crowded around the tea tray as their waitress, one of the plump, dark-haired Benoit daughters, cut it into thin slices.

Rebecca pulled her camera from her bag and stood up. "Everyone at home made me promise to take a lot of pictures. They even gave me ten rolls of film at a farewell party."

"Well, you'd better start snapping then!" insisted Claire, whose cheeks were bright red in the overheated and crowded dining room.

Rebecca aimed the camera at the children, their faces lowered happily into pink and white pieces of cake.

"You might take the lens cover off first," Richard suggested.

While the adults lingered over coffee, cognac and cigarettes, the children grew tired and bored. Too soon, thought Miriam, the dinner would be over and they would have to abandon the convivial atmosphere of the evening.

As the adult inhabitants of Les Bluets paid the bill, gathered up the children and prepared to leave the restaurant, the drunken revelers at the next table who were still singing stopped, stood also, and bowed in the formal but friendly French tradition, wishing them all "*Bon soir!*"

Miriam slumped down on the back seat and let her head rest on Simon's shoulder during the drive home. Through her satiety and weariness, Richard and Rebecca's periodic conversation in the front of the car sounded like formless mumbling. "I think I'll sleep in my room tonight with Rebecca," she said to Simon. "It's her first night."

155

"You don't have to give me a reason," he replied softly. Then he put his arm around her and kissed her.

Miriam had been about to explain that, in light of her very vocal and rigid position on consorting with men in the past, she felt she should have a talk with her old friend about Simon before Rebecca had to ask.

"God, what a meal!" groaned Rebecca as she slid into her sleeping bag.

Miriam was nearly asleep. For half an hour she'd been waiting for Rebecca to perform her nightly ritual of washing, applying creams, and brushing her hair, and now she was sufficiently alert only for the bare minimum of communication. She turned on her side, toward Rebecca, although she couldn't see her face. "We can talk more about this tomorrow, but there's something I wanted you to know right away."

"You mean that you and Simon are lovers?"

Suddenly Miriam was wide awake. "Is it that obvious?"

Rebecca laughed. "You never have been any good at concealing that sort of thing, Miriam. But I'm curious as hell about how it ever happened."

"Well, Ellen was here." Miriam had already decided that Ellen was the catalyst in her relationship with Simon, the conflict that had united them, opening their eyes to each other. She tried to tell the story without criticizing Ellen excessively, but Rebecca had known her as long as Miriam had and could fill in the gaps.

"I always knew Ellen would be good for something someday," replied Rebecca caustically. "Don't feel guilty about asking her to leave, Miriam. She would have made everyone miserable." She dismissed Ellen permanently by changing the subject. "I like Simon. He's nice. He'll be good for you."

"I know," Miriam agreed, trying not to sound too self-satisfied.

"About time," Rebecca said, yawning. "This is really a great place, Miriam. I'm so glad I came."

"So am I." Miriam remembered with pleasure the times that evening when they'd exchanged mutual thoughts in a glance and was happier than Rebecca could know to have her there.

They fell silent then and she listened as she did each night to the creaking of the house as the wood beams cooled. Somewhere a door left slightly open bumped softly against the doorjamb. She wondered if Simon was asleep and knew he was. She turned away from Rebecca and pulled the sheet liner of her sleeping bag up to her chin.

Les Bluets/8

The day Jack and Simon had business with the notary in Annonay, Miriam and Rebecca went along to explore the town. The narrow cobbled alleys that wound around the hill on which Annonay had first been built culminated in a fortress and Simon assured them that the view from the top of the *ancienne ville* was well worth the strenuous climb.

Jack stopped the car in the bus station parking lot and let the two women out. He pointed to a cafe, Des Cordeliers, across the street. "We'll pick you up there in a couple of hours, eh?" An overflowing beer mug had been painted on the cafe's one large window. *"Pression,"* it said. Hanging above the open door was a wooden planter of red roses in full bloom.

As the Citroen disappeared around the corner, with Simon's arm waving out the window, Miriam turned to Rebecca. "Well, we're on our own. How about some coffee to fortify us for the climb?"

Rebecca sighed with contentment as they sat down at one of the small round tables crowded between the cafe and the sidewalk. "I feel so sophisticated — even though we're only in a town square."

The proprietor stepped briskly toward their table, smoothing his black wiry moustache, and Miriam ordered for them. *"Deux cafés au lait grandes, s'il vous plaît."* She leaned back and yawned, not fully awake. They'd left the farm in too much of a hurry that morning for her to linger over her usual second cup.

Neither of them tried to make conversation. Rebecca was distracted by the unfamiliar details of the environment — the morning bustle of the shopkeepers sweeping the sidewalks, the small boys in short pants kicking balls down the center of the street — and Miriam was entertained by her friend's curiosity.

The large white cups of strong coffee, topped by layers of creamy foam, were set before them with a flourish. *"Mesdames!"* Both of them sat up straighter, surprised out of their respective musings. The day promised to be hot and, without an umbrella over the table, the sun was mitigated only by the remaining morning coolness. Brushing her hair back, Miriam noted that she was already perspiring and nearly regretted her caffeine addiction, until she took the first fortifying sip.

"What are you thinking about with that pleased smile on your face?" Rebecca asked finally.

"I was remembering how Martin used to drink about twenty cups of coffee a day no matter how hot it was," replied Miriam.

"Martin!" exclaimed Rebecca. "That was a long time ago."

Miriam nodded. "You know, all these years I've told myself Martin didn't love me and I've been going around feeling unloveable and cheated. Now I see that, in his own way, however he was able, he did love me."

"I always thought he did," said Rebecca.

Miriam smiled. "I'm much happier, realizing that."

"Could it be Simon?" Rebecca teased, not being one to pry.

Miriam gave Rebecca a serious look. "We're friends too, and it's making all the difference."

Rebecca stirred and swallowed the thick residue of coffee and milk in the bottom of her cup. "You probably don't know this, but I've been involved with a man for several months. His name is Stephen. He's a lawyer."

Miriam paused, uncertain of how Rebecca wanted her to respond. "I thought so," she ventured. "You've been referring to 'a friend' and I finally figured it must be a man since I wasn't ever meeting this friend." After a moment she decided to risk hearing something unpleasant. "Why didn't you tell me before?"

Rebecca shrugged self-consciously. "I thought maybe you'd write me off."

Miriam winced, remembering the heated arguments they'd had about the logical conclusion of the feminist position, with Rebecca taking the liberal, more humanist view.

Rebecca continued, "Your involvement with Simon has made it easier for me to tell."

Unhappy with herself again, Miriam sighed and looked away toward the passengers boarding the bus across the square. She didn't want to be a person who lacked compassion. I haven't been a very good friend."

"Oh, I wouldn't say that."

"But you couldn't be sure of my loyalty."

"Only in terms of Stephen," Rebecca said.

"It's not loyalty then." As they gazed at each other across the table, what Miriam saw were all the years they'd been friends, and how she'd limited that friendship, had even threatened its existence, by her political rigidity. She was overwhelmed by the realization that she hadn't measured up very well against her own expectations of friendship. "I've been a stupid fool," she concluded.

"Oh, Miriam," Rebecca cautioned, "you're always so hard on yourself."

Miriam shook her head, refusing to be exonerated. "I'm sorry I made it hard for you to trust me, that's all – because of some abstract, theoretical notion I had."

Their fingers were nearly touching across the small table and Rebecca laid a hand over Miriam's. "It's all right. Besides," she gloated, "my theory has won *you* over!"

With their shared laughter Miriam knew she was really forgiven but she still resolved silently never again to subject her friendships to political scrutiny.

Suddenly Rebecca, glancing at her watch, jumped up from the table. "Hey, let's go! I want to see as much of this town as I can in the next hour and a half!"

They leaned exhausted and breathing hard against the thick stone parapet of what had once been a defensive fortress for the town, and inspected the streets and shops of Annonay below.

"You know what I still ask myself though?" Miriam turned to Rebecca, shielding her eyes from the bright sunlight with a raised hand. "Why, even when I knew better, did I go on with Sasha?"

With hardly a pause to consider, as if she'd answered the question before, Rebecca replied, "Because there was something you had to learn and that's how much time you needed."

"But what did I need to learn? What could have required that much misery?"

"Sorry, I can't answer that one," Rebecca said casually. "That's only for you to know." She continued to watch the traffic, the smaller European cars, the old men in dark jackets and berets, the women in cotton dresses with their shopping bags, now full, winding through the narrow dark alleys on their way home to prepare lunch. "Once you asked me a similar question," Rebecca began again. "It was when your marriage to Martin was virtually dead, but before you met Sasha. You asked me what I thought would be better, a relationship based on friendship or one based on passion."

"I remember that evening!" Miriam exclaimed. "We were sitting in front of the fireplace at Mt. Hood Lodge after hiking in the snow." Miriam paused. "Your answer was 'Why Choose?' " The two years since then passed through her mind rapidly. She saw herself falling in love with Sasha's beauty and charming gaiety, her own disillusionment and anger, her attempts to reconcile their differences, and finally her disgust. She and Sasha had never been friends. "You can't build an enduring relationhip on passion," she concluded.

Rebecca was focusing her camera to take another picture. "True," she said. "On the other hand, friendship alone won't sustain a sexual relationship."

Miriam avoided comparing her romance with Simon to Rebecca's difficult standard. It was a new love, she reasoned, and it would continue to grow.

The circular descent from the fortress was much less taxing but they walked slowly anyway, enjoying the revolving scenes of town life as it lay peacefully within the surrounding lush valley and beyond that, the mountain wilderness. Rebecca looked back occasionally at the fortress, its massive walls broken by time and neglect into remnants of stone. From a distance she could compose better snapshots of it.

"Rebecca, are you happy with Stephen? Do you have any regrets?" Miriam asked the questions hesitantly, not wanting to appear judgmental.

Rebecca gave her a shrewd look, then smiled. "An emphatic yes to the first question. As to the second, well, I never believed — like some people I know — that love between women was superior to love between men and women."

"Oh," laughed Miriam, mocking herself, "I only believed that for about a month, until the first time Sasha was unfaithful to me."

Perhaps I expected too much of a political movement, without taking into account the individuals and their diversity within it. A year or so ago I read an essay about the ways in which oppressed groups oppress each other by internalizing the methods of their oppressor. I concluded that, as long as some women treat other women the way men treat them, women's lives will be no better. I suppose I'm disillusioned about lesbianism as a better way to live the same way I was disillusioned about the peace movement in the sixties. Only certain people, men or women, are better.

Jack and Simon pulled up in front of Des Cordeliers just as Miriam and Rebecca arrived there, both exhausted by so much walking in the midday heat. Climbing into the back of the car, Rebecca begged, "Quick, home for a cold beer!"

Simon was unusually silent as he drove, glaring at the pavement ahead. Miriam wondered if he'd had some adverse report from the notary. She knew they were preparing to make the final payment on the farm that year and, French property laws being as intricate and confusing as they were, an unfortunate hindrance at the last moment wasn't totally unlikely. While Rebecca discussed their sightseeing tour with Jack, Miriam tried to catch Simon's eye in the rearview mirror but he seemed to be avoiding her.

"Is something wrong?" As she helped carry the lunch dishes outside, Miriam blocked Simon's entry into the hallway.

Though he smiled at her, his eyes had an unstable look like blue skies gathering clouds for a storm. "No, of course not," he replied quickly, letting Richard come between them with a platter of cheese. Throughout the meal he remained quiet, speaking only when someone addressed him and then in distracted monosyllables.

Miriam, though she sat opposite Simon, could not get him to meet her eyes. This unaccustomed emotional distance between them frightened her.

After the table had been cleared, Simon remained there alone, looking out over the valley, and refilling his glass from the liter of beer left in front of him.

Miriam and Claire washed and dried the dishes together. Then Miriam stood in the entrance to the yard for a few minutes, staring at Simon's back. She wondered, with no good reason, if she were somehow the cause of his withdrawal, or if Jack, in his time alone with Simon, had criticized their affair. Finally she sat on the edge of the retaining wall where, if he cared to look, he could not help seeing her. Being emotionally isolated from Simon was a shock. Lack of communication had often been a problem in previous relationships, but she'd thought it would never occur with Simon. All their interactions as lovers had had such a wondrously fresh and unfamiliar quality that it seemed no old patterns of behavior could intrude from either of their pasts. Now the fear of being unloved and unloveable rose in her again, and that unwelcome reminder of a pain she wanted to escape hurt most of all. She drew her knees up, rested her forehead on them, and watched several small black ants dragging a dead bee across the hot stone between her feet. Then she felt a hand on her head.

"Hello in there." Simon's voice was apologetic, trying in turn to coax her out of a silent withdrawal. When she looked up into his face, he gave her a sad smile and wrapped his arms around her. "I'm sorry," he whispered into her hair. They remained like that for a few minutes before Simon spoke again. "How about a walk down to the creek? This heat is killing me and it'll be much cooler there."

Until they entered the deep green shade that marked the entrance to the woods and separated them from any view of the farm, they held hands but did not speak.

"I'm glad you finally saw me," Miriam said.

"Oh, Miriam, sweetheart, I'm sorry." Simon sighed and squeezed her hand. "I was so lost in myself I didn't even realize I'd hurt you until I saw you sitting there like that."

"I was thinking of old unhappy times."

"I was too, today," he said.

She glanced at him. The tension that still dominated his face made her decide not to ask any questions.

When they were seated on the large flat rock above the creek and occasionally dipping their bare feet into the icy water, Simon broke the companionable silence between them. "Last summer I was involved with a local woman named Gabrielle. Quite involved. I even thought I wanted to marry her." He paused for a long moment as though the subject had already become too difficult.

Miriam considered revealing what she'd already been told by Richard to make it easier for Simon but knew instinctively that nothing she said could do that.

Staring blankly into the dense foliage before them, Simon finally spoke, haltingly and with some obvious effort. "I made a total fool of myself over her. I was crazy about her, and everyone on the farm and in Garance knew it, and she knew it. I thought she felt the same way." He shrugged. "Maybe she did for a while. One day her ex-husband came back for a visit — they have an eight-year-old son. She began to change toward me after that. Sometimes she still loved me wildly, like in the early days. Other times she treated me like I was nothing to her. I won't go into all the ways she did it. In spite of all that, I couldn't break off with her. I would for a day or two and then we'd run into each other in Annonay and it would start all over again. The last time I saw her was in the cafe in Garance. It was near the end of the summer

166

— thank God — but in front of nearly the whole goddamned village. She got very drunk and began yelling at me to leave her alone and stop bothering her, that I was boring her to death."

When he fell silent again, Miriam knew he was reliving the memory with all its painful emotions, a process with which she was too familiar. His voice, when he spoke again, was choked with tears. "I thought I'd never be able to come back here again, never live at Les Bluets again. I couldn't face anyone."

Miriam realized that for Simon such a self-inflicted banishment would ultimately have been more agonizing than the failure of the romance. It was no wonder to her now that he interpreted the return of the hawk as a favorable sign.

"I saw Gabrielle in Annonay this morning for the first time since that night." Simon looked at Miriam significantly as if this statement were the conclusion of his story.

After a few moments, she prodded, "And?" Inside she was almost afraid to know any more.

His face took on a concentrated stare. "Well, I think we saw each other at exactly the same moment, across the vegetable stand where Jack was buying some things for Beth. Gabrielle lives in Garance but she owns a florist shop at that corner of the market in Annonay." He laughed nervously. "When I saw her, I wanted to run but I couldn't even move. I just stood there speechless. I must have looked like a moron — but it was so strange, Miriam. I've never had a physical sensation like that — a cold tingling in the base of my spine, a sudden nausea, a tightness in the chest. I couldn't take a deep breath and my heart was pounding like mad."

Simon frowned as he recalled his experience again, still trying to understand it. "She came over then and said hello to me and Jack, smiling as if nothing had ever happened, as though we'd never been lovers or ex-lovers, just neighbors. I have no idea what I said, or if I said anything, but finally Jack grabbed my arm and we walked away. The tingling, nauseated feeling lasted awhile though. I guess that's why I wasn't saying much when we met you and Rebecca." He turned to look at her. "Since then I've been trying to figure out what triggered such a reaction in me."

"Fear," Miriam replied simply. "Gabrielle represents hurt, embarrassment, potential loss of everything that means the most to you, Les Bluets. The arousal of fear is a way of protecting yourself from getting too close again to someone who once had the power to cause those things — and probably still does."

He shook his head. "I wouldn't say she has any power over me."

Miriam gave him a wry smile. "You're kidding yourself. There's a chemistry between certain people, and I don't think it ever loses its energy. You're still attracted to her and you know it."

"I really thought I had it licked," he said, "until I saw her. Then everything I'd told myself over and over about her — how terrible she'd been — just vanished from my mind."

Miriam laughed at the disconcerted look on Simon's face. "All this time you've been giving me advice about Sasha that you should have been giving yourself!"

"I have been," Simon replied. "I'm ahead of you by a whole year, remember." After a moment Simon laughed too. Then he put his arm around Miriam, drew her toward him and kissed her. "Aren't we funny?"

"Hilarious," Miriam said. She had no doubt that Simon loved her, not Gabrielle. She knew, from her own experience with Sasha, that his residual feelings for Gabrielle were involuntary, and her knowledge prevented any jealousy. "But now what do we do?"

Simon reached out and grabbed Miriam, tumbling them both backward into the grassy slope, where they lay a long time in each other's arms kissing. After awhile Miriam, leaning on an elbow, gazed down into Simon's blue eyes, now happy and free of worry.

"I guess that's one good answer to my question," Miriam said. "But according to your theory, in order to rid our psyches of Gabrielle and Sasha, you must become sophisticated and entertaining, and I must become beautiful and charming. How will we tolerate each other?" she asked him, and she was only half joking.

"Maybe there's another way," Simon suggested, smiling into her eyes. "Maybe it would help just to love the right person."

Miriam nodded thoughtfully. "We've both been fighting the same battle, Simon, but on separate battlefields. You could call it 'the battle of misdirected love.'" Miriam was suddenly almost as sorry for Gabrielle and Sasha as she was for herself and Simon, because they probably hadn't had what they wanted either. "Has the whole world lost its instinct for what's good for it — or is it just us?"

Simon sighed, caressing the curls that hung down the sides of Miriam's face. "It's not just us, but it's us we have to care about now. We aren't on separate battlefields anymore."

Miriam leaned down and kissed Simon until they were both out of breath.

Later in the afternoon, when it had begun to cool, Miriam left Simon sleeping in the loft room and went outdoors. At the table Jack was engrossed in another spy novel and Tina was playing quietly with a box of old costume jewelry.

Across from them Rebecca was writing postcards. "I figured I'd better get these written and mailed before my visit was over."

Miriam sat down and poured herself a glass of beer from the cold liter bottle on the table. "I make a point of not buying postcards for that very reason," she said.

After a moment Tina looked up at Miriam and pointed at her hand. "Miriam, can I look at your rings?"

"Sure, but they're not nearly as pretty as those." Miriam removed the three silver rings she always wore, one of which was the reproduction of a theatrical mask.

Tina began to try each of the rings on her own fingers, frowning to herself when they didn't fit.

Rebecca believes it's possible to have a deep loving friendship and a powerful sexual attraction for the same person. That hasn't been my experience, or Simon's. With Sasha I had overwhelming passion. I don't have that same kind of passion for Simon but with him I can have the real love and commitment that I didn't have with Sasha. With Simon there is hope for a future happiness, while with Sasha there was only recurring betrayal. With Simon there is growth and stability and goodness. I've been saying I wanted a common life, commonly lived, and we could have that together.

169

Les Bluets/9

Miriam was relieved when Rebecca and Richard decided to tour the neighboring chateaux and vineyards for a couple of days. While she was willing to accept some responsibility for the quality of her friend's first trip to Europe, Miriam herself had no desire to travel any farther from the farm than Annonay.

Everyone stood around Richard's blue station wagon as Simon loaded luggage. Beth added more items to the lunch she'd prepared and Richard finally located the map he needed to guide them on the local roads.

Rebecca took possession of the map. "I'll navigate because I'm certainly not going to drive."

"I know you're not," agreed Richard.

Miriam waited for him to make some remark about women drivers but he only pushed his sunglasses firmly back on his nose and climbed onto the driver's seat. Catching Miriam's eye over the top of the car, Rebecca sighed audibly and got in too.

Simon leaned in and gave Richard a friendly punch on the shoulder. "Don't be too hard on her, mate," he said and they both laughed.

The children were not pleased that Richard was leaving them story-less and stuck their arms through the open windows as if the sight of their familiar brown limbs could make him stay.

"Now there," admonished Claire, "we'll read you some stories and even if they're not as good as Richard's, I'm sure you'll survive until he returns."

"Will we survive though?" groaned Beth as she set the picnic hamper in the back of the station wagon.

Richard drove slowly out of the yard and everyone waved. Jack shouted, "Cheerio, mate!" The three children followed the car up to the main road still begging Richard not to go, but returned to the yard already arguing about which story Claire should read first. Peace settled upon them once more after the station wagon disappeared over the curved hill above the farm.

Simon and Miriam were planning a surprise birthday party for Richard the evening he and Rebecca returned, and after lunch they drove to Annonay arguing amicably about possible gifts.

Their first stop was at the best bakery in town. They weighed the merits of each cake, its composition, size and decor, and ordered one with blue and yellow icing, edged with cornflowers. Simon, over

Miriam's protests, insisted on purchasing thirty small blue candles.

They searched for a gift in nearly every shop along the cobbled streets, stopping occasionally for cold bottles of brown beer. Finally, as they were standing across the street from a hat shop, discouraged and a bit drunk, Miriam focused on the Basque beret at which she'd been staring blankly.

"Hey, about one of those?" She pointed at the navy blue circular object.

Simon's face broke into a grin. "That's it! He'll look smashing!"

Then Miriam sensed defeat once more. "But what size does he wear?"

"Oh." He frowned but only momentarily. "Look, I'll try some on and when we find one that's too tight, that's the one," he proposed, crossing the street. Then he paused and, noticing Miriam's puzzled look, explained, "His head is slightly smaller than mine."

Miriam giggled as she imagined the confusion of the salesperson when, after trying on piles of berets, Simon bought the wrong size. It was definitely the best idea they'd had though and she hurried to catch up with him.

They entered the narrow dim shop, the only customers. A middle-aged woman with curled hair and too much makeup came briskly through a curtained doorway. *"Oui, Monsieur, Madame?"*

Miriam asked to see some Basque berets. It was difficult to move around much due to the numerous hats hanging on the walls and on racks in the middle of the room. Simon began trying the berets, making faces at himself in the mirror. Miriam's eye was caught by the feminine fragility of the wide-brimmed straw hats, what her mother had called "picture hats." She stared at herself in the full-length mirror, a tall suntanned woman in faded jeans, sandals, and one of Jack's old white shirts with the sleeves rolled up high, wearing a straw hat with a white satin ribbon and artificial gardenias around the crown. As she turned slowly, the long white ribbon hanging down her back lifted in the breeze coming through the open doorway and waved jauntily at her.

When I was sixteen, my mother bought me one of these, with many different colors of ribbons and flowers that could be changed to match my dresses. She tried hard to make me into an attractive feminine partner for some man, yet encour-

174

aged me at the same time to be intellectually superior to them all. She obviously didn't realize that even if such a combination could be achieved, the opportunities in which it would be fully appreciated were definitely limited. I only wore the hat a couple of times. Changing the ribbon was too much trouble.

Miriam looked across the room where Simon was still trying on berets, and smiled. Here was the man, she thought, who accepted both her intellect and her femininity. Not exactly the kind of man her mother had probably had in mind, not a doctor or a lawyer, and not a Catholic. Simon's personality had a strong streak of feminine in it too and, as she watched him inspecting the wool of the berets, Miriam realized how much that had to do with her attraction to him.

"Miriam, I think this is the one. What do you think?" He held one of the berets out to her. "Don't *you* look lovely!" he exclaimed in surprise.

She laughed. "Like this?" Her gesture called his attention to the incongruity of the hat with the rest of her attire.

He nodded. "Even like that."

Miriam blushed with embarrassment when she noticed the saleswoman's critical frown but was still pleased by Simon's admiration. She glanced back at herself and flashed a quick smile at the mirror.

The shopkeeper was watching them with obvious irritation as if she thought they weren't serious about choosing a hat and were merely wasting time. Perhaps, since she moved nervously to stand between them and the door, she questioned their ability to pay.

This unfriendly suspicion made Miriam want to finish their business in the shop quickly and be out in the sunny street again. She took the beret from Simon and laid it on the counter, explaining to the woman that they were buying it for someone else and that it might have to be exchanged if not the right size. The clerk nodded curtly with pursed lips, understanding the situation but not liking it. Miriam replaced the straw hat on its hook.

"Shall I buy that one for *you*?" Simon asked, as the saleswoman wrapped the beret in some tissue paper.

Miriam shook her head. "I wouldn't wear it enough." She looked at the hat again. "It is beautiful." An attraction, sometimes involuntary, to beautiful things was what she'd inherited from her mother, and she was determined to control it. She gave the hat a last glance of appreciation, then turned to smile at Simon. "No, that's not the hat for me," she concluded.

They paid for the beret and left the shop holding hands, pleased with themselves and their purchase. On the way to the car, they stopped at a corner novelty shop where Miriam bought a birthday card with a large bouquet of flowers on it. When the card was opened, the flowers stood out from it three-dimensionally, like the old-fashioned cards she'd seen often as a child but which were no longer popular in the States. In addition it was strongly perfumed.

"Hardly the card for a man," Simon commented.

"It'll be good for him," replied Miriam, a glint of mischief in her eyes.

By the time they arrived back at Les Bluets, it was late afternoon. Miriam wrapped the beret in some gold foil paper Simon found in the cupboard and hid it in her room. Simon set the bottles of champagne down carefully into the cold water of the trough and covered them with the dozen liters of beer routinely kept there.

After Miriam helped Tina chase the ducks and chickens into the big barn for the night, she sat outside watching the stars emerge twinkling in the growing darkness. A half moon rocked, cradle-like, among the clouds. The inhabitants of the valley below were settling into their private evening rituals and the lights in their homes glowed warmly. Up the hill a dog barked and someone called its name.

Though the scene was one of rustic contentment, encouraging a peaceful mind, Miriam was distracted rather than seduced by its appeal. She pulled her sweater more closely around her and sighed audibly. In her adolescence and even in her early twenties, she'd often gone to her mother for help in analyzing and understanding her emotions. Judith always had illuminating insights into her daughter's problems. Self-doubt and mental restlessness were nagging at Miriam now and she couldn't perceive the source.

The gas lamps shining through the windows behind her didn't break the enclosing darkness. She heard the wind in the forest rising up toward her like some ghostly conversation. When there was a footstep behind her, Miriam jumped.

"It's me — Claire. May I join you?" She sat down on the bench with her hands wrapped around a cup of hot tea.

"That looks good," said Miriam.

"Water's still hot if you want some." Besides the tea, Claire had fortified herself with a down jacket and wool cap. She glanced up at the sky. "Were you pondering eternity?"

Miriam smiled but didn't answer immediately. "I was thinking about my mother."

"You think about her a lot, don't you?" asked Claire.

"I suppose I do," admitted Miriam. "She was the central character in my life until I left home. I didn't have many friends as a kid."

"What was she like?"

Miriam laughed sardonically. "Basically indifferent. I've often wondered if she even wanted me."

Claire said nothing for a moment, then responded in a soft, compassionate voice. "Miriam, that's terrible, my dear girl. I'm so sorry."

"In spite of that," Miriam went on, "I can't seem to talk about certain things with anyone else. Now I have to deal with them alone."

"Have you given up on all of us then?" Claire's concern mitigated her admonition.

"No, of course not." Miriam turned to face Claire. "I've been accused of being aloof, but I see myself as vulnerable. I believe I'll be misunderstood so I don't try."

Claire tilted her head, looking at Miriam slightly askance. "Even with Simon?"

Miriam shook her head, smiling. "I've found myself telling him things that surprise me."

"What do you think will happen?" Claire spoke with a gravity that suggested she'd been planning to ask the question for some time. "What do you want to happen, Miriam?"

"I'm not sure," Miriam replied. "I admire Simon so much. He's one of the finest people I've ever known. And I love him, of course." She was silenced then by her own uncertainties and by her desire to be absolutely truthful with Claire.

"You've made him very happy," Claire said, her heavy-lidded blue eyes studying Miriam's troubled face.

"I'd like to make the happiness last for a long time – not just a few weeks."

"And you're not sure about that, are you?" Claire probed.

Miriam paused before answering. "No, I'm not." She didn't have a reason but some inner doubt or fear was preventing her from making a more definite statement. "I know I need him though. We need each other."

177

Claire sighed. "A relationship that's based on need, even a mutual one, can't survive, Miriam. Perhaps you're not as much in love as he is." Miriam began to protest but Claire went on. "You're a powerful person, Miriam. People are drawn to you. That's an advantage, but you're responsible for it too. I'm sure you realize that."

Miriam remembered saying often during conversations with friends, "The one who is the less emotionally involved has more power in the relationship." She didn't want an emotional imbalance between herself and Simon. "I certainly don't feel powerful!" she exclaimed.

Claire laughed. "Because of you, Simon won't let Beth do the children's laundry anymore."

"Maybe Beth can put that time to better use," said Miriam.

Claire leaned toward Miriam and patted her on the arm. "Don't worry. The point wasn't lost on her though sometimes old habits die hard." Claire sipped the hot tea cautiously. "You're very demanding of yourself too, Miriam."

"So I've been told," Miriam replied, shivering as a cold chill ran up her spine.

"That mother of yours must have been quite a taskmaster," commented Claire.

"A perfectionist." Miriam laughed. "She always said, 'If you're going to dream, dream big.'"

"Do you want to be like her?" Claire's tone was curious rather than judgmental.

"Oh, no!" Miriam cried, realizing she'd given Claire the wrong impression. "My mother was a failed artist. She never achieved a thing! She died of cancer, guilt-ridden and bitter. She was a loser!" This unexpected outburst, revealing attitudes toward her mother that she'd never admitted, nearly brought Miriam to tears. "Oh, God," whispered Miriam, putting a hand over her mouth.

Claire touched Miriam's hair sympathetically the way Simon so often did, brushing it back from her face. "But you're always comparing yourself to her and finding yourself lacking. I don't understand that."

Miriam sighed. "I don't either."

"You must let yourself go a little," advised Claire. "Be yourself, not the perfect, obedient little girl your mother wanted you to be."

"That's what I thought I'd been doing since I got here," Miriam replied. "That was my intention. 'Decadence,' Richard said on our way

178

over."

"Maybe, but you're still a very restrained person. You have a big investment in your dignity, Miriam." Claire paused to smile at Miriam's embarrassment. "I've been watching you," she admitted.

Miriam's eyes widened in surprise at this subtle surveillance.

Claire smiled. "Old people and children — we both see much more than we're given credit for." She grew serious again and brought her face close to Miriam's. "I see a passion burning in you that wants to be released. There's no good to be gained in trying to suppress it. That passion won't allow you to go against your ultimate best interest without suffering and regret." She stared hard into Miriam's eyes. "I just hope your best interest will coincide with Simon's."

I want to create a union of the personal and the artistic, like the dark and light sides of the moon — the union that has been nearly impossible for women to achieve, except at the cost of their sanity or their level of production. Lesbianism seemed the obvious solution to the contradictions in the lives of women artists.

Can I reach my goals if I'm in a relationship with a man? There are worthy models for that life too — Mary Wollstonecraft, George Eliot, Virginia Woolf. Virginia Woolf, the writer whose work I admire most, and who, I should remind myself, walked into a river with the pockets of her coat filled with rocks.

The wind was beginning to sing down in the deep woods and blew Miriam's hair around her head. "There's going to be a storm tonight," predicted Claire.

Miriam was stretched out in her sleeping bag but restlessly awake when Simon knocked softly on the door. He sat down on the edge of the bed. "Are you all right?" he asked.

"Of course," she said. "I just felt like sleeping alone. You don't mind, do you?"

"Not much!" he said lightly, joking. After a moment he leaned down and kissed her and she could taste the whisky warm on his breath. "Are you sure everything's all right?"

She nodded.

179

"Between us?" he added.

She laid her hand on his cheek, then ran one finger around his lips. She knew he would accept her ways and reasons but would never really understand them. "I have this *weird* craving for solitude sometimes," she said, smiling up at him, "but I love you anyway."

He laughed. "I love you too, you weirdo." He kissed her again and then stood up. "Good night, love."

"Good night. Sleep well," she answered.

The clouds had momentarily moved away from the face of the moon. Its light was shining through the window and, as she fell asleep, began to move across her body.

During the night she was awakened by the wind howling around the house and among the nearby trees. Rain was dripping from the slightly open window onto the floor and she jumped up to close it. As she stood there a moment, enjoying the fresh smell of wet earth, the lightning flashed, illuminating her in the window like a pale nude figure within a frame.

Les Bluets/10

While they were still lingering over breakfast, Martha's shouts summoned them all out into the yard. "Look, mum! Look, daddy! You can see the Alps!"

"You certainly can!" Jack responded to his daughter's excitement with good humor.

Everyone stared at the awesome snow-covered peaks and Beth took a photograph. "It won't turn out though," she said to Miriam. "Never does."

"Daddy," cried Martha, pulling on Jack's arm, "can we hike to the ridge today? You know, the one where we went last year."

Tina and Davy began jumping up and down shouting too, while Claire tried to quiet them by putting her hands over her ears.

Jack looked around at the others. "Well, if we're going to do it at all, it had better be today." He gestured at the mountains. "Those bloody things will disappear again tomorrow."

While the discussion continued, Simon explained to Miriam that the year before they'd found a ridge about fifty kilometers away from which the view of the Alps on a clear day was spectacular.

Claire took sides with her grandchildren. "This is probably our only good look of the whole summer."

"But I bought a big pot roast for tonight and I don't want it to go bad," protested Beth.

"Oh, mum!" wailed Martha. "Please! Nobody cares about any stupid old pot roast!"

"Well, *I* do," corrected Beth. "Rebecca and Richard will be here for dinner tonight too, remember?"

Miriam and Simon exchanged a silent communication and then Simon spoke, "Look, Beth, Miriam and I won't be going with you so we can cook the pot roast."

"The whole dinner, of course," interjected Miriam with a nod of reassurance.

"With a little instruction from you before you leave," added Simon.

Though she seemed to be doubtful of their culinary talents, Beth surprised Miriam by agreeing easily to this plan, and the children cheered.

"Why aren't you coming along then?" Claire asked her son.

"Because, *ma mère*," teased Simon, putting an arm around her, "we're going into Annonay to get the *gateau*." He was trying to conceal Richard's surprise birthday party from the children.

"Oh, yes, that's right," said Claire, remembering.

An hour later, after Beth had instructed Simon and Miriam in the mysteries of pot roast and settled the rest of the menu, the family, dressed for hiking and carrying a substantial picnic lunch, drove away in the Mercedes. Miriam and Simon went in the other direction in the Citroen.

On their return from Annonay, it fell to Miriam, as she'd suspected it would, to put the thirty candles in some geometrical pattern around the edge of the cake. Simon escaped into the fields to gather flowers. In spite of the tedium of the chore, Miram considered the finished product worth the effort and was only slightly irked at paying the price for Simon's childlike enthusiasm.

When they'd decorated the dining room with a profusion of flowers, they tackled the problem of the pot roast with grim determination and strict observation of Beth's handwritten notes. They worked together silently except for mutual assurances after the completion of each step in the process.

Simon interrupted the measurement of some essential seasonings to look at Miriam. "You know, it just occurred to me, the summer's almost over." He emptied the contents of the measuring spoon into the bowl and then looked up at her. "Miriam, why don't you come to London with me and let's get married?"

Miriam laughed. "You can't be serious!"

He shrugged. "Why not?"

Miriam was nonplussed and panic-stricken for a moment. "Marriage — that's a bit of a leap, isn't it?"

"Some people think it's a terminal disease," Simon said sardonically.

"And I may be one of them," Miriam said, raising her eyebrows for emphasis.

Simon smiled. "I may be too, if it comes to that." After a moment he spoke more seriously. "Come to London and live with me then."

Miriam tried to imagine what that would be like. As Simon's partner she would have family, people who cared about her, she would be loved. She would come back to Les Bluets, would attend the catered dinners, would tend the fire in the hearth. Simon would encourage her to write. She studied Simon and the familiar interior of the room, aware that she was being drawn forcefully toward a life she'd rejected and had often criticized, with good reason.

Simon interrupted her thoughts. "Miriam, I'm just asking you to think about it."

She reached out to Simon and they held hands for a moment across the table. "I *will* think about it," she promised.

Simon was completely serious now. "Neither of us love lightly, Miriam. I think we've established that. Did you think I was going to say, 'Thanks a lot and cheerio!' at the end of the summer and return to London without a backward glance?"

Miriam smiled at him coyly. "Well, I could hardly suggest that you sell your business and move to the States."

"You could," he replied, grinning, "but I think we'd have more fun in London, visiting that George Eliot Memorial and eating Scotch eggs and hanging out in pubs."

While Miriam and Simon were still imagining the fun they'd have together in London, Richard's dusty car rolled into the yard and Rebecca, hot and tired, nearly fell into Miriam's arms. They'd driven three hundred kilometers that day, and both agreed to immediate naps. As she and Simon returned to the preparation of the pot roast supper, Miriam couldn't completely dispel the sadness that had invaded her at the thought of their approaching departure from the farm.

They were in the kitchen, deep in Beth's final instructions when the family arrived home from viewing the Alps. The children bombarded them with details of the day as Beth checked the state of the food.

"Well," she announced, "I can see I'm not needed around here! Just look at this roast!" she said to Claire.

The smells from the cast-iron pot permeated the kitchen and everyone insisted at the same moment that it was time for dinner. Martha ran upstairs to wake Richard and Rebecca.

The substantial meal of meat with potatoes, and vegetables cooked in the gravy, was eaten slowly amid tales of Rebecca and Richard in search of the perfect white wine. Richard had bought some samples and the two bottles were immediately consumed. The dining room grew dark quickly after the sun set and finally Simon began to stack the dirty dishes.

During the confusion of clearing the table, Miriam disappeared into the music room with Rebecca, and Simon ran to the troughs for the three bottles of chilled champagne.

The two women tried to light as many of the candles as possible with a single match and singed their fingers repeatedly, giggling in their haste. "So how did you enjoy Richard's company?" asked Miriam, concentrating on the tiny wicks.

"He was very decent for the most part," Rebecca assured her. "Actually, I had a very good time."

"No conflicts?"

Rebecca laughed. "Oh, of course!" She paused and raised her head to look at Miriam. "His personality is oddly composed of compassionate humanism and conservative morality."

"So is mine," Miriam reminded her.

"Yes, I know," Rebecca replied. "Maybe that's why you two irritate each other so much."

They smiled wryly at each other, acknowledging the complexity of human nature and an occasional resentment toward its irritations.

Rebecca continued, "We had a discussion in which I almost got him to admit one of his most glaring inconsistencies."

Miriam glanced up in wonder.

"Richard enjoys the company of intelligent women but doesn't want them to disagree too strongly with prevailing opinion," Rebecca noted. She was describing a male trait that had always angered both of them, but mostly during their college years.

"He means *men's* opinions," Miriam countered sarcastically. "How did he react when you pointed out the inconsistency?"

Rebecca sucked on the end of her burned finger. "He just stopped talking and I told him that was one for me."

Both women hooted with laughter at Richard's wounded male vanity. They left the music room together, still sharing the glow of Rebecca's small success.

Everyone was seated again in the darkened dining room waiting for the "surprise dessert." Miriam carried the blazing birthday cake through the main room, walking very slowly so that the candles would remain lit. The children shrieked and clapped when they saw her. Richard, his face flushed with alcohol and then with astonishment, beamed at this unexpected act of remembrance. Miriam set the cake before him with a flourish and a quick kiss.

"Oh, isn't it lovely!" exclaimed Claire.

"Not bad," agreed Jack, as Davy wriggled off his lap and crept close to Richard for a better look.

In loud voices they all sang "Happy Birthday" followed by "For

He's a Jolly Good Fellow." Rebecca dashed around the crowded room, trying to capture each person's response to the radiant dessert, and Richard's speechless delight.

"Well," he said sheepishly after a few minutes, "I know I can't blow out all these candles by myself." He glanced quickly around at the children who were barely controlling their excitement. "I think I'll need the help of at least three other people but they'll have to be small ones to fit next to me and this huge cake." At that invitation Martha and Tina jumped forward to stand beside Davy. The adults cheered and whistled, shouting "Bravo!" as the thirty flames disappeared into smoke.

Simon uncorked all the bottles of champagne at once and Miriam passed around clean glasses. Even the children were allowed to have some. Soon the table was crowded again with dirty dishes. When everyone had been served, Simon brought in the gift-wrapped beret.

Richard at first teased the children by pretending not to be at all interested in opening the gold foil package. When he finally tore off the red ribbon and the paper with one great pull, however, his own pleasure was unrestrained. "My God, I've wanted one of these bloody things for years! My God!"

Miriam and Simon glanced at each other and were gratified. Richard adjusted the beret on his head of thinning hair. To Miriam's amazement and Simon's relief it fit perfectly.

"I guess you know Richard's head as well as you know your own," whispered Miriam.

"Better, he knows it even better," said Richard, overhearing the remark. "Eh, mate?" asked Richard.

"As it should be," answered Simon, and the two men grabbed each other's hands affectionately.

Rebecca took several pictures of Richard in his hat — front, back, and profile — and then it was passed around so that everyone could inspect its genuine Basque label and try it on.

When the card from Miriam was handed around, Jack took the opportunity to taunt Richard about one of his well-known prejudices. "Seems that she thinks you're a 'poofter,' my good man!" The laughter in response to this remark was weak and Beth gave Miriam a quick nervous look.

By the time the sugary dessert was consumed and the bottles of champagne were empty, it was clear that the adults had indulged to excess and the children were yawning, ready to be put to bed.

Wearing his beret, Richard settled in front of the fire, spared the usual dishwashing in honor of his birthday. After she'd swept the dining room floor and wiped the table, Miriam brought the bottle of whisky to the couch with her, refilled Richard's drink and poured one for herself. She clinked her glass against his. "To your health, my friend," she murmured.

"Are we still friends?" Richard inquired, glancing up at her with a cynical smile.

She sat down beside him, returning the smile. "Never a doubt has crossed my mind," she joked. She was determined not to argue with Richard anymore, mainly because, she told herself, it wasn't worth it. When Claire joined them, Richard turned toward her with a welcoming gesture. "And how did you like that cake, Mrs. Claire?" he boomed in his jovial manner.

"Lovely, just lovely," Claire replied, patting her stomach. "Miriam and Simon obviously think a lot of you."

"Well, we go back a few years now, don't we?" Richard exchanged a friendly look with Simon who was passing through to the dining room with clean dishes.

Realizing that Claire was looking at her, Miriam agreed. "Oh, yes, we certainly do, to the Dark Ages." She gazed at Richard and laughed. "And thank God those are over."

With glasses of brandy Jack and Simon joined the silent group in front of the fire. Beth took her guitar down from the top of the cupboard, tuned it and began to play "Summertime," humming along. The blank meditative stare on her face indicated that her mind must be elsewhere.

Miriam stared into the fire, smoking a cigarette. She sensed that both Claire and Beth were observing her now in Simon's best interest and, though she believed they liked her well enough, they were probably slightly suspicious of her independence and anti-domesticity. She was estranged from Richard and almost totally unknown to Jack, as he was to her. Miriam recognized the sense of restless claustrophobia that was invading her and, following her weeks of contented happiness, she was disappointed and sad. The murmurs of slow-paced conversation hovered around the edges of the music. Miriam finally moved to sit on the arm of Simon's chair and he put his arm around her waist.

Jack turned casually to Simon. "We stopped at Charlu's on our way back today. He won't be caretaking for us this winter."

Simon's acknowledgment of the unpleasant news was an anxious nod. He was waiting for Jack's explanation.

During the time he took to light a cigarette, Jack assured himself of everyone's attention. "Seems Annalise has run off with some woman she met in Lyon," he said simply.

In the surprised silence that fell over the room, Rebecca looked over at Miriam, rolling her eyes in mock dismay.

Beth stopped strumming the guitar. "Run off?" she asked doubtfully.

Jack glanced at his wife. "Well, moved to Lyon," he explained coolly. "Charlu's taking the two kids and going to his brother in the States."

Simon took a long swallow of his brandy, then cleared his throat nervously. "I hate to sound calloused, but who the hell can we get to watch the place and feed the chickens this winter?"

Jack chuckled, apparently amused by Simon's unabashed selfishness. "Charlu's a good guy — he's already arranged for his cousin Roger to take over for him. In fact, Roger was there at the time and we settled it."

Simon nodded gratefully and leaned back in his chair again. With his momentary concern for the farm assuaged, he could relax. "Poor Charlu," he muttered.

"Rotten luck," Richard commented lightly.

Miriam was wondering what kind of husband Charlu had been and she knew Rebecca was thinking the same.

"Hardly luck," said Jack. "What was Annalise doing running into Lyon every week for that feminist consciousness-raising stuff?"

"Maybe she was unhappy," said Rebecca with an irritated edge in her voice.

"Oh, come on!" argued Jack. "Just because you're unhappy that doesn't give you the right to go in for perversion."

"Jack!" exclaimed Beth. "What are you talking about?"

"Oh!" Miriam cried out before she could stop herself. Her heart had begun to pound so hard that she could feel the pulse in her temples.

"Jack, do you mean it would have been all right if she'd run off with a man instead?" Simon's tone was both curious and incredulous.

"We all know what's right and what's wrong, don't we?" Jack's gaze slid over Miriam's pained face before giving Simon a hard look.

"Do you know any gay people?" Rebecca asked Jack innocently.

For the sake of everyone in the room, Miriam wanted Jack to realize that he might, and how close he was to sounding silly and ignorant.

"Now, why would I be hanging out with gay people, Rebecca?" Jack responded, almost sarcastically. "What would we have in common?" Both he and Richard laughed.

A quick despairing look passed between Beth, Rebecca and Miriam, and Simon glanced critically at Richard.

Miriam swallowed and tried, in lowering her voice, to sound calm and rational. "Jack, you might want to consider that sexual orientation isn't something you choose. It's something you're born with. You didn't choose to be heterosexual any more than —" Miriam stopped just as she saw herself heading toward a statement that she could no longer make. "— Any more than Annalise chose to be what she's finally realized she is."

Jack nodded. "All right, Miriam. Say she didn't choose. Say she was seduced."

Miriam was no longer so angry with Jack; suddenly she was amused. "Are you talking about sin?" she asked, leaning toward him.

Jack turned on her. "I'm talking about a person being seduced away from the most important responsibilities in life — family and children!" he shouted.

Rebecca laughed. "Maybe she was seduced by the truth then."

Only Miriam, watching Jack's face from her advantaged position on the arm of Simon's chair, had seen Jack catch himself and turn pale, had seen him realize the self-condemnatory nature of his statement.

Beth stood up to put her guitar away. "You're hardly the one to talk about being seduced away from familial responsibilities, are you?" She glared at her husband.

Richard coughed and began to whistle "Summertime" softly through his teeth.

Jack rose to refill his drink and passed close to Beth. "Have some dignity," he muttered to her but the others heard him too.

Beth grabbed Jack's arm and forced him to look at her. "You talk to me about dignity? That's a laugh! Ha, ha!" Though she began laughing almost hysterically, there were tears of rage glistening in Beth's eyes. "I agree with you about one thing: Adultery's the commonest, the most disgusting, the most embarrassing denial of personal responsibility there is. How dare you criticize Annalise! You, adulterer!"

With the tears finally streaming down her face, Beth turned and ran through the doorway and up the darkened stairs.

Everyone could hear Claire's sharply drawn breath. A few seconds of silence followed, then Jack quietly left the room as well. The long silence of shock enveloped those who were still sitting before the fire.

When Simon and Miriam were alone in the dark of the loft, lying close and ready for sleep, Miriam sighed. "Well, I doubt if Jack will be thrilled to have me in the family if he finds out about my past."

"To hell with him then," said Simon. He was rubbing the small of her back with the palm of his hand the way she liked. "Besides, he'll come to see that it just doesn't matter."

"But it does!" Miriam insisted.

"What do you mean?" Simon leaned on an elbow and looked down into her face.

Miriam sighed again, discouraged. "I don't know." She stroked the side of his chin where the beard was already growing back though he'd shaved just a few hours before. "Sometimes I feel separate from everyone — even you," she confessed. "I was glad to have Rebecca here tonight though."

"Why?"

She shrugged. "We just look at each other — and know. We see and hear things in the same way. We've been around each other long enough to recognize what the other is probably thinking."

"I'm jealous," Simon admitted. "I want to be in on it, I guess."

"But you have that kind of friendship with Richard," she exclaimed, "and I'll never be in on it! We're bound to be separate in some things," she concluded.

"Maybe you need more separateness than I do," Simon suggested.

"No one can be everything to another person, Simon," she tried to explain. "You get things from Richard that you don't get from me."

Simon chuckled. "And vice versa."

Miriam laughed too. "I know what you're thinking!" Then she poked him. "You see? Just give it time!"

"We don't have time, Miriam." He sounded angry and she wondered if her honesty had been inopportune and a bit harsh. She suspected harshness in a woman would be as unattractive to Simon as it was to Richard.

"Of course we do!" she maintained firmly, so tired that she believed it herself. She snuggled closer to him, burying her face in his neck, and closed her eyes.

Les Bluets/11

While they insisted it was a treat for the children, the adults planned the excursion on the steam train with equal anticipation. Simon, Claire, Rebecca, Miriam, and the children would ride the train one-way, driving Richard's station wagon from Les Bluets to the station in Tournon. Later in the morning, Jack and Beth would drop Richard at the car on their way to Lemastre, the train's destination, and he would drive on alone, following the Mercedes. At one o'clock they would all rendez-vous for lunch in the cafe where they'd eaten the previous summer.

This system of sightseeing was too confusing for Richard. For several days he'd been shaking his head at the unnecessary complexity of the trip, certain that he would lose his sense of direction on some winding local road. "What's happening here anyway, a scavenger hunt? Where are the clues?"

Miriam spread the regional map out on the hood of the car and Simon explained the route again in case Richard lost sight of the other car. "It's really quite simple, mate," Simon reassured him. "I don't think you stand a chance of getting lost."

"Right," nodded Richard unbelieving. He had a visible hangover, and propped his head up with one hand. "It's daft, really daft."

Rebecca was standing in the doorway focusing her camera on the three of them. "Maybe he wants to get lost," she said innocently. No one denied the possibility but she and Richard exchanged an antago-nistic smile.

It suddenly occurred to Miriam that Richard's supposed incompe-tence was merely an attempt to solicit Simon's attention. She'd never known Richard to lose his way on any kind of road, and this new coy-ness puzzled and irritated her.

Simon, on the other hand, seemed to be enjoying the game and he finally slapped Richard firmly on the back, saying, "See you there, my friend!" He slid into the driver's seat of his car. "You kids pile into the back, okay?"

After some halfhearted whines, Martha, Davy and Tina agreed to sit in the carpeted trunk area, leaving the back seat to Rebecca and Miriam. Claire sat in the front with Simon.

The sky cleared as they descended from the cloudy mountain top where Les Bluets nested. They left their pastoral isolation and entered the lush, more heavily populated Rhone valley. Winding through small villages much like Garance, bumping along the cobbled streets, they

195

eventually began to follow the river on a main road that passed through larger towns and market squares. Hotel and restaurant signs dotted the sides of the road. No one had much to say as the car sped through the changing countryside; the children were too preoccupied by the unfamiliar sights to fuss. Rebecca's attention was held by the vineyards on the sides of the mountains, the ruined fortresses and other structures that even from a distance were clearly of historical interest. Claire and Simon occasionally spoke to each other in the front seat. Miriam was thinking of how much she was going to miss France, Les Bluets in particular.

It's so beautiful here and I know that's why I don't want to leave. I want to live surrounded by beauty. When I think of Portland, I remember only volcanic dust and hurt feelings and a general sense of disgust.

My mother addicted me to beauty at an early age. Not only was she beautiful, she made beautiful things. Our house was beautiful. She surrounded me with music, art, elegant dining, sophisticated conversation, and emphasized a reverence for aesthetic values as a kind of religion in itself. I'm glad she did that. I'm the one who has mistaken that aesthetic for emotional attachment and confused myself.

At Tournon, Miriam negotiated the purchase of the tickets and the children scrambled eagerly aboard to find seven seats together. Ultimately, no one wanted to sit down anyway, preferring to hang out the windows. Rebecca took pictures of them from the platform and just as she hopped up the iron steps and into their car, the whistle blew signaling a punctual departure.

Young and old, everyone cheered as the train pulled away from the station. The passengers were nearly all tourists which gave a festive air to the occasion, and around her Miriam could hear other languages besides French and English being spoken excitedly.

As she glanced at the unfamiliar faces, Miriam found herself staring at another woman nearby whose short, very blonde, almost white, hair contrasted sharply with a deep tan. In khaki pants and white shirt open low at the neck, she had the rugged, healthy aura of a misplaced safari guide. The woman's wide gray eyes returned Miriam's stare with a mixture of curiosity and arrogance, and caused an unbidden rush of sexual tension to flow through Miriam.

Instantly turning away to locate Simon, she was disconcerted to find him at her elbow. He put an arm around her and she relaxed against him. The children were hanging out the windows as far as they could while being monitored by Claire who was certain they would lose either a nose or an arm before they reached Lemastre. Climbing the steep incline slowly, the train shot increasingly thick clouds of steam into the air. At every curve, where the whistle blew loudly, the passengers could lean out and see both the front and the back of the train, as well as the faces of the other passengers.

Miriam abandoned the view after a few minutes to study the interior of the steam train. One of the last of its kind, this one was a well-preserved antique with wooden seats and highly polished slats around the windows and across the ceiling. With all the windows open and the fresh scent of pine trees filling the cars, it seemed that they were actually outside, yet the interior was dim. Miriam continued to watch the blonde-haired woman surreptitiously. She was standing about six feet from Miriam on the same side of the car, talking and laughing with a group of friends, several women of various ages who seemed to know each other well. Miriam wondered about them and wished she could think of a reason to introduce herself.

Though she knew it was a bad example for the children, Miriam hung her hands and head outside the window to enjoy the warmth of the sun, so close to the trees and boulders she could touch them if she stretched far enough. Up ahead she saw the engine following another bend in the track. Shifting her gaze in the opposite direction, she encountered, three windows away, an unimpeded view of the blonde woman's face. Squinting against the bright sunlight, her short hair swept back by the speed of the train, she was looking once again directly into Miriam's eyes. Rather than being seductive, the sudden physical magnetism Miriam felt toward this woman disconcerted her. That a sexual attraction could be so strong, with Simon standing two feet away and in spite of the knowledge that she loved him, was devastating to her emotional equilibrium. She felt herself blushing as if she'd been caught in a lie.

Then the scenery began to change radically. The lush green corridors of trees were gone and on both sides were rugged canyons, the rivers that ran through them in the winter dried almost to a trickle now. This looked so little like any European scene in her memory that

197

Miriam was reminded instead of the desert landscapes of eastern Oregon. As she and Simon gazed down into the steep canyons, the height gave Miriam a sense of vertigo. Tense and claustrophobic in the crowded car, she realized she was also feeling slightly faint in the increasing heat. Like a number of other small children on the train, Davy was asleep on one of the wooden seats, the blue sweater under his head for a pillow. Tina and Martha were clammering to go out onto the platform between the cars, but Claire refused saying it was too dangerous. Miriam saw her escape and a momentary distraction from her troubled thoughts. "Rebecca and I'll go out with them," she said suddenly to Claire. "It's really safe enough if we both hang on to their hands. And there are chains on each side."

They stood on the platform with the girls between them. Miriam's feet tingled as they always did when she looked down from a great height, but the momentary panic had eased as she took deep breaths of the thin mountain air. With Tina holding onto her belt, Rebecca moved to the other side and snapped some pictures of a village perched precariously on the nearby cliffs. After a few moments the door opened and Miriam heard a woman's voice address Rebecca.

"You take a lot of pictures." She had a haughty voice and a Scandinavian accent.

Miriam knew without looking that it was the blonde woman. She decided not to turn around immediately but eavesdropped on the conversation instead.

Rebecca laughed. "Yeah, I guess I'm the typical American tourist."

"Not only Americans take pictures. I have a bagful." She explained to Rebecca that she'd never been in France before and that she was traveling with some women she'd met at the International Feminism Conference in Copenhagen.

"How wonderful!" exclaimed Rebecca.

While still in Portland, Miriam and Rebecca had discussed including the conference in their summer plans but Miriam had declined: "I want to avoid political obsessions and musical beds for a while," she'd said bitterly. Now she wished she hadn't been so emphatically opposed.

Rebecca finally introduced herself and then added, "This is my friend Miriam."

Miriam turned to face them, her hand on Martha's shoulder.

"I'm Kristin," the blonde woman said. She held Miriam's other hand a moment or two longer than was conventionally acceptable.

198

Miriam received the unspoken message and the involuntary physical thrill of it left her in an even more complicated mental state. She both desired and was annoyed by Kristin's attentions.

Kristin was speaking again of the conference, directing her remarks to Rebecca, describing some of the workshops and the all-night discussion in various bars with the guest speakers. Studying the pale shiny hair, the smoky gray eyes beneath proud arched brows, the arrogant mouth, Miriam hardly listened. Kristin glanced only occasionally at Miriam but it was an aggressively inviting look that made no promises.

Rebecca and Miriam noticed simultaneously that Claire was motioning for the children to come inside but it was Rebecca who pushed them quickly before her, leaving Miriam and Kristin on the platform alone.

Kristin's eyes studied Miriam coolly before she asked, referring to Simon, "Is that your husband?"

Miriam was gratified that Kristin had watched her so closely. "No. Not yet anyway."

"That would be stupid."

This rude and unsolicited judgment irked Miriam and she considered going inside too. Yet as she gazed back at the soft tanned skin and the sensual lips left slightly parted, she knew Kristin was right.

Then they were plunged into the total darkness of a tunnel. As Miriam was smiling to herself at Rebecca's subversiveness, she felt Kristin's hand touch her and stepped forward instinctively. The two bodies came together quickly, magnet-like, and their mouths met and fused. They wrapped their arms around each other tightly. Miriam was still aware that they were very close to one of the chain guards and that the tunnel wall was a foot away but it didn't seem to matter much. She let herself bend and dissolve into the sensations of the embrace, pressing forcefully against Kristin and inhaling the tweedy sophistication of her scent. As their hands moved over each other's breasts, she heard Kristin moan. A frenzied desperate longing to be naked against Kristin's naked flesh, for a deeper union, rose in Miriam. Her entire body trembled and her crotch ached and it became difficult to remain upright.

Then through closed eyelids, closed from habit rather than necessity, Miriam perceived that full daylight was only seconds away and that they would be very visible to the passengers inside. With difficulty she separated herself from Kristin. They looked at each other in the sudden light, both wide-eyed and breathless.

"Have lunch with me!" Kristin whispered in an urgent voice. "We can get rid of these people. We can find a place, somewhere private." Her own behavior during the previous two minutes had been so capricious that Miriam was stunned and speechless. She had no doubt about the powerful attraction of Kristin's invitation, of her own desire for it, or of the physical pleasure it promised. Yet she didn't view herself as the sort of woman who engaged in romantic escapades with strangers, male or female. What she had done frightened and confused, as well as excited, her. "No, I don't think I can do that," she heard herself say.

"Too bad," replied Kristin sarcastically.

From inside someone shouted, *"Kristin, nous sommes arrivées!"*

Kristin inclined her head to Miriam like a chivalrous knight, but one corner of her mouth was turned downward critically. Without a word she left Miriam standing alone on the platform.

Miriam saw Simon watching her intently as she walked through the crowded car toward him. She couldn't bear just then to see the affection in his eyes and busied herself with helping Claire collect the children's belongings.

As they left the hot noisy train, Rebecca and Miriam fell behind Claire and Simon who were being pulled along by the impatient children. They saw Kristin stride past them, talking excitedly with one of her friends, arms linked in the European fashion among women.

Miriam and Rebecca looked at each other without speaking and Rebecca slipped her arm through Miriam's. "Attractive but probably fickle," she commented, her left eyebrow lifting slightly in disapproval.

Miriam agreed silently, remembering the disdainful look Kristin gave her when she refused the offer of a private tête-à-tête. She no longer had any interest in romantic games that ended by complicating life and destroying emotional stability. She wanted it simple now.

"Besides," Rebecca reminded her appropriately, "you're already involved." Her smile, though affectionate, challenged Miriam's self-proclaimed dogma of fidelity.

"So I am," replied Miriam, smiling too though her thoughts were anxious. While she recognized it was only a flirtation, the encounter with Kristin had resurrected a part of herself she couldn't ignore. Her love and admiration for Simon hadn't eradicated her passionate attraction to women and at the first opportunity she'd surrendered to it. The

200

incident put a barrier between Simon and herself where she'd believed none existed — something she was unwilling to share — and she didn't know how to break it down.

When they arrived at the restaurant, Richard was sitting alone drinking a beer at a long table protected by large bamboo umbrellas.

"Where's mum and daddy?" Martha asked him, her small brow wrinkling with sudden worry.

"I've been wondering that too," he said. "I passed them up just shortly after we left Tournon."

"Well," said Claire with an edge of irritation in her voice, "I suggest we order without them. They'll turn up and I think we're all starved."

The restaurant meal progressed like any lunch at the farm, slow, conversationally stimulating and alcoholic. Richard and Simon traded Scottish and Australian jokes respectively and kept the other three adults entertained and sometimes shocked.

Halfway through the main course, Beth and Jack arrived, laughing and holding hands. "Sorry, sorry!" they both cried, eyeing the food. "This looks great!" exclaimed Beth, a bit out of breath. She and Jack sat down next to each other, their shoulders touching, and began filling their plates.

"Well, where have you two been?" asked Claire mischievously.

Jack shrugged, his mouth already full of bread smeared with Camembert. "We just decided to take our time." He looked around the table, obviously pleased with his decision. "I mean, what's the rush?"

Richard leaned forward and pointed his finger at Jack. "Why are you such a bloody slow driver?" he joked.

After a moment of surprise, Jack pointed at Beth. "It's her!" he cried feigning innocence.

Beth made a face at him. "He got lost," she said archly. Though everyone laughed, no one believed it.

Beth was sitting opposite Miriam and finally glanced up from her food. Her face was still flushed and smiling, and she returned Miriam's quizzical look with one that was hopeful. Something, though not everything, had been resolved between Jack and Beth on the drive to Lemastre.

When the children got restless they chased each other around the park beside the restaurant and were allowed to order as much ice cream as they could eat. The adults lingered after the meal, consuming several bottles of a chilled regional white wine.

After the coffee was ordered, Simon moved around to the other side of the table and sat down next to Miriam. "Richard was saying that there's some sort of religious festival in Louvesc today. Might be interesting to go that way and stop in."

"The four of us, you mean?" asked Miriam, including Rebecca.

"Right-o," he grinned and kissed her lightly on the mouth.

When they arrived at Louvesc late that afternoon, the church was empty, but in the dimness hundreds of candles still flickered. All the altars were smothered in flowers, and the smoke of recently burned incense lingered in the air. From some hidden place the slow strains of organ music trembled around them. After only a few moments inside, Richard wanted a cold beer, and he and Rebecca left the church for a bar they'd seen down the street. Simon stood in the center aisle staring at the low sunlight through the stained glass windows where it made bright squares on the walls and floor.

"Amazing," he whispered. "What made people build these things? All the work! Decades — even longer sometimes."

"Faith," Miriam replied.

"More than that."

"Passion?" She couldn't seem to escape the word.

"Yes," Simon nodded thoughtfully. "It had to be."

They walked up and down the side aisles looking at the statues of the saints who had prayed and suffered. The organist was playing the "Regina Coeli" very slowly, never the way it would be sung, but the way Miriam remembered hearing it at the end of the weekly Holy Hour in convent boarding school.

The son of two devout atheists, Simon was fascinated by her background of Catholic ritual and paraphenalia. He asked her questions, wanted to know how if had felt to believe.

It was difficult for Miriam to remember something so intangible, something she had rejected so resolutely in the past and that was still unacceptable to her in the present. "We believe things and then we stop believing them," she said finally. A perfectly clear image of Sasha stopping and turning to be kissed as they walked single-file through the autumn woods together obscured Miriam's consciousness for a moment, but it didn't hurt so much any more.

"Does something else take its place?" Simon asked, separating her from her past.

Miriam smiled at him. "I hope so."

They came out onto the porch of the church. Directly in front of them, beyond the stone wall of a lookout point and its telescope, the sun was dropping brilliantly into the canyon as though it were a huge orange that would roll away along the dry river bed. The sky was streaked with layers of blue and gold.

Simon took her hand and they sat down on the top step to watch the last few moments of the sunset. "I think the kind of passion that could inspire such dedication and skill must be worth dying for," he said softly.

"Yes. Are you planning to?" she teased.

He tightened his hold on her hand but continued to speak seriously. "I worry sometimes about not being passionate enough."

"For what?"

"For life. For you."

She smiled. "And I worry about being *too* passionate."

"Not for me, my love."

Miriam thought of how much Simon trusted her and of how she'd betrayed that trust. By kissing Kristin with such desire, she'd been unfaithful to him already. She wanted to want Simon so much more than she knew she did. Perhaps she wanted too much. At that moment she wondered if it wasn't better to take what was offered by life and be grateful, rather than to hold out too stubbornly for what could never be achieved.

"It makes you a mystic, I think, don't you, having a passion for life?" asked Simon. "A seer of visions," he mused aloud, "a maker of fates and inseparable unions."

Inseparable unions, thought Miriam ironically. Yes, she knew about those.

They stood and went down the steps. From an outdoor table at the bar, Rebecca waved to them.

"Do they have to be mutual — the unions?" she asked Simon, as they walked slowly toward their friends.

"How else?" he replied, glancing at her with a confident smile, as though she were still teasing him.

Les Bluets/12

Preparing for his return to London, Richard piled his sleeping bag and clothes on the front step of the farmhouse. Miriam stood watching him. She wanted to find the words that might ease the tension they'd built between them during the last few weeks, while recognizing that such things couldn't be done in the final hour.

"Back to the grind, I guess, eh?" Richard's smirk revealed the cynical attitude he'd adopted in relation to her.

"You don't mind driving all that way alone?"

"I prefer it," he replied, arranging his belongings in the back of the car. "It's a good way to make the transition between the tranquility of this place and the insanity of London. I drive straight through without sleeping and when I get there, I'm as ruthless and crazy as the rest of them."

His anger and bitterness disturbed Miriam because, in spite of the unpleasantness between them and his macho encouragement of Davy, she'd always considered Richard as gentle a soul as Simon. "Will you write to me?" she tried to inquire offhandedly.

"Probably not." He looked at her puzzled, as if they hardly knew each other. "Oh, I suppose I will, once a year when I'm drunk enough."

"Maybe that's the best time since you'll be too drunk not to tell me the truth."

"I always tell you the truth, Miriam." His tone of voice was even cooler than his statement.

"Tell me now then," she challenged, holding his gaze with her own.

They studied each other for a long moment during which it was obvious to Miriam that Richard was debating something within himself. Then he spoke, visibly hardening toward her. "You've come between me and Simon, you know, as friends — and the funny thing is, ultimately, you won't give a damn about either of us. Too bad Simon doesn't know that now."

Miriam's eyes narrowed critically and she wished she'd confronted Richard's insecurity earlier. "That's ridiculous, Richard. You've chosen to separate yourself from both of us."

"You asked, Miriam, didn't you?" He glared at her accusingly a moment, shrugged, and resumed stowing his gear in the car.

Davy stood on the porch, holding with both hands the camera Richard had left in the dining room cupboard. "Are you really leaving today?" he asked sadly.

Richard took the camera. "I certainly am, Bionic Dave! It's time for this lazy bard to go earn some money!" He grabbed the little boy and swung him around in the air and Davy's sadness was temporarily forgotten.

By this time everyone had gathered near the car. All three children hung on Richard's arms and legs as he tried to make his farewells. Taking one of her hands in his, he bowed gallantly to Rebecca. "Thank you, dear lady, for being such a pleasant traveling companion. May we meet again!"

Rebecca returned this formal leavetaking with good-natured mockery twitching at the corner of her mouth. "Thank you for being such a willing guide — and chauffeur." Then she whipped her camera out from behind her back and snapped a close-up of his surprised face. Her gesture broke the tension of the moment and everyone laughed.

Miriam stepped toward Richard and put her arms around his neck. It was her last attempt, the only way she could imagine finally, to make contact with him. His mind and heart were clearly shut to her.

He put his arms around her loosely, as if reluctant to touch but unwilling to create an embarrassing situation for anyone, participants or observers. He moved away quickly without meeting her eyes and slapped Simon on the shoulder. "Ring me when you're back and we'll get together for a round at the King's Head."

"Sure will, mate," promised Simon. After Richard had adjusted his beret and settled himself in the driver's seat, Simon stooped down toward the open window. "Safe journey, my friend."

Richard lifted his hat to Simon but ignored Miriam who was standing beside him. He left the farm exactly as he had arrived, tooting the horn and waving an arm out the window.

Beth agreed to wring the necks of the three ducks that afternoon and prepare them for the evening meal. She'd waited because of Richard's aversion to that particular meat, but now Claire and Jack were both begging for what they considered the specialty of the house. Rather than have the children witness the actual kill, Jack took them for a swim in the heated pool at Annonay. With Beth and Claire studying the cookbook in the kitchen and Rebecca doing her laundry, the house and yard were strangely quiet. Miriam sat at the outdoor table sipping a glass of cool beer. Normally Richard would have been sitting with her, watching the uneventful stillness of the valley, or waiting for the clouds that obscured the distant Alps to clear away.

I came here to save my own sanity and because I know that the world is a dangerous and precarious place that it is easy to lose each other irretrievably. Not only through physical death, but because we change and forget, allow ourselves to be distracted and too busy. I didn't want to lose Simon and Richard that way.

Now Richard and I have confronted each other's ideological differences so defensively that we've created an ever-widening and probably irreparable rift. As far as our friendship is concerned, it would have been better if I'd stayed home.

It seems that we devote our lives to all the wrong things. We know, if we are asked, what is most valuable, but we do not live as though we accepted it in our hearts. After all the political arguments, after all the awkward silences, isn't the real life between any two people best measured by the times they've laughed together, dried each other's tears, the times they've clinked glasses together and wished each other well? What can be more valuable, can redeem the sadness of this life more, than a good friendship or a faithful love?

Simon approached noiselessly and sat down on the bench letting his arm lie beside hers, barely touching. "Are you all right then?"

She didn't look at him directly but was grateful for his presence. "Oh, I suppose so. I was wondering where Richard is by now."

"Well, if he stayed on the motorway since this morning as he planned, he'll be on the boat by the time we finish dinner." He reached out and took her hand.

Miriam sighed and smiled weakly at Simon. "When I arrived two months ago, I was exhausted by the politics of human relationship and determined to escape from all that. I guess it's just not possible — not for me anyway."

"That's a good name for it, 'the politics of human relationship.' I suppose you win a few and lose a few." He caressed her fingers for a few moments. "You won me, Miriam. I hope it's been worth it."

Miriam laid her other hand over his. "You know it has." For a brief second Sasha's face and then Kristin's floated before her. "Maybe we shouldn't view it in terms of winning or losing," she continued.

209

"There are only changes." Considering what all her friends except Rebecca would say if they saw her holding hands with a man, she laughed aloud. "And have I changed!"

"So have I," Simon agreed, preoccupied with his own self-examination. "I have to question everything I once took for granted."

Suddenly Miriam turned toward him, sitting sideways on the bench. "Simon, I'd like to stay on here at the farm, just for a while." Until that moment she hadn't been conscious of the possibility and, only as she suggested it, did she know it was what she wanted most.

"Alone?" Simon asked, his mouth twisted in a discontented frown.

Already imagining her approaching solitude, Miriam nodded happily. "Is there some reason why I can't?"

"No, of course not." Simon shrugged, considering the practical. "There's a full supply of wood in the big barn, and the gas tanks have just been refilled. The car is running as well as it ever does." He looked at her, still frowning. "You wouldn't be afraid though?"

"Afraid of what? Being alone?" She knew she could never be as alone as she'd been the last few months, and still was on some unreachable level, but wouldn't say that to Simon; he wouldn't be able to understand her emotional isolation any better than she did. The difference was that she was ready to confront it now, to struggle for the repossession of her sense of self, like the medieval knight in a trial of virtue.

"There are degrees," he insisted. "Why make life more difficult than it is?"

She didn't disagree with this argument but was compelled along the path she'd just chosen. "I think it would be helpful for me to spend some time by myself, that's all, physically alone and totally dependent on myself." This explanation sounded familiar and she remembered immediately how sincere Sasha had looked as she delivered it to Miriam in February.

"I'll worry," Simon contended, already anxious.

"I'll phone you every week from the post office." She ran her fingers through her hair nervously. "I haven't done much writing lately, you know, not like I planned. What I'm really afraid of is looking at that wretched book again after so long." A tremor of self-doubt made her heart beat faster.

"You're so compulsive, Miriam," Simon said, smiling. "I thought this was supposed to be a vacation."

210

"And the vacation's almost over. When your family disappears over that hill, and you and Rebecca head for Paris, I'd like to wave good-bye and settle down to something!" she exclaimed impatiently.

Simon stared at her fingers. "Well, okay, but when you've done this writing, will you come to London instead of going home?"

"I'll have to come to London in either case since my ticket is written for Gatwick," she reminded him gently. Her eyes were sparkling with victory.

"You know what I mean." His gaze was fixed on hers with serious intent as if he could make her agree.

Her thoughts returned unbidden to the encounter with Kristin on the steam train; it had shaken Miriam's confidence in her future possibilities with Simon. She glanced away, realizing guiltily she might always be dreaming of some woman, actual or imaginary, and that Simon would be the loser. Remembering Kristin's smooth skin, the soft rounded breasts beneath the well-cut shirt, she worried that she couldn't be emotionally satisfied for long with any man.

She could almost visualize the scenario ahead if she lived with Simon: the philosophical difficulties she'd have in adapting to the heterosexual couple's way of life, the secret sexual fantasies, and finally the inevitable infidelity. It would hurt Simon much more if she left him then, after they'd established a life together, than if she said no to him now. At this point, so far, there was only one furtive kiss in a dark tunnel violating their relationship; up ahead there could be much worse transgressions. What minimized these doubts was the strength of Simon's love and her own need for it. She believed that Simon loved her more than anyone ever had, more than any woman had. To refuse that love would be foolish, she argued with herself. She looked back at Simon with a sad smile. "I can't decide anything right now," she said finally.

He leaned forward and kissed her. "It's not like I have a choice whether to love you or not. I just want to be able to give it to you, that's all."

Simon was offering his life to her and the choice was hers. He was mellowing her with his love, winning her by not trying to win. This was a new way of loving, what she'd always thought she wanted. For once someone was waiting for *her*. Miriam studied the angular masculinity of Simon's face and the intelligent openness that gave it such individuality. She felt her love for him flow out between them.

In a companionable silence they looked out over the valley. Once again she found herself imagining the two of them as ruling monarchs overseeing their realm. She realized, when Beth called Simon to help round up the ducks and he was gone, that the time for them to sit together was quickly running out. Overcome by sadness for a moment, she nearly changed her mind about remaining at the farm alone. Then she went to find Rebecca.

They borrowed Simon's car to drive to the post office in Garance. Rebecca wanted to make a transatlantic call to Stephen and asked Miriam to speak with the clerk there who would assist in placing it. "I know I'm being silly," she explained as they drove away from Les Bluets, "but I just want to hear his voice before I get on another jet."

"You're not being silly at all," Miriam reassured her. "I was going to suggest getting away for a while anyway. I don't want to watch Beth and Simon kill those ducks."

"Oh, I know!" agreed Rebecca, lighting each of them a cigarette. They drove silently, passing the familiar houses and pastures, until Rebecca spoke again, her voice soft and sentimental. "You know, I'm really going to miss all this. It's so beautiful and I've been so happy here. By the time I get back, I'll wish I was still here."

"And what about Stephen?" Miriam teased, rolling her window all the way down for more fresh air.

"Well," Rebecca replied firmly, "he's the only good reason I can think of right now for going back."

Miriam considered for a moment how differently she and Rebecca were responding to the men in their lives. "Simon wants me to go with him to London — to live with him or marry him or something."

Rebecca smiled at Miriam affectionately. "I figured he would." Then, apparently pondering what she knew of Miriam's probable conflicts about that, she became serious again. "What are you going to do?"

Miriam sighed deeply. "I don't know. I guess we could try it for a while — if there were no expectations."

"That might be difficult — for Simon," Rebecca noted, sounding critical.

"I know." *That's what Sasha's wanted too*, Miriam thought, *no expectations. It's a heartless thing to ask from someone in love.*

"Do you really love Simon?"

Miriam glanced quickly at Rebecca. "Of course!" she replied unhesitatingly.

"But not like Sasha," Rebecca reminded her.

Miriam nearly replied that she'd never be able to love anyone that much again, but suspected it wasn't true. She concentrated on a tight turn into the first of the village's narrow streets and muttered, "Thank God."

"Are you being honest with Simon?"

Like a devil's advocate, Rebecca was questioning Miriam's motives. The pointed query unwittingly criticized Miriam too for the strict standards by which she'd often judged others. As Ellen had reminded her already, Miriam had written and talked a lot about emotional honesty between women but never until now had she seen that it must apply to all intimate relationships.

Miriam pulled the car sharply into the tree-lined square and parked it in the shade. As she turned off the ignition, she faced Rebecca. "I've never believed anyone could change his or her sexual orientation and still don't, but I'm not going to give Simon up until I'm sure one way or the other."

Rebecca smiled at her sympathetically. "I guess I've been confused about it most of my life."

"Are you now?" asked Miriam, wanting a clear answer.

"Sometimes," replied Rebecca and laughed.

Watching Rebecca inside the phone booth, Miriam saw that there was no answer on Stephen's end of the line. Over a drink at Benoit's, Rebecca was despondent, her conversation dulled by frustration and disappointment. She re-read what Stephen had written in his last letter. When she'd replaced the thin blue envelope in her handbag, and, after a long stare into it, raised her head, there were tears in her eyes.

Miriam stroked Rebecca's hair as the tears spilled over. "He can't be sitting in his apartment night and day in case you might call," she reasoned, trying to comfort her friend.

Rebecca nodded. "I know. He should be home now though." She gulped half her glass of beer and blew her nose. "Stephen and I talked about marriage once." She smiled wryly. "I want to and he doesn't. His family life was so bad as a kid. His dad's one of those alcoholic shrinks and his mother had the occasional black eye and constant bridge party. He doesn't want to take a chance on repeating it, he says."

"Does he think only married people treat each other like shit?"

213

Rebecca sniffed. "Good point."

A half hour later when they placed a second call to Stephen's number, he answered and Miriam saw Rebecca's face light up with joy inside the dim phone booth. She signaled that she'd wait outside and walked across the small square to sit on the steps of the church. She suspected that, in spite of her doubts, it was easier to be in her position than in Rebecca's, easier to be in Sasha's position than in Simon's. Yet she still believed that the ultimate determinations must be made in the arena of ethics, no matter what one's position.

Richard's departure created a void at the dinner table that no amount of lively conversation and wine were able to fill. Even the children were unusually quiet and reserved. As promised Beth had prepared a delicious meal: *petit pois* — a French delicacy they all loved — and crunchy pieces of potato and other vegetables that had been roasted with the ducks.

Miriam stared at the crusty brown bodies in the roasting dish and knew with a unique kind of certainty that those feathered creatures with whom she'd spent the previous few weeks no longer existed in the world. They wouldn't be flapping their wings and quacking the next day as they bathed in the rocky bottomed stream, nor poking their bills aggressively into the refuse pile they shared with the rooster and two hens.

When she glanced up, her eyes met Rebecca's and she knew her friend was having similar thoughts. Simon handed her the platter of meat. As she put a slice of duck on her plate, Miriam was a bit disappointed in herself. She'd thought she would refuse to help eat the ducks, that her somber reflections on the proximity of life and death would make it impossible. Now, she reasoned, only the ones who had lost their lives would appreciate her concern, and they were much too far removed for that. She experienced a twinge of guilt with the first succulent bite. She would have offered condolences to the surviving relations but there were none.

"Well," said Jack, cutting some meat for Davy, "our leftovers were put to good use this year."

"Oh, daddy!" complained Martha.

"Listen, my dear," he admonished, "the living go on living and don't waste their time mourning the dead."

Miriam considered arguing against such simplistic theorizing but in-

214

stead refilled her wine glass. Beneath the table Simon pressed his knee against hers and they smiled knowingly at each other.

Martha turned to Miriam. "Are you going to marry Uncle Simon?" she asked loudly.

Everyone glanced around nervously and Beth's look apologized to Miriam. "Well," said Miriam, with a glance at Jack, "I'm so prickly that I'm not sure your Uncle Simon could stand it."

The children's laughter infected everyone at the table, as Martha explained the joke.

"I guess I'll have to grow porcupine quills of my own in self-defense," laughed Simon.

"You'll need 'em, all right," said Jack with a smile that wasn't totally sincere.

While the others played pinochle, Miriam and Simon sat before the fire as they had on so many other evenings. "It sounds ridiculous to say I'm going to miss you," he murmured, and Miriam could hear the sadness in his voice.

"Yes," she agreed. Longing, waiting, missing — her vocabulary lately had been full of such words, her life full of unsatisfied desires. She knew she could change that now by saying yes once more, but she wanted that affirmation to include the rest of her life. As they went upstairs together earlier than usual, she reminded herself that what she needed was time.

Les Bluets/13

On the day everyone but Miriam planned to leave Les Bluets she woke up unusually alert, as if she'd been subliminally awake for hours. She heard Jack drive into the yard with bread and milk, and the children arguing over priorities in the bathroom. When she tried to rise without disturbing Simon, he groaned in his sleep and rolled over into the warm hollow where her body had been. She pulled the white caftan over her head as he stretched an arm out to her and mumbled, "Where are you going?"

"Downstairs," she replied softly. "I want to spend some time alone with Rebecca."

"What about me?" he demanded, opening one eye.

"Don't worry." She bent over and kissed him. "You'll get yours."

"Not enough. Never enough," he complained and slid back into sleep.

She managed to get past the bathroom unseen by the children and found Rebecca already awake but still in her sleeping bag, staring blankly at the far wall.

"How's the view?" joked Miriam, climbing into her own bag for warmth. She leaned on an elbow and studied Rebecca's sensitive profile.

"I was listening to the activity in the house," replied Rebecca after a moment. "When I first got here, I couldn't sleep at night and woke too early because the unfamiliar sounds bothered me so much."

Miriam nodded, indicating that she had felt the same.

"Now it's all so friendly." Rebecca turned toward Miriam suddenly. "I think I'll be back someday."

"No doubt," agreed Miriam. They smiled at each other reassuringly. "I'm wondering if my decision to stay on is just a silly whim and if I'll really accomplish anything."

"Oh, come with us to Paris then!" Rebecca urged. "We'll have a great time! You can be the official tour guide!"

Miriam could tell that Rebecca really wanted this, and she was tempted to say yes because she could already visualize them there, eating Italian ice cream and climbing the steps of the Sacre Coeur. After a few moments Miriam became aware that she was staring at the small vase on the window sill that she'd kept filled with cornflowers. The sunlight was spilling over the delicate blooms and onto the floor. She quickly recovered confidence, the doubts dissipated by that single image. "There's something I have to do here. I must stay," she replied firmly, more to herself than to Rebecca. "It's just a feeling I have." She glanced across at Rebecca and shrugged. "I can't explain."

"You don't have to. I can see the attraction of it." Rebecca climbed out of her sleeping bag a bit disappointed but willing to accept Miriam's decision. "Anyway the drive to Paris with Simon is some compensation."

"Yes," conceded Miriam. She was trying to remember what kind of person she'd been, how she'd been living, so long ago when she left Portland and last saw Sasha. There'd been a crazy woman in her body then, a woman possessed. The demons were nearly gone and she knew the last ritual of exorcism must be a solitary one. She extricated herself from the sleeping bag but continued to sit on the edge of the bed, tapping her bare feet on the dusty floorboards. "I want to write again, Rebecca. I want to get started on something."

"That's good. I'm glad," Rebecca said quietly. In addition to the intense look on Miriam's face, the air in the room vibrated with diffused energy. "How is Simon taking it?"

"My staying on here? Okay, I think." Miriam smiled. "At least he's keeping me on this side of the Atlantic." She watched Rebecca who was standing by the open window brushing her hair, the small firm breasts under a pale lavender tee shirt, the expensive lacy panties she always wore. She looked like a model on a very appealing erotic postcard.

Rebecca went down to breakfast, but still Miriam was slow to begin her day. She wanted to savor and store carefully away the rhythm of voices making conversation downstairs. Rebecca's possessions, clothing and souvenirs, strewn around the room were comforting. Half dressed, she went into the bathroom to brush her teeth and found Beth gathering all the toilet articles that normally littered the sink and shelves into a plastic sack.

"I got up when Jack left for Garance and I'm nearly finished with the packing," Beth said triumphantly. She looked hot and tired already.

As usual Miriam was disturbed by Beth's industrious and cheerful servitude but didn't comment on it. "If you have a minute, stop by my room," she said. "I've got something for you."

Awhile later Beth knocked softly at the open door. "Meditating?" she asked.

Miriam, who had been standing in the middle of the room contemplating her worn-out sandals that needed replacing or repair, turned abruptly and laughed. "Come on in." She began searching through her notebook until she found a sheet of paper which she handed to Beth.

It was a long poem that took several minutes to read. Beth looked up at Miriam finally. "You wrote this after the night we sat outside together when the moon was full."

Miriam nodded. "That copy's for you."

Beth read through the lines again quickly. Miriam could see that she was moved by the sentiments expressed but was uncertain of the appropriate response.

At last she said shyly, "It's a wonderful poem. Thank you." Beth folded the piece of paper and put it in the back pocket of her Levi's.

"I take it you and Jack have made peace with each other," Miriam said, trying to sound casual.

Beth sat down on the edge of the bed. "A conditional one."

"Meaning?" Miriam asked as she began brushing her hair.

"Meaning I want Jack to start taking more responsibility within the family and around the house, in other words, doing his share so that I can do something else once in awhile."

Miriam sat next to Beth but didn't speak, though her raised eyebrows revealed how doubtful she was about this plan.

Beth shrugged. "I'd really like to take some classes — or something — I don't know. I want a life of my own separate from him and the kids."

"I think that's a great idea," Miriam said, putting an arm around Beth's shoulders and hugging her. "You have my full support."

"I know," laughed Beth, then she was serious again. "When Jack raced out of the room after me that night, it was because he *did* recognize his own mistakes in the criticism of Annalise. He was embarrassed and angry at himself. In spite of his other faults, he isn't a heartless, stupid man."

"Well, he needs to learn something about gay people," Miriam said.

Beth gave her an apologetic look. "I know. I felt terrible about that."

Miriam stood up and slipped on her sandals. "Nothing new about his attitude though," she said bitterly.

As they went down to breakfast, Miriam stopped on the stairs. "Shall we write to each other?"

Beth was obviously pleased by the suggestion. "I'd like that! You probably won't get anything from me though until the kids have started back to school."

"Well, I'll be here," Miriam replied. "You know the address." Then she added, with a contrite smile, "I promise to be better as a correspondent than I was as a conversationalist."

"Don't worry," Beth said, in a low voice that already suggested sisterly confidences. "I haven't abandoned all hope."

Miriam had settled into her chair and was breaking open a piece of baguette, trying to decide between strawberry and apricot jam, when Tina appeared at her elbow waving a blue airmail envelope. "Thanks, sweetie," she said, taking it from her. She noted from the handwriting that it was a third letter from Sasha. She was curious, but for once her heart didn't rise unbidden into her throat. Determined to let nothing distract her from this last day with Simon, she put the letter in her pocket unopened.

"How long do you think you'll stay, Miriam?" inquired Claire as she cracked Davy's boiled egg for him.

"I don't really know," Miriam replied. She started to qualify her uncertainty but saw Claire glance briefly at Simon and didn't.

"She'll stay until the first time the Citroen has a flat tire," commented Jack.

Rebecca cleared her throat and set her coffee cup down loudly on the table.

Jack continued, addressing Miriam in a bantering tone. "You'd better learn to bat those long eyelashes. You know, life can be hard around here."

"Oh, Jack, stop!" complained Beth. She gave her husband a stern, irritated look.

"I'm sure Miriam will do fine," said Simon tensely. He changed the topic of conversation then to the care of the chickens and other matters of keeping the farm.

Miriam noticed that Beth was eating hastily in order to finish her packing before the two taxis arrived to take them to the Lyon airport. She leaned forward and said, over the children's excited chatter, "I'll take care of the cleaning up, Beth."

Claire made two fresh cups of coffee. "Take a stroll with me," she suggested, handing one of the cups to Miriam.

The only ones not bustling about elsewhere, they walked out into

222

the uninhabited and quiet yard, and stood by the retaining wall gazing into the woods. It was a warm morning in spite of a slight breeze, and the bees were already buzzing in the flowers below them. The two hens scratched beneath the table, searching for bread crumbs. Everything was exactly as it had been on so many other mornings, yet Miriam sensed that, when the chaotic activity of leavetaking was accomplished, she would be alone in a completely new landscape.

She and Claire sat down on the retaining wall after a moment and faced each other. Having learned that Claire was no sentimentalist, Miriam wondered a bit nervously why she had requested this friendly tête-à-tête.

"What are you going to do here all alone?" Claire asked, with an ingenuous smile that encouraged the absolute truth.

"Try to decide about the future," Miriam replied simply. "And try to write. I think they're connected." She remembered again with a sense of failure the abandoned novel upstairs. "I've been blocked for several months."

"Why?" Claire probed with her usual sincerity.

"I don't really know." Miriam no longer believed that the fault was Sasha's.

"Do you let yourself write about whatever's on your mind?"

Claire's question seemed casual enough but had an ominous sound to Miriam, who laughed nervously.

"What I'm thinking about probably isn't all that interesting," Miriam concluded. Actually she considered autobiographical writing to be a cheap shot.

"Searching for the *perfect* material?" Claire smiled at her playfully.

It was true, Miriam realized, and the sudden realization made her feel foolish. Perhaps her doubts and self-criticism were only a form of procrastination.

Claire stood up, laying a hand on her shoulder. "It's a cause and effect world, my dear. In the end we only get what we're willing to work for. That's how we *know* what we really want."

After Claire was gone, Miriam pondered her speech, taking long sips of the fragrant black coffee and frowning at the pine trees, the invisible creek, and the chiseled faces of the viewpoint rocks that stared implacably back at her across the valley.

While the luggage was being stowed in the trunks of the taxis, Simon hugged Claire, Beth, and the children, and shook hands with Jack, each several times. Miriam hugged the children, exacting promises from them to send her some postcards. She shook Jack's hand, recognizing that he probably viewed her as an unwelcome challenge. She knew that next time he would approach her cautiously, as a potential foe in the field of moral issues. She hugged Beth warmly reminding her that they'd agreed to write, and Rebecca thanked her for being the "Julia Child of Les Bluets."

Claire kissed Miriam on the cheek. "Take care, my dear. Now, you won't stay on here if it's too much for you."

Miriam gazed into the penetrating blue eyes so much like Simon's, choosing to accept Claire's concern as friendly rather than maternal. She was just becoming aware of a liberating distance from Judith, her own demanding Fury of a mother, a sense that the emotional umbilical cord was being slowly severed.

As the taxis disappeared over the hill, the children waving customarily until the last curve was rounded, Miriam turned to Simon and saw that he was close to tears. "You're sad."

"Sure am."

"Is there anything I can do?" She put out a hand to touch him.

He shook his head, walking away from her in the direction of the big barn. She suspected he was going to the hayloft where the chickens often roosted in bad weather. It had a single large unshuttered window that opened out over the valley. They had made love there one warm humid afternoon surrounded by the sweet musty perfume of the sunlight on the hay.

She didn't follow, knowing that Simon would not want any comfort but the venting of his own sorrow. Instead she went upstairs with Rebecca and watched her finish packing. The house was silent and empty around them. Miriam lay on top of her sleeping bag as Rebecca walked around the room placing her neatly folded clothes in the suitcase, toilet articles in the side pockets. Sitting back on her heels, she turned to Miriam suddenly, a thoughtful crease across her forehead. "I feel like we're leaving you to some Fate."

Miriam laughed. "Well, of course!"

"No, I mean something mysterious. Leaving you alone with all this — Nature!"

Miriam sat up on the bed. "I don't think it's Nature we should fear. It's other human beings who do the damage." She stopped, hearing her pedantic tone. "I know what you mean though. It might be easy to disappear into Nature. People have."

"I guess that's it. Please don't disappear, okay?"

"Okay," Miriam agreed.

Simon reappeared at lunchtime. Seated on the same side of the table facing the woods, the three of them ate a simple meal of bread, cheese and fruit, and drank the last bottle of the elderberry wine. Each surrendering to personal memories, plans and emotional states, no one said much.

Finally Rebecca broke the silence. "I think I'll hike to the 'viewpoint' when we've cleaned up. Just a final look. Do we have time, Simon?"

"Oh, sure. I'm in no rush, are you?" He gazed at each of them steadily as they shook their heads. For a moment it seemed as if someone would surely suggest that they stay exactly where they were, forever. Then Rebecca rose and began stacking the dishes.

A half hour later, Miriam and Simon sat in their same places at the table and watched Rebecca walk down the dusty tire tracks leading into the woods. Miriam expected her to turn around and wave to them just before she entered the thick green shade but she didn't.

"Well," said Simon taking her hand, "I guess this is it then."

"For a while anyway." She almost wished he were staying with her but knew the wish was produced only by her fear of the unknown.

"You will call?"

She nodded. "And write." Facing him, she demanded petulantly, "Will you though? You're a terrible letter writer — I know!"

"I'll write back the same day I hear from you," he swore solemnly. It was a moment before he spoke again, and when Miriam glanced at him, his eyes were clouded with apprehension. "You know, Miriam, I've always wanted kids — and you've always said you didn't."

"I still don't," she replied bluntly. "Simon, I know I haven't seemed very serious about my writing lately, but I really do want to make books, not babies."

Simon laughed, then grew serious again. "Well, I guess I'll have awhile to give that some thought, eh?"

Miriam nodded but didn't reply, knowing they were on sensitive ground.

"I want you to be happy, Miriam. I want us both to be happy.

Christ, I love to hear you laugh!" He gestured across the valley. "The way I love to hear those church bells ring over there, echoing through the hills like a whole symphony." His voice broke then and his eyes narrowed in a concentrated effort as if he were bracing himself against the coming separation, not from Miriam, but from Les Bluets.

Miriam gazed at him, studying the features of his face slowly one by one, the intense serious eyes, the slightly crooked mouth. "I've been happier here with you than I've ever been before," she said. She remembered Claire's words of encouragement and faith in her, and felt an inner resolve solidify. "I'm sorry that I can't be more definitive about a future for us." She looked away from him. "There's something I have to do — I don't even know what it is — before I can make any plans."

He nodded, but she knew his acceptance didn't make him less unhappy with her decision, only more willing to be patient. He caressed her hand with both of his. "Would you like to go to the loft with me?"

Miriam nodded and smiled at his euphemism all the way up the stairs.

His suitcase was packed but the purple sleeping bag was still open on the bed.

"Will you leave the typewriter for me?" Miriam asked as she stepped out of her shorts.

"Sure will. Anything else of mine you want?"

Miriam helped Simon gather belongings that had become scattered around the house. He was like a small child darting here and there, searching for sunglasses, science-fiction novels, his favorite running shoes that he crammed, swearing, into the bulging suitcase.

"Simon, if you've forgotten anything I can always mail it to you," Miriam reasoned.

"I'll leave the radio for you too," he said, taking the extra batteries out of the glove compartment of the car. "You don't know how quiet it can get here at night when you're alone."

Miriam watched him closely, trying to memorize every nuance of tone, every gesture, realizing only in the last minutes how much of her heart she'd given to him.

Rebecca, in her well-organized way, needed no assistance, merely threw her luggage into the back of the Mercedes and finished shooting the roll of film in her camera.

They made their farewells quickly. Miriam hugged them both, kissing Simon on the mouth and Rebecca on the cheek. Like Rebecca, she believed they would all be together again and wasn't sad. Through the clouds of dust the car raised on the gravel driveway to the main road, they waved and called out repeatedly, "Good-bye! Good-bye!"

When she knew at last that she was alone, Miriam stood in the center of the yard, moving in a slow circle, stretching out her arms as if extending the sphere of her power through her fingertips. Then she sat down to read Sasha's letter.

She says she's broken off with the Other Woman and is waiting for me. I'm not surprised. Most people would be discouraged by now if their letters hadn't been answered but Sasha lives for this sort of contest. What will it take, she asks herself, for me to be convinced that I'm her one and only again?

What I'm convinced of is that I could have a great adventure without taking even one step from where I am. Unlike Simon, I will not accept that to love passionately means to lose free will. Such a state can hardly be called any kind of love at all. I want to love where I choose, not by some unconscious dictate.

Listening to her footsteps echo around her, she walked slowly along the hallway of the second floor. The rooms were empty except for the beds that had been stripped bare and the antique wooden armoires. The air was warm, and was vibrating with the streaks of light lying across the unvarnished wood floors that had been swept clean. She checked the latches on the shutters in each room, though she was certain Jack had already done that, and tested the doors as she shut them behind her so that there would be no banging in the night. She moved all her belongings to the main room downstairs and carried Simon's typewriter from the loft, placing it at one end of the long dining room table. She locked the shutters in the loft room as well and, with a final glance at the forsaken double bed, closed the door tight. She found a chamber pot Beth had used in the children's room and set it with a roll of toilet paper in the tool closet next to the music room. Her last preparatory gesture was to bolt the door in the entry hall that led up the wooden staircase to the second floor. She wouldn't go upstairs again except to bathe. Everything she needed was close at hand. She was ready to begin.

PART FOUR

> I am quite the French farm woman after a week alone here, with my *pot-au-feu* on the stove and the long apron I found in one of the dining room cupboards. I've cleaned the scullery, the main room and the dining room thoroughly and I know where everything is in my little world. Outside, where I spend most of my time since the weather remains hot and sunny, is a larger universe waiting to reveal itself. The longer I am here, the more I feel a part of the place, moving within its framework like any single piece of an intricate clock, knowing my exact function and not wishing to disturb the perfection of the whole. Like the hawk that flies over Les Bluets, I am circling closer and closer to my own center.

By noon each day she completed the daily chores of the farm, the cleaning, laundry, stacking of wood by the hearth, and after lunch she sat with her notebook at the outdoor table. She began slowly and uncertainly to write again, influenced by Claire's parting remarks about emotional spontaneity. After a few days she perceived some progress. The words still came slowly, but more easily than the previous spring when she couldn't manage even one coherent paragraph. Her perspective on the material had changed. She sat in the sunlight with an eager hand, only occasionally glancing up at the woods or the valley.

> I've learned that it's necessary to find the significance within the material of our lives. The part of me that creates, that makes words coalesce on the page into meaning, also absorbs my life. The one grows out of the death of the other. I believe that the part that is created will be greater than the part that is destroyed. In this case the whole is greater than the sum of its parts.

She stopped for a beer at Benoit's whenever she was in the village for groceries or to mail letters. Madame Benoit brought the bottle outside to Miriam and stood for a moment wiping her big red hands on a soiled apron. "You are alone, mademoiselle, at Les Bluets?"
Miriam tilted her sunglasses back and smiled. "Yes, madame."
Madame Benoit frowned and shook her head. "Not good."
"Why, madame?"
The short bulky woman shrugged. "One must pay attention, you

know, in the mountains. It can break you." As she began to turn away, she paused. "You come to see me sometimes, eh? So I know you are all right."

Miriam agreed gratefully. The sound of another human voice was pleasant as long as she could control its duration.

After starting the fire in the main room, Miriam ate her dinner of soup and bread at the outdoor table and watched the tree boughs and the flowers sway in the rising wind. Though it would be daylight for another hour, she locked the gate and chased the chickens into the big barn. She lit the gas lamp just at sunset and the room was suddenly full of newly acquired and still unfamiliar shadows. After pouring herself a generous glass of cognac and adding more wood to the fire, she curled up inside her sleeping bag with the copy of *Middlemarch* Beth had finally finished and left behind. It was only in those long evenings as the house creaked around her, as the days shortened and she had to spend more time indoors, that Miriam was occasionally lonely. Yet she didn't want human company and could hardly bear the thought of leaving Les Bluets. She turned on the radio and flooded the room with music instead.

The days became weeks and her routine of physical work and writing did not change. The pages in her notebook were filled and she purchased a larger one. The flowers gradually disappeared and some of the trees began to turn color, others to lose their leaves. She spoke to no one except the merchants who sold her supplies. Once a week she called Simon from the post office in Garance.

"How is everything?" he asked.

"Wonderful! But why haven't you written?" Miriam accused him. "You're as terrible as ever!"

"I've been working twenty hours a day, that's why," Simon replied in an exasperated voice. "One of the fools who's working for us crashed the lorry two days ago and a leak in the roof wrecked a whole shipment of books."

"Oh, Simon, I'm sorry," Miriam said, conscious of her own peaceful and uncomplicated situation.

"Wish I were there."

She could tell he was feeling nostalgic and sad. Miriam tried to keep the romantic content of the phone calls to a minimum. She was so immured in her creative solitude that she wouldn't have wanted even Simon's company and she saw no good for either of them in the constant expression of unsatisfied desires. "Have you seen Richard?" she asked, changing the subject.

"Couple of nights ago for a few pints."

"And?"

"Well, it's going to be awhile. He's a stiff-necked old bugger."

"Yes, I know," replied Miriam, with an irritated sigh, "in spite of his pretensions to apathy."

"Listen I'll get a letter off to you tonight, okay?" Simon always promised at the end of the conversation.

Miriam lay a long time each night before sleep would come, thinking of people she'd known. She tried to go as far back as she could, to even the minor characters — to her second stepfather's sister Greta, a child prostitute with long blonde braids who gave Miriam her first book, *Little Women*; to the grocer on the corner, Mr. Silverstein, who made fried egg sandwiches for her that were so greasy that she threw up afterward but felt too guilty to complain; to Miss Mitter, the elderly spinster who'd worked with her at her first job, in the public library, had been there forty years and still lived at home; to a college classmate Brian who'd been asked to leave the seminary because he was discovered to be gay, who took too many drugs and fell accidently off of "Suicide Bridge"; to a co-worker named Gary with whom she'd gotten very drunk one night and taken to bed only to be so revolted by his hairy chest that she ran away clutching her clothes; to the Indian woman who wanted to be a poet and whom she tried to encourage. The memories were thick with characters about whom she wanted to write. She slept fitfully, awakened repeatedly by faces and scenes. Some made her laugh. Others made her cry.

One night she had a vivid dream about Les Bluets. There was a woman floating in a brilliant blue sky above the farmhouse and waving to her, a woman wearing a black evening dress trimmed in fur with very full sleeves that were billowing out in the wind like her long black hair. In a friendly and inviting manner, she related that she'd once lived at Les Bluets and that she now watched over it, protecting those who lived there. As the dream began to fade, she leaned down toward Miriam. "No regrets in this place," she said, stretching out a hand, "no regrets."

Miriam woke suddenly while it was still dark outside. Simon was right, she thought, there is a guardian of the manor. The parting admonition given her by the benevolent ghost reminded Miriam that she must eventually decide whether to stay with Simon or not, and that realization made her nervous and apprehensive. Unable to resolve her dilemma, she lay awake in her sleeping bag until daylight chased the shadows from the room. She'd become attuned to the songs of the birds, gradually recognizing which ones sang first and aroused the others into a diverse, but not unpleasant, symphony. Outside a dense mist was curled around the house but it would lift by mid-morning.

Miriam decided to ride the bicycle into Garance for the few groceries she needed instead of driving the car. The sky was blue, the air crisp as she pedaled up the inclines and coasted down the slopes of the road.

She arrived in the village tired and chilled and wishing she'd driven the car. Deciding that she needed a coffee before she could begin her errands, she stopped out of curiosity at the other cafe, not Benoit's. The only customer, she purchased an espresso, and sat down near the small wood stove that was glowing with warmth in the corner. The dim room, smelling of stale tobacco, was silent except for the ticking of the clock. This cafe was smaller than Benoit's and furnished with worn red velvet chairs and stained marble topped tables. Such shabby elegance seemed out of place in the village and she wondered what sort of people frequented Coco's, as it was called.

After a few moments the door opened letting the cool air in and blowing the ashes of her cigarette out of the ashtray. The customer was a petite, dark woman with high cheekbones and large black eyes. She'd twisted her hair into a low bun and was wearing a maroon skirt and matching cape with high boots. She ordered a *café au lait*.

As he prepared the coffee, the bartender, a heavy-set man with a long black moustache and a nose with prominent red veins, conversed with the new arrival in a low voice. A young boy in knickers came in, nodded at Miriam, and shoved more wood into the stove.

When she'd paid, the woman in maroon brought her coffee to Miriam's table. "May I join you?" she asked in good English but with a distinct accent.

"Of course," answered Miriam politely, though she wasn't particularly interested in conversing.

"My name is Gabby Gautin." The woman smiled warmly as she threw her cape backward over the chair.

Miriam shook the hand held out to her and introduced herself.

"You are an American?" Gabby had a full sensuous mouth. Her black eyes, heavily lashed, shone with curiosity.

Miriam nodded, aware that she was on guard against something. As she sipped the hot coffee cautiously, Gabby studied Miriam's face. She smiled again and leaned forward confidentially. "And what are you doing in our little village?"

"I'm writing a book," Miriam replied simply. "I've – rented a place near here so that I can work undisturbed." Miriam was surprised to hear herself lie about Les Bluets but was unwilling to share too much about her current situation with a stranger.

Gabby's eyebrows rose with interest, though the large dark eyes didn't look away for a second. "And what's it about, your book?"

The two women gazed at each other intently as if measuring each other's strength, and Miriam caught a brief reflection in the mirror of past experience. "Beauty and goodness," she replied finally.

"How do you mean?" Gabby asked without a moment's pause as she stirred the milky coffee.

Miriam quickly considered the several ways she might answer the question, then chose the most abstract. "When human beings are attracted to something or someone, they perceive that object as beautiful," she explained. "They insist that it's good for them to love that beauty. That's how human beings hurt themselves, because, in fact, it's only good to love goodness."

"And beauty is only in the eye of the beholder?" asked Gabby coyly.

Miriam nodded. "And the eye cannot perceive goodness."

"How is it perceived then?"

"With the heart, of course."

Gabby looked puzzled, frowning, and her mouth gathered into a pout, but Miriam knew she understood. "I've never thought of love that way before," Gabby said softly, almost to herself rather than to Miriam.

After a moment Miriam finished her coffee and stood up. "Well, I'd better be going."

Gabby reacted with surprise and a gesture of protest at this impending departure and she stood up too. "Miriam," she said quickly, "why don't you come home with me for lunch? My flat is nearby. She put a hand on Miriam's arm. "You must get tired of eating alone all the time. Besides I – I would enjoy talking more with you about this beauty and goodness. And I'm a very good cook." She laughed lightly and squeezed

Miriam's arm. "Please say you'll come."

Miriam considered Gabby's arguments, all of which were suddenly very persuasive. She *was* lonely, and tired of her own simple, almost spartan, meals; she could allow herself a brief diversion. "All right," she replied, smiling back. "That sounds very nice. Thank you for inviting me."

They walked along slowly, Miriam wheeling her bicycle and listening to Gabby relate the geneology of her family in Garance.

"Come in! Come in!" Gabby cried. She ran ahead of Miriam up a long flight of stairs attached to the outside of a gray stone building.

The bright sunny flat was decorated in pastel colors and vases of half-wilted flowers stood everywhere, filling the place sweetly like a perfumed sachet. Miriam noticed a child's jacket and a soccer ball on the pale pink couch.

"Oh," said Gabby, anticipating Miriam's question, "my son's with his father for the weekend."

Suddenly Miriam realized that this was the Gabrielle of Simon's failed love affair. "Damn!" she murmured. She watched Gabby stretch to pull the drapes, shutting out the glare of the midday sun through the large windows. She could appreciate how attractive Gabrielle must have been to Simon, how attractive she would be to anyone she chose.

Without a word Gabby took Miriam's jacket, hung it up in the hall closet, and disappeared into the kitchen. Now that she had Miriam in her own environment, she seemed distant and self-contained.

Uncomfortable in the silence between them and continuing to chide herself for not recognizing Gabrielle sooner, Miriam followed and stood leaning against the doorjamb. The kitchen was white and modern, and Gabby was efficient in it.

"I hope you like omelettes," she said, cracking two eggs into a bowl. She flashed a radiant smile at Miriam. "This one will be special."

Miriam was wishing she could think of an excuse to leave. "How flattering," she replied, smiling back, though she'd lost her enthusiasm for the shared meal. Panic had risen and settled beneath her rib cage. Something about Gabrielle, and not just that she'd been Simon's lover, frightened her.

Gabby had been truthful about being a good cook. The meal was attractive and delicious. The white wine they had with the omelettes and salad relaxed Miriam and she began to view the encounter as an ironic twist of fate rather than a punishment. Since Gabrielle didn't know of their mutual connection, Miriam decided that she held the winning hand in any manipulative ploy.

Conversation flowed easily between them again, though Miriam steered away from personal detail and kept to abstract subjects which fortunately Gabby seemed to enjoy. Over coffee and brandy, Gabby talked about flowers. Miriam, as she sipped her brandy, watched Gabby, her lips, her hands, her eyes, all the most expressive parts of a woman. Gabrielle, she decided, was lovely and soft and dark, and the afternoon of gentle laughter and low voices in a sunny fragrant room passed quickly and unnoticed.

Miriam heard the six o'clock Angelus bell ring and remembered with a guilty start her conversation with Simon: "And the Word was made flesh." "I should go," she said suddenly. "I have to get home while there's still some light and it's ten miles."

Gabby raised the shades and they both saw Venus twinkling in the early evening sky. She turned toward Miriam, her face hidden in shadow, "You won't make it — not on a bicycle." Then Gabby lifted her hand to the back of her neck and released her hair. It fell, heavy with waves, to the middle of her back, hanging partly over one shoulder. "You should just stay," she said very softly.

Miriam heard a small voice arguing inside her but hushed it. Her heart was pounding and there was a rippling wave in her diaphragm moving rapidly downward. In the warm stillness of the pale room they could hear each other breathing deeply. After a moment Gabby, unbuttoning her shirt, moved soundlessly toward Miriam and stood between her legs. Miriam's hands caressed Gabby's body, beginning with the hips and moving upward. Gabby leaned down, her hair surrounding and sheltering them, and Miriam pressed her lips into the white flesh between Gabby's breasts.

In the morning they lay in Gabby's large featherbed with its pale green sheets and drank freshly ground coffee. The bedroom was pastel too, shades of green and gray. A gray leather armchair dominated one corner.

Gabby laid her head on Miriam's shoulder and sighed happily. "Next time I'll cook something for you that's very French. When shall we do it?"

"I don't know," said Miriam. "There may not be a next time."

Jerking herself up on one elbow, Gabby stared at Miriam, then she smiled. "You're not serious."

Miriam laughed. "But I am. I mean, who knows? I don't even know how long I'll stay around here," she concluded, shrugging.

"But *I* know!" exclaimed Gabby. "You'll stay forever!" She kissed Miriam lightly. "You're beautiful! You're wonderful! I love you!"

Recognizing the echo in her head, Miriam turned away and lit a cigarette.

"Don't you love me too?" asked Gabby in a petulant voice.

Though she remembered asking as well as answering that question in such situations many times, Miriam could not reply in the affirmative. "We haven't even known each other twenty-four hours," she replied. "Do you think love is that easy?" Gabby responded to this question with a kiss and Miriam laughed softly, pulling her down onto the pillows again. "I'll admit I want you."

Gabby pushed away, resisting, and Miriam released her. "You *are* serious," Gabby said, frowning.

"About love, yes," agreed Miriam. "It's absolutely necessary to be honest," she added, sitting up on the bed. "I learned that the hard way, Gabby, and the hurt feelings were mainly mine."

"I'm honest," insisted Gabby. "I love you."

Miriam smiled. "That's your prerogative."

"What does that mean?" Gabby was still pouting.

"You have the right to feel any way you want, regardless of how I feel," explained Miriam, "but I'm not going to let myself be convinced, either by you or by myself, that you love me."

Gabby eyed her thoughtfully, chewing the corner of her mouth. "You are a lesbian, aren't you?"

Though amused by the irony of the situation, Miriam considered the question seriously. She thought about Simon and Kristin and what Rebecca had said about her own ambivalent sexual identity. Then she looked at the seductive, yet vulnerable, beauty of Gabrielle and was suddenly sure. She began to laugh. "Oh, yes, I am a lesbian! Yes! Yes!" she repeated, laughing loudly and hard and throwing herself backward on the bed in happy relief.

Gabby leaned over her, puzzled by Miriam's response and plainly uncertain of her own.

When she'd stopped laughing and wiped the tears from her eyes, Miriam gazed back at Gabby. The smudged makeup and long tangled hair reminded her of the previous night's erotic pleasures and she

238

jumped up before she could be tempted to stay longer. "I've got so much work to do. I must hop on that bicycle and dash!"

"I could drive you," offered Gabby.

Miriam shook her head and began searching for her clothes. "No, riding the bicycle back will do me good." For Simon's sake as well as her own, she didn't want Gabrielle at the farm with her. Actually, she didn't want anyone there.

"At least tell me where you're staying," Gabby said, kneeling naked in the center of the bed.

Miriam glanced at her, then away. "At Les Bluets. Simon is a very close friend of mine."

The look on Gabby's face was a mixture of embarrassment and fear; she knew Miriam knew everything. "You, shit," she said in a low angry voice.

Miriam stared across the room at Gabby in innocent surprise. "Should I have said no last night?"

Her return to the farm on the bicycle was slow. She was deep in thought and tired from lack of sleep. There was little traffic in either direction and she saw the smoke from every chimney along the narrow road before she saw its house. The weather, like the day before, was clear and brisk, and she knew her nose and cheeks were soon bright red. Her feet and hands were nearly paralyzed with cold when she was only halfway to Les Bluets. She remembered the hot, sunny weather in September and of the long walks she'd taken through the neighboring fields. There'd been moments during those languorous wanderings when she'd imagined that Simon was with her, holding her hand, gathering flowers, laughing.

A line from Eliot's "Little Gidding" came unbidden to her: "This is the use of memory: /for liberation — not less of love but expanding/ Of love beyond desire, and so liberation/From the future as well as the past." A wave of melancholy swept over Miriam and she felt herself close to tears. If she could have made a life with any man, it would have been Simon. From him she would have had the love, security, and support she'd been wanting; but now she knew that it would never have worked. Both of them would have been miserable.

The night spent with Gabby had shown her clearly that she would never be satisfied with less than her passion demanded. Even the knowledge that Gabby was Simon's ex-lover, that she'd hurt him deeply, almost irreparably, didn't stop Miriam, and that told her a significant truth about herself.

For months she'd been condemning Sasha for not loving her, though Sasha's only real fault lay in pretending that she did. What Sasha had felt for Miriam was what Miriam had felt for Gabby — sexual passion. Though she recognized it was not love, she vowed never again to deny her passion for another human being. It was clear to her now that this kind of passion was as necessary and as worthy as love. By refusing to see it as a potential good, she had been denying a part of herself and so could never distinguish between passion and real love.

By spending the night with Gabby she had begun to heal the crippled part of herself that would never be satisfied with less than love *and* passion. Perhaps there was some woman like herself, who hoped and dreamed as she did. Perhaps they were moving toward each other. Now at least Miriam would be able to recognize her.

Claire had seen the suppressed passion in Miriam long before she herself could, the passion that is the source of energy, firing the mind as well as the heart. A passion for the moment and a passion for continuity. *And what is the creative life,* Miriam asked herself, *if not a passionate striving?*

Finally she spotted Les Bluets' chimney in the distance and wished there were a warm fire waiting for her inside so that she could begin writing immediately. Staring hard, she stopped pedaling, then blinked and stared again. Something was suspended in the sky, hovering in midair over the woods. It appeared to be a woman with long hair, wearing a full-sleeved dark gown, waving to her. A soft voice whispered, "It's all right now, my darling. Everything is all right." Perhaps, she thought, it was even her own voice. Recalling her dream, she smiled, accepting the message, and a deep sense of well-being and harmony flowed through her.

Whistling the "Alleluia Chorus" loudly, and breaking occasionally into wild, ecstatic laughter, Miriam pedaled as fast as she could toward the farmhouse. A hawk circled the roof of Les Bluets, dipped down into the ruins and then, crying once over the quiet valley, returned to her nest in the hidden heart of the woods.